CORPSE

by
Philip McCutchan

MAGNA PRINT BOOKS
Long Preston, North Yorkshire,
England.

British Library Cataloguing in Publication Data.

McCutchan, Philip
CORPSE

A catalogue record for this book is
available from the British Library

ISBN 0 7505 0309 2

First Published in Great Britain by Hodder & Stoughton Ltd., 1980

Copyright © 1980 by Philip McCutchan

Published in Large Print 1992 by arrangement with the copyright
holder

Printed and bound in Great Britain by
T.J. Press (Padstow) Ltd., Cornwall, PL28 8RW.

11.95

CORPSE

CORPSE

Two dead bodies branded with the letters CORPSE suggest something more than homicidal maniac to Commander Shaw and 6D2.

Shaw and Miss Mandrake find themselves fighting a Rightist backlash set to take over Britain. CORPSE's idea of persuasion is to poise nuclear waste-bearing vessels around the ports of the United Kingdom.

Shaw's hunt for the centre of their operations takes him to Torremolinos and to a curious religious sect called the Flood Fearers. The pursuit is complicated when 6D2's old adversary, the left-wing group called WUSWIPP arrives in the unlovely shape of Polecat Brennan; Shaw and Felicity Mandrake find their own lives in a countdown to megadeath.

CHAPTER 1

The girl was stone cold dead; so much was obvious at first glance, even the casual glance that in the red glow had revealed the body to me as I waited at some traffic lights on the outskirts of Peterborough. I was alongside a building site. It was, I thought, a hell of a place to be found dead, and not just the fact of the building site either: Peterborough is a fine old cathedral sadly isolated in a glut of any-old-High-Street shop names over featureless fronts. It was late at night and not much traffic around. I reversed until I was clear of the lights, parked, and ran back to the body. It had been some while dead. I scrabbled away at what looked like the contents of several generations of dustbins, all mixed in with broken bricks, mortar, wood and concrete, what the building industry uses as a sort of basic filler to make a foundation. At first only the girl's head and chest had been visible to my torch, but I cleared enough rubble to see the cause of death staring me in the face: the stomach had been penetrated by three evenly-spaced bullets.

7

I stood up, breathing deep. I had an immense fellow-feeling for that girl. It wasn't so long since I'd fought a battle with a building site down in Woolwich, only I'd been intended to suffocate below ground and had been lucky enough to be rescued by the friendly neighbourhood bulldozer. This looked different. There being nothing else I could do, I went back to my car and went in search of the nick, where I identified myself and quoted 6D2 at the law, stressing that I was tired and wanted to go to bed. They said they would investigate right away, and where could I be found if needed?

'Talbot House Hotel, Oundle,' I said.

'Under your own name, Commander Shaw?'

I laughed at that. '6D2's not MI5 or whatever, Inspector. Often enough we're cloak and dagger, but not when on leave.'

I saw the law note down 'on leave'. A few minutes later I was driving out of Peterborough again, back past the awful anonymity of Boots, Dolcis, Currys, The Co-op, various building societies, and Freeman, Hardy and Willis, with the cathedral spire rising rather pathetically over the dismal view. Oundle was thankfully different: ancient serenity unruined by progress, with a first-class hotel complete with old courtyard and walled garden alongside the calm

8

cloisters of the famous school. Oundle was dignity, charm and individuality...I was thinking about that girl, though. Dignity had been far away from her at the end, and it had been impossible to tell whether she had had charm or not—the police were going to have a hell of a job of identification, though she just might check with their list of missing persons.

I went up to bed; the bar had closed long since. I passed Felicity's room, hesitated, but didn't knock. I knew Miss Mandrake would be willing, because Miss Mandrake nearly always was, but with that pathetic young body on my mind I couldn't raise the enthusiasm. To us, the field men of 6D2, the dead come, I suppose, easy, for they're largely our stock-in-trade; but when they're young and female it's different and not all the women's libbers in the world will ever alter that fact. One still does not associate girls with violent death and never mind the swelling ranks of rapists who provide the statistics that prove the opposite...

In my room bed beckoned but the telephone burred and it was Peterborough police. 'Commander Shaw? You'd better come over, sir, if you don't mind. Something's come up.'

★ ★ ★ ★

Leave is given, and leave is all too often taken away when the world's affairs beckon. Focal House—the HQ building of 6D2 Britain—was on the line early. After virtually no sleep because of the police—and following upon a bachelor party earlier that night with a former 6D2 man in Grantham—I didn't fancy driving all the way to London, so Felicity Mandrake drove the Scimitar while I filled her in on the night's events.

'Why,' she asked as she headed out of Oundle towards the A1, 'the police phone summons? Come to that, why Focal House?'

I said, 'I'm not sure about FH. The police... they found a brand mark. Burned in with a red-hot branding iron.'

'On the body?'

'Yes. Beneath the right breast. Before or after death, I don't know. CORPSE, in capital letters.'

She gave a hard laugh, no humour. 'Appropriate!'

'You could say so. She was far gone,' I added. 'It was only just visible. I missed it, first time round.' I paused. 'The other body was a lot fresher.'

She turned and stared. '*Another* body?'

'Yes. With CORPSE, just below the right nipple. Stabbed in four places. A man this time, in a car parked in the town.'

'What does it mean—CORPSE?'

I shrugged. 'I've no idea at all, Felicity.'

'I don't suppose it means anything—in our sense. Does it?'

I said, 'I don't know, but it could be why FH wants me. We'll know about that soon.'

Felicity frowned, and shifted gear as she came up behind a mobile haystack blocking the road, which was narrow. I liked Miss Mandrake when she frowned—liked her at any time, but somehow the furrowed brow added something, I don't know why. I hadn't met her until she'd been assigned to me on my last job —assigned as my field assistant, notionally secretary, although she in fact outranked me in the 6D2 hierarchy, which was something she was apt to dwell upon at times. Since getting back from the Chinese mainland, though we hadn't worked together again, she'd become a habit in off-duty hours. Max, Executive Head of 6D2 Britain, hadn't commented; but his general sourness and his forebearing looks indicated that he knew, all right. Miss Mandrake spurted in third past the farm vehicle and raced up the road, swinging back in just before a corner; I didn't really like her driving, but never mind... She asked, 'Had the police any ideas?'

'None as yet,' I said. Last night could have

been time wasted; on the other hand I had a feeling it wouldn't rest there, and not just because I'd been ordered in to FH on the heels of it. It was the whole set-up and above all that curious brand. CORPSE in faded, decaying royal purple beneath the breast of a dead body is not commonplace. The fact of death does not normally require the literary support of a branded statement. We live in a world of silly initials: NATO, ASLEF, COMAIRPAC, NUPE...it all started after the last war, of course, probably as a direct result of SWALK. In my book, CORPSE had to mean something, and something nasty at that.

★ ★ ★ ★

Miss Mandrake took the A1 at a hurtle and then the London traffic reined her in and we entered the City sedately and drove into the underground car park at Focal House, forty-two storeys below the helicopter landing pad on the reinforced roof. We were met by a uniformed commissionaire, one Horridge, late Company Sergeant-Major in the Black Watch. He was an elderly man with a wooden leg acquired in Aden when attached to the Argyll and Sutherland at Crater.

'Good morning, sir and madam.' Horridge

saluted, real parade-ground smart. He still respected my naval commission, ex though I might be. 'You're wanted in the suite, sir,' he said, the reference being to Max—who was known just as Max throughout 6D2, it not being his real name of course, but CSM Horridge had told me once that it went against the military grain to refer to a CO by a mere Christian name, so he'd found his own way round that one. 'Word's just come down.'

I asked irritably, 'How did he know I'd got here?'

Horridge released a faint smile. 'The suite, sir, has long ears.'

'Plus built-in radar,' I said. 'He'll have noted Miss Mandrake breaking the speed limit all the way down the A1.'

Horridge coughed; he didn't approve of officers criticising one another in front of NCOs. He asked formally, 'Shall I inform the suite you're on your way up, sir?' He departed from attention for long enough to tweak at the ends of his moustache.

Gravely I said, 'If you please, Horridge,' and he marched away to his official kiosk where he used the internal telephone. Miss Mandrake and I went into the network of corridors and staircases, lifts and offices that formed the vast warren of Focal House. I murmured the

13

obvious to Miss Mandrake: the nick at Peterborough had been in touch with Max, so maybe
something else had emerged. We went for a lift,
walking past the underground armoury, the
Physical Fitness Room known as the tough-up
chamber, the sound-proofed firing range, the
series of cell-like apartments, all padded, where
the field men were put through the interroga-
tion-accustoming routines in front of blinding
lights. The lift hoisted us fast past the various
floors where you could find the many sections
that made up the Britain organisation: Foreign
Office Liaison, Police Liaison, CIA Liaison,
FBI, Interpol...you name it, we had a liaison
officer plus team. We were big, yet we were
strictly unofficial, non-Establishment, independent of but backed by the various Western
governments, and all that gave us immense
freedom in operation. No accounting to parliament or the People—that was 6D2 Britain, and
the same went for 6D2 North America et cetera
et cetera. And here in Britain, God was called
Max and sat haloed upon a swivel throne of expensive tulipwood padded with plush velvet.
He was well protected by five secretaries, the
chief of whom was named, inaptly, Mrs Dodge
—the one thing you couldn't do was to dodge
her. But this morning she was in an ushering
mood.

14

'Good morning, Commander Shaw, Max will see you right away.' She bustled to her intercom, spoke briefly to Max, then went to his door and swung it open and in I went, Miss Mandrake staying behind to take tea with Mrs Dodge unless and until sent for; she was really not germane to the Peterborough business but if there were to be developments I intended to ask for her services on personal attachment.

'Ah, Shaw.' Max didn't get to his feet: his stomach was a heavy one and he tended to be ashamed of it. He kept it behind the desk, which was of tulipwood like the chair and was estimated to have cost at least fifty thousand pounds.

I asked, 'Has Peterborough been in touch direct?'

'Yes,' he said. 'Reason—and the reason why you're here—is that the male body was a VIP. Or at any rate, a pretty high civil servant. More about that soon.' He fixed me with a look. 'I don't in fact have built-in radar,' he said, from which I knew he'd had his bug pressed, 'so perhaps you'll tell me what you've been up to with Miss Mandrake?'

I glared. 'Do you really want to know?' I asked.

'No.' He waved a hand. 'Sit down and fill

me in, leave nothing out. About the bodies.'

'If the police—'

'You heard what I said. I want your own words.'

I did as bid. Max listened closely, his piercing eyes on me all the time, not even a blink so far as I was aware. When I'd finished he sat back in his chair and stared at me over the tips of his interlaced fingers. He said, 'CORPSE. H'm.'

'Do we know what it means?' I asked.

'No. And I gather the police have no views. Or clues either.'

'Correct. It's difficult to see what the girl would have looked like in life, of course, and up to the time I left the station after my second visit they hadn't tied her in with any of their own missing persons. Or the man. It's yet to be checked nationwide,' I added. 'The man—'

'Quite. And is being. I've been on to the Yard personally. All fingers out in regard to the girl.'

I raised my eyebrows. 'Is she that big?'

'How should I know—yet?' Max brought out a cigar case. He didn't offer it to me, but lit up himself; the lighter was gold. He said over the smoke, 'There are pointers that must be taken seriously.'

'Where do they point?' I asked.

Max shrugged. He said, 'I'll take the girl first. Peterborough police gave me their guess at what happened in her case—I'll come back to that in a moment. Forensic had finished their autopsy—death took place a matter of weeks ago, they can't be very specific but suggest three weeks. Cause clear enough: gunshot. The murder weapon—they found a bullet lodged in the spine—fired an A.22 cartridge, the standard small-bore target round. Many different types of gun could be involved as you'll be aware, but the weapons experts believe this was fired from an automatic rifle made by Hammerli of Switzerland. Nothing new about it—'

'I'm familiar with it,' I interrupted.

'What do you know about it?'

I said, 'Weight forty ounces—'

'We've gone metric.'

'I haven't,' I said, 'but if you insist, 1,134 grammes, eighteen inches—forty-five centimetres—in length.'

'Anything else?'

'Yes,' I said, as it came to me all of a sudden. 'A whopping great grip. When used criminally, it's been strictly for assassination only. But if that's what you're getting at, then I don't see why. Murder's murder, and just because—'

Max interrupted. 'I'm not necessarily getting

at anything, Shaw, but it has made me think, and what I think is this: the particular weapon used is *not* the sort any ordinary professional criminal would be likely to use, nor would a jealous boy-friend, nor would the common or garden amateur mugger. Added to which forensic is positive she hadn't been killed on the building site. This does not look like any chance killing by a would-be rapist on the loose, according to Peterborough CID. Now here's their guess: during the day before, deliveries of rubble are known to have been made by contractors who are probably being questioned at this moment. In recent months, recent *weeks*, a number of decayed properties have been demolished in Peterborough. The police view is that the unknown girl could have been killed in one of these properties, the body was left, the bulldozers moved in, and she was carted off in the rubble.'

'And just tipped?'

Max nodded. 'Just tipped, Shaw, and almost certainly a matter of hours before you spotted her. It may be odd she wasn't found sooner, but men delivering rubble to building sites are not customarily on the watch for bodies. And the rubble could have shifted on its own after work had packed up for the day.'

I said, 'Yes, it holds together as a theory,

all right. But I find nothing to suggest it's our job rather than an ordinary police one—except for CORPSE, that is, and we could be reading too much into that.'

Max shook his head. 'I don't like the sound of CORPSE, Shaw. Let us now come to the male body.' He leaned forward, stabbing a finger at me. 'I have an identification—it came in only just before you got here, made from the tailor's labels in the suit—Savile Row, as you may have seen for yourself. His name was Chartner. He was forty-nine years of age...and he was a Deputy Secretary at the Department of Industry who'd been assigned to an investigation on a political level of a dispute affecting the Adger-Craby chemical complex at Corby.' Corby was in Northamptonshire, not so far from Peterborough. 'The car, by the way, was not Chartner's—a check's been made with Swansea's wretched computer. I regard it as an accolade that it was made to work fast.'

* * * *

It was to be, in Max's words, what the police call a long slog. Already Max had been in touch with Whitehall's mandarins and 6D2 had been presented with the job. There would be a clamp on the press. There would be liaison with the

19

police, but we'd been asked to take the responsibility, largely because of Max's own expressed anxieties as to the meaning of CORPSE. Like me, his mind had flown to all those silly sets of initials, the laborious shuffling of words to make up something that stuck in the mind. No one would ever have heard of NATSOPA if it hadn't juggled itself, though the AUEW seems to get away with it somehow. Anyway, CORPSE had begun to have overtones of a political involvement and a nasty one, and I, aided at my request by Miss Mandrake, was to root it out and see what made it grow. A long slog, yes—many people to talk to, all manner of clues to follow up if and when they emerged, basically of course a police job and one that failed to engage my enthusiasm. But naturally at that stage I had no idea how far this thing had spread already, had no conception of what was involved, of what was to be dredged up from below the tip of the iceberg that had shown in Peterborough, of clandestine but world-wide movements taking place even then against the security of Britain and the continuance of life for so many millions of British people, of the insidious threat about to move in from somewhere that could be anywhere between the coasts of far Japan to the Statue of Liberty off Manhattan by way of the Middle

East, from the frozen waste of the South Polar icecap up to the waters of the Denmark Strait between Greenland and Iceland... CORPSE had gathered way unseen, silent behind the cloak of brilliant security.

I collected Miss Mandrake from Mrs Dodge. The two of them had been nattering away like grannies over their knitting, and Mrs Dodge remarked to me that Miss Mandrake looked bonny, with a healthy colour in her cheeks. 'It must be the air out of London,' she said rather wistfully, and I agreed that indeed it must, though I knew of other things that gave Miss Mandrake that bonny look. We left Mrs Dodge to supervise her secretarial team and went down again in the lift. I gave Felicity the gist of my interview with Max and told her she was back on my personal staff, taking demotion to the field once again. She seemed happy enough; I believe I'd become a habit too.

'Where do we start?' she asked.

I said I hadn't the faintest idea but something would come to me. In the meantime I needed some clean shirts and so on, and so we drove to my flat.

CHAPTER 2

Miss Mandrake produced a late breakfast efficiently and then I took a nap, which refreshed me. I'd just woken up when FH came on the closed telephone line with information that the owner of the car, the one in which the second body had been found, had been contacted by Peterborough police: a food chain's rep who had been blotto after a night out in Stamford and had emerged to find his car had been nicked. A man on whom the police had nothing. All the same, since I intended visiting the Midlands again after contacting the Department of Industry, which I would do that afternoon, I asked FH to have the police keep the car owner available—just in case. He might have something to yield up, something that might click with me though it might pass over the police.

I gave Felicity lunch at a small Greek restaurant near my flat, then I took a taxi to the Department of Industry in Victoria Street; a phone call just before lunch had got me an appointment with one Fishlock, the late Chart-

22

ner's boss. Fishlock was very prim, very precise, with gold-rimmed spectacles and a dark suit. He also had a somewhat forbidding manner. He said crisply, 'I have the facts already, of course. Your HQ was in touch as soon as this most unfortunate affair came to light. What can I do for you?'

I said, 'A run-down on what Mr Chartner was to do at Corby.'

'It's classified, you know.' It sounded stupid and was, but we're a furtive lot these days.

'Sure,' I said sardonically. 'So am I.'

He looked very slightly disconcerted. 'Yes, yes, I understand.' There was a pause. 'Well, it's quite straightforward really. A question of threatened industrial action over redundancies. Chartner went down to keep a finger on the pulse. We deplore strikes, of course, we do strive to keep management and unions together on these matters, to keep the dialogue going—'

'Naturally,' I broke in, stemming the Civil Service flow of meaningless verbiage right from the start. 'Anything political involved, do you know?'

Fishlock smirked: how brainless could the sleuths get. 'My dear Commander Shaw, is not politics always involved in industrial disputes today? It's not just pay and conditions any more, is it?'

I said, 'You know what I mean, I think, Mr Fishlock.'

He looked down at his blotter. 'Well, yes. Yes, I do. Extremists. On this occasion I don't believe so. It's purely the redundancies...the work force seeking to protect itself. That's natural, and no one realises that more than we do. Equally naturally, their representatives—the shop stewards, you know—stand up for them.'

'But somebody killed Chartner.'

Fishlock sucked in breath, sharply. 'Surely there's no connection?'

'I don't know,' I said. 'I'm trying to find out. Had Chartner any political associations?'

'Certainly not. We don't, in the Civil Service —that is, we don't *militate* about it. I happen to know he'd been a lifelong conservative voter.'

I nodded. 'Enemies?'

'Not to the extent of murder! No *enemies* that I know of—no. He didn't get on with every-body, but who does?'

'Who indeed?' I murmured, then asked, 'How long had he been in the Peterborough area, Mr Fishlock?'

'He went up the day before...the day before he was found. He'd not actually been over to the Adger-Craby complex, in fact I imagine he'd done little beyond settling into his hotel, which was the Great Northern...'

I let Fishlock talk on for a while in case something emerged, but he got me bogged down in Whitehallese and circumlocution and finally I cut in with a glance at my watch and a request for a breakdown of Chartner's career from start to finish. He sent me along to Establishment Senior Staff Management Division, where I browsed through Chartner's confidential file. It was ordinary enough: born 4 September 1931 in Hounslow, educated at a preparatory school and Haileybury, then Cambridge—Emmanuel—1949 to 1952. He'd taken a BA degree in Modern History and had subsequently entered the administrative grade of the Civil Service via the War Office. He had held later appointments in the Ministry of Defence before being seconded to Industry. Very ordinary indeed. A conscientious civil servant, married with two children, no blemishes on his character. There being nothing outstanding about him, he had probably—I read between the lines—reached the zenith of his career. A conscientious plodder, with patriotic and Tory parents: he'd been hopefully named Stanley Baldwin Chartner. All in all, he seemed somewhat too cosy to merit murder by CORPSE. Whatever CORPSE might be...

★ ★ ★ ★

Late that afternoon we headed north into the Midlands again, Felicity and I. I drove up the A1 in blinding rain, a real cloudburst that almost had me aquaplaning at times. I turned off on to the A15 for Peterborough and in due time squelched to a stop at the nick. Nothing fresh; still no line on the dead girl. The nation-wide missing persons check hadn't yet produced a thing. There was, it seemed, no one to claim her. I was given the food chain rep's address at a Stamford hotel, and we got carborne again. I found the rep in the bar with a woman, and I got rid of the woman tactfully by getting Felicity to buy her a drink, but it was no use: the rep was drunk again and in a belligerent mood because his car upholstery had been desecrated with Chartner's blood and there was a dent in the wing and anyway he'd lost the use of it because the effing fuzz were hanging on to it and it was all my effing fault. No help there: he was just a boozy bum bacon flogger who'd had his car nicked in the interests of murder and that was all. His effing was better employed elsewhere, so I released him to his woman after extracting the one piece of hard information that he seemed capable of, and that

26

was that his effing car had been effing nicked while he'd gone into a public convenience for a pee. He refused to admit, since it was a firm's car, that he'd left the keys in the ignition, but I knew damn well he had. The theft had taken place at approximately three p.m the day before the body had been found in Peterborough. I reminded him that he'd told the police he hadn't discovered his loss until the next morning, and that shook him for a moment. He told me to eff off and I made the assumption that at the actual time of loss he'd been breathalysable and hadn't wished to mention it to the police. Even boneheads have a sense of self-protection when their livelihoods are at stake, and, I say again, it was the firm's effing car anyway...

I rejoined Felicity and reported.

'Where now?' she asked.

I said, 'It's getting late, but I'm going to snoop around the Adger-Craby works—outside, just a familiarising look-see. After that, Oundle.'

'Talbot House?'

I nodded. She made a sound of pleasure. We headed out of Peterborough for Corby. Wet roads and the daylight going with the overcast ...I put on my headlights and they beamed out over hedges and fields and trees, raising the occasional luminous sparkle from cows' eyes. I took a wrong turn somewhere and after a while found I was heading towards Oundle. Getting back on track, we passed through some delightful villages, with clustered cottages built in what looked like Cotswold stone, and nice old churches. Very rural, surprisingly so when we were on the fringe of the industrial Midlands...and suddenly it changed. Way ahead we picked up the lights of the Adger-Craby chemical plant and as we came up to the complex we left country scenes behind us for the gates of hell. Corby was colossal, it was hard black beneath brilliant light, it was smelly, it was all clang from what was left of the British Steel Corporation's presence and there was also a lot of closed-down dereliction. Once, it had been all steel and iron: I dare say it had had a City Slagheap instead of a City Centre. It was Port Talbot plus, or had been. I felt much sympathy for all those areas where the steel plants had shut down totally, drawing fires for the last act. At the same time I was glad I was not a steel worker forced to live in a steel town.

I drove around for a while, just looking, pausing when the road ran past entry gates to the once-busy steel works, peering within through binoculars, glimpsing the environs of job-loss, the sort of thing, I supposed, that might be about to hit Adger-Craby. There was some activity; steam and smoke rose like a pall, and there was the clang, clang too; the steam and smoke was like a heavy mist at times, as it was held down by the pouring rain. There was a sulphurous sort of stench; my heart bled for Northamptonshire and its quiet villages and lanes and woody fields. It could well be glad to see the withdrawal of British Steel. And what about Adger-Craby? Redundancies there, too, and some who liked Corby as it was, those who didn't want to be made redundant and who'd been innocently, or maybe not innocently, responsible for bringing Chartner up here to be stabbed to death. *Was* there a connection? Had someone else a vested interest in ensuring that Chartner brought about no reconciliation, someone who was out for industrial trouble that would shut all the activity down? Socialist Workers Party, National Front, Trotskyites from somewhere beyond Britain?

'Well?' Felicity asked. 'Are we getting places, or not?'

'Not,' I decided. I'd come because it's always been my policy to get to know the geography, feel the feel, get worked in and acclimatised. Not because I'd expected to pick up the killer at the works gate or anything like that. Tomorrow I would come again, on an official visit to the management. I said, 'Next stop Oundle, and a drink, and dinner if it's not too late. And?'

'Almost certainly yes,' Miss Mandrake said in a prim voice like Fishlock's. I got going and went fast out of desolation towards friendly countryside, back through the snug little villages of rural England. About fifteen minutes after leaving Corby behind I picked up something astern that shouldn't have been. Just a blur in my mirror really, but a blur that stuck and was becoming faintly visible as the rain stopped and the night lightened just a little. I told Felicity to look behind, and she turned in her seat.

'Nothing there.'

'Sure? Keep looking.'

She did; a few minutes later we came into another village and as I took a right-hand bend out of it again, she said suddenly, 'I've seen it, a car without lights.'

'Right,' I said, 'We have a tail.'

'So we shake it off?'

'No. Sometime we have to make contact with someone. The sooner the better. We haven't spotted it.'

'Okay,' she said, and turned round and settled back in her seat. I could feel the tension in her: there is a nasty feeling in a tail and you never quite get used to it. I kept my speed steady and soon after that we were coming into Oundle. In my rear-view mirror I saw lights behind: my tail had no doubt switched on for Oundle and if we went further would switch off again. But we were going no farther than the war memorial in Oundle's centre, and having reached it I turned left and left again into the Talbot House Hotel's narrow yard where once the stage coaches had shed their loads. I parked up at the far end, saw no sign of our tail, and went with Felicity to check in at Reception. We carried our grips up, then rendezvoused for a drink. No one in the bar looked like a murderer. The only discord came from a public school youth with shoulder-length hair who was haranguing his long suffering and visiting parents with a statement that he wished to be a dropout rather than take A-levels. Officially dinner-time was past but the hotel laid on food all the same and afterwards we went straight up to our respective rooms. Half an hour after I had turned in, there was a tap at the door. Playing safe, I had my automatic handy when I pulled back the door catch, but, as I'd expected, it was Felicity. I took her in my arms and kissed her and we retired for the night. It was daylight when I woke, and it was the soft burr of the telephone

31

at my bedside that woke me. I glanced at my wrist-watch and it showed a few minutes after eight. I yanked the receiver off the hook, disengaged Miss Mandrake's arm, and said, 'Yes?'

A woman's voice, a nice one but full of strain, asked, 'Commander Shaw?'

I caught Felicity's sleepy eye, and I didn't answer. The voice went on, 'This is Mary Chartner—'

'Chartner!' I sat up straight.

'Yes. I came up yesterday...to see my husband. To see the—'

'Yes, all right, Mrs Chartner. I'm Shaw. I'm terribly sorry...is there something I can do?'

She said, 'There's something you ought to know, I think. Not on the telephone, you'll understand that.'

'Yes, I do. The police—'

'Not the police. I was wondering...I'm sorry to be a nuisance...would you come and see me about ten o'clock this morning?'

I temporised. 'Where?'

'I'm staying with friends near Alconbury. Tenbury House—it's on the outskirts of Barham. You take the Thrapston road from Oundle, and turn left a little before Thorpe Waterville. Thank you so much, Commander Shaw.' She rang off abruptly—too abruptly for

32

a refusal. In fact I didn't know whether I would have refused or not. I fancied she was genuine but I'm not grass green and I knew it could be a trap. On balance, though, I tended to believe she was on the level. Peterborough nick could conceivably have told her where I was staying, and I suppose she was entitled to know I had been assigned to the job. Chartner had ranked high—his relative rank in, say, the Foreign Office would have been Assistant Under-Secretary of State or thereabouts. His widow would be treated with trust and respect. Anyway, I rang Peterborough. Yes, they told me, Chartner's wife had formally identified the body and had asked to be put in touch with me, and they had given her the hotel's address and telephone number. I said they might have warned me, and they apologised. They thought a call had in fact been put through to me from the nick earlier.

I rang off.

I told Miss Mandrake that we would head out for Barham immediately after breakfast and that was what we did. After a close scrutiny of the road atlas I had the route fixed in my mind: that left turn before Thorpe Waterville would head me on to very minor roads for the village of Barham. When I took the left turn I found just how minor they were, and after I'd turned again in the hinterland they became more minor still. There wasn't much traffic but what there was had got stuck in my vicinity: I had two cars behind me, keeping close, the leading one being a powerful Volvo driven by a girl with long blonde hair. Ahead of me, blocking the whole narrow road and ambling at an infuriating pace, was a huge pantechnicon with its rear doors hooked open. It was empty but for a youth leaning back against a mattress hung against the near-side bulkhead. The youth was reading a copy of *Fiesta*. I was close enough to read the title over the top of the tailboard and to see the nude on the cover. They youth glanced up from his stuides, saw the impatience in my face, and gave me a reversed V sign. However, after a while the pantechnicon gathered some speed and more or less tore away from me. As the blonde behind crowded me impatiently and used her horn in a long blast, I put on a little speed too. After that things happened fast. The youth released the tail-board and swung himself up to the top of one of the doors, and simultaneously the pantechnicon braked hard. A man of quick reactions, I braked too and hoped fleetingly that the Volvo blonde would be as fast as me. My brake pedal went flat to the floor, no resistance at all, and I swept willy-nilly up the pantechnicon's tail-board, bounced on the flooring, and smashed forcefully into the reinforced bulkhead behind the driver's cab. My engine went, so did a lot of other things including the radiator. There was a burst of steam and boiling water. Felicity and I had been saved only by our seat belts...as I sat somewhat stunned, the daylight went: the doors had been closed. Looking sideways I stared right into the little round hole in a revolver held by the youth. He was grinning like a satisfied tom-cat. I twisted to the rear: four men and the blonde, all armed, had crowded in behind. The pantechnicon, having trapped me, had stopped for a moment, presumably to embark the posse from the Volvo and the other car behind, but was now under way again and moving fast and we were swaying about like a ship in a heavy sea.

I looked stonily at the youth. 'My brakes,' I said. 'What happened?'

'Didn't effing answer, did they?'

'That,' I snapped, 'is obvious. Why didn't they? Who tampered with them—and why didn't they fail earlier?'

He grinned on. 'Effing things got bled, didn't they, and refilled with water.' I listened aghast as he proceeded with his technical exposition: it was clever, all right, and of course it had all begun with that tail from Corby. In the brooding peace of a dark night the work had proceeded without interruption once chummy's master key had gained him entry to my car, and the use of automatic bleed nipples had meant that just the one villain had been able to eject the brake fluid and refill. On went the nipples and with one of them open chummy sat in the driving seat and pumped the footbrake, emerging now and again to fill up the master cylinder with more water and to open up the nipples on the other three wheels. Once I was on the road, gentle braking would only warm the water up and I would notice no effect whatever; but the moment I slammed the brakes on hard for an emergency, as in the case of the pantechnicon, the water reached boiling point, and wham. Total brake failure, and me in the van. The explanation given, the youth was joined by another man, a man wearing dark glasses and a lot of hair under one of those grotesque blue fake nautical caps with peaks. He, too, thrust a revolver at my face and told Felicity and me to sit tight, keep quiet, and all would come clear in due course. He motioned the youth away and as he did so the blonde came up on the near side of my imprisoned car and out came yet another gun, this time a small handbag automatic, a prewar Sauer & Sohn

6.35 mm. This covered Felicity, I looked at the man in the funny cap and said, 'I presume we're not going to call on Mrs Chartner after all?'

He grinned: his teeth were good and white. 'Correct, Commander Shaw.'

'And she doesn't exist—up here, that is.' I kept my eyes on him. 'How did you fool the police?'

'They fooled themselves. Mrs Chartner's up here, all right, and she wanted to see you. That was genuine.'

A tap on the hotel's line, I thought, and said so. The answer was no, and if I was thinking—which I was—that my non-arrival at Tenbury House would be notified to the police at Peterborough, I had better forget it. The woman who had called me was not Mary Chartner, she was the blonde currently holdling her automatic where it would blow Miss Mandrake's brains out. Her looks belied her voice. Mary Chartner had intended calling in person at my hotel.

'How did you know all that?' I asked.

'Use your brain,' the man said, and laughed. I suppose it was really quite simple: the real Mrs Chartner would have been taken either to the interview room at the nick, or, more probably in view of her husband's status in life, to the Chief Superintendent's room. It would

37

be tricky, but not impossible, for phoney workmen or such to place bugs in both rooms, and the ordinary police forces don't often think in terms of bugged nicks. Nevertheless, I was wrong. The man, who seemed to be a mind reader, laughed once again and said, 'You can forget bugs too.'

'Then what—'

The revolver moved a trifle closer. 'You'll find out. For now, wrap up.'

I sat silent, thinking and getting nowhere. There was, of course, no possibility of a breakout. There were too many guns...and, as if once again reading minds, the man with the blue cap told me to fetch out my own gun and Felicity's and pass them through the window. If I did not, the end would come for Miss Mandrake. We complied, and the guns were passed back to the other three men in the rear by the doors. The pantechnicon drove on, accompanied no doubt by the Volvo and the car that had been behind it; the Volvo would be under the control of another driver in place of the blonde. It was easy to assess the moment when we joined the Al: the traffic sounds and the increased speed gave the clue. And the route was south; so much had been physically transmitted to me by the direction of swing and the pause in what was obviously the central reservation. It was equally easy to assess when we began to enter the big city, which for my money was London. But from then on, of course, I was lost. When at last the pantechnicon stopped and the engine was switched off, I had no idea where we might be. And when the rear doors were swung open and we were pushed astern to roll powerless back down the lowered tail-board, I was none the wiser. The surroundings were anonymous and enclosed—a big warehouse with its doors shut and a lingering smell of, I fancy, baled wool, though there were in fact no wares of any description in sight.

'Out,' the blue-capped man said, and we climbed out into a ring of guns. There were no other vehicles; the Volvo and the second car had evidently peeled off somewhere en route. My car, once we were out, was rolled away to the far end of the warehouse and I watched it disappear down a ramp. Whatever happened to Miss Mandrake and me, I didn't expect to see the Scimitar again, but then, like the bacon salesman's, it was the effing firm's car and no skin off my bank balance or insurance. Gun-surrounded, Miss Mandrake and I were led away towards the side of the warehouse, through a doorway, along a passage, down a flight of greasy stone steps to be halted by a large trap door set into concrete. One of the escort pushed past me and operated some mechanism and the door swung up silently on a counter-balancing weight.

We were ushered down a vertical steel ladder like a ship's. We went into a stench of sewers and another passage, one that dripped water: maybe we were not so far off the river, or maybe the surroundings really were leaky sewers. The man who had worked the trap door went ahead again and reached up and did something to the left-hand wall of the passage, and amazingly a section of it lifted, as silently as the trap door, into the overhead regions to emit blackness. As we came abeam the blackness was replaced by bright electric light and we entered yet another passage with a door at the end. This door was opened and the whole party went through. It was a very ordinary and sparsely furnished room we entered—it stank like a drain, but it was ordinary otherwise—and scarcely a fitting backdrop for the extraordinary cloaked and hooded apparition that sat behind a cheap deal desk: an enormous figure that, had its wrapping been of white, could have passed for a ghost. But the covering, hood and all, was of a royal purple hue. Two slits in the hood showed eyes, and these seemed to flicker from side to side in the bright light while the rest of the purple mountain remained quite still. It was somewhat like, I suppose, being brought before Cardinal Wolsey with his biretta pulled down over his face.

Pressure of gunmetal urged us towards this seated figure, and it spoke. The voice was deep and I fancied I could detect a trace of a German accent. The English was otherwise flawless, though I admit the opening statement gave little scope for a full judgment.

The figure said, 'I am CORPSE.'

'Yet you speak, therefore you live.'

The hood moved slightly. 'We shall dispense with jokes, Commander Shaw. The time for that is past, as your country will discover.'

I apologised.

'I am the Chairman of the Committee of Responsible Persons for Selective Eradication... CORPSE.'

'Yes, I see,' I said.

'You do not, and you should not be flippant. CORPSE has remained unknown until now. Whilst unknown, it has grown large and powerful. The time has come for CORPSE to be known to the world. What it means to do cannot be done secretly, as you will soon understand, and it would be better that it were not done at all. If your government can be made to understand, to appreciate the power of

41

CORPSE, Commander Shaw, then it will be well for Britain.'

A hand appeared, very white against the all-over purple, and made a gesture. The light changed: it went purple, like the garment. It was really quite dramatic. The hooded figure, so large, weirdly emanating so much power, seemed to become one with the atmosphere, with the underground room itself. Somehow —as, of course, was intended—the change of lighting leant weight to the words that emerged from behind the hood. In spite of that muffling hood the voice seemed to boom out at me, to surround me as though in stereo. It was a grotesque situation, and the purport of the figure's message, the message of CORPSE, was no less grotesque; but I had no doubt of the sincerity, the determination behind the doomful words, nor did I doubt the ability of CORPSE to put their threat into terrible effect.

* * * *

No harm came to us; we were treated with consideration and politeness, for we were to be the messengers of CORPSE, the heralds who were to bring the truth home to Whitehall and the British people. Naturally, CORPSE knew all about 6D2, even had a fairly comprehensive knowledge of Focal House; and they had respect for our organisation as being more effective and more readily listened to than the official organs of government: no red tape, no political reputations to worry about, no need to woo the voters. No bullshit. And they knew me: CORPSE had my career taped from the word go till the moment I was brought before the Chairman. CORPSE were good at their horrible work. Miss Mandrake and I spent upwards of an hour listening to the boss, then we were led away, back along the same underground route for a while, then along a different track that also ended in the warehouse but on its other side. The pantechnicon had gone, and a plain mid-blue van awaited us. Still under the guns of three men, we were embarked and we were driven around the streets of London for one hour and fifteen minutes approximately, twisting and turning just to make sure that any sense of direction I might have, which I hadn't, was well and truly fouled up. Then we stopped, the guns were kept out of sight, and we were told to step down. I had no idea even then where we were, but after walking a while after the van had moved away into the traffic, various signs told me we were in the borough of Hackney.

'Now what?' Miss Mandrake asked. She was

moving in a dream, as though she couldn't bring herself to believe that CORPSE was real and was embodied.

I said, 'The nearest tube, and FH.'

Outside the tube station, when we found one, was a news stand and the early editions of the evenings were already on sale. Catching sight of a headline, I bought the *Standard*. BODY, it read, IN LONELY FEN. Felicity and I read the report together while London milled about us, pushing and shoving and smelling of summer sweat. A body, so far no name released by the police, had been found dumped in fen country between Ramsey and Chatteris in north Cambridgeshire, near Forty Feet Bridge. It had been a woman in her forties and she had been run over by something heavy: face unrecognisable. And below the right breast had been branded the single word CORPSE, which was a piece of information that certainly shouldn't have reached the press. Murder most foul, and doubtless, I felt, preceded by a little persuasion to talk...I made a guess as to the body's identity that later proved accurate and decided I knew, now, how the man in the nautical cap had got his detailed information re the movements and wishes of Mary Chartner.

CHAPTER 3

Max, of course, was livid: certain government departments had failed him. The directives to the press hadn't gone out on time; no blame attached to the *Standard*, but Max was going to have some Whitehall official's guts for garters. He said as much in my presence, down the telephone to Whitehall. He had not wanted CORPSE to reach print, and I was right with him. Neither Max nor I were believers in too much openness; it doesn't help efficiency in tracking down the villains, and in the long run it doesn't help the public either. They're better left to suck their lollies, distribute their litter and watch American domestic-situation funnies on the telly with their heads buried in the soporific sands of technicolor...what the heart doesn't grieve over, the professionals can get on with and solve.

It was Max who gave me the confirmation of the latest victim's identity: it was indeed Chartner's wife, or widow. 'Nothing else known,' he said briefly. 'Can you help?'

'Not very much,' I said. 'I've met the man

who must have authorised the killing, but—'

'For God's sake, that's—'

'But I don't know where he is, or rather I couldn't ever hope to find the hide-out again except by the sheerest chance. In the meantime, I have a lot to report and it can all be said to impinge on Mrs Chartner.'

He nodded. 'Go ahead, then.'

I did. I filled him in, in detail. I'd met CORPSE in person, I said, and CORPSE was to be taken deadly seriously. Deadly was the operative word.

'How deadly, why, and to whom?'

I said, 'Well now, I'm only just taking in the implications myself. It's big...to begin with, CORPSE is the enemy of WUSWIPP. At this stage WUSWIPP is not in fact involved, though personally I believe they could come in against CORPSE if *we* are not seen to be hitting back effectively. On the other hand, CORPSE is out to strike hard if we don't play along with *them*. We're between two stools— or we could become so.' I was aware of Max reflecting on WUSWIPP, which is the World Union of Socialist Scientific Workers for International Progress in Peace, the progress and peace part being sheer bull. I'd personally had far too much war with them to be taken in by that, and the same went for Max. I told him

46

what CORPSE stood for, adding that although 'selective eradication' could perhaps be a term applicable to Chartner, and possibly, in developing circumstances, to his wife, the unidentified girl in Peterborough looked, on the face of it, like a chance shot of non-selection albeit for some purpose so far unknown. Max said peevishly that that depended on her identity. Then I came to what CORPSE meant to do, and put in a few words it sounded as dead simple as I knew, in fact, it could be.

'Nuclear waste,' I said. 'The stuff that's already going to the storage ponds at Windscale for reprocessing eventually, even though they've not yet started building the main plant.'

Max looked shaken. 'Be more precise,' he said.

'Right, I will be. A shipload—many shiploads in fact—sailed into British ports, with nuclear devices set ready to be triggered by remote control.' I added bleakly as Max stared back at me, 'The area of actual destruction would be very great indeed, the area of nuclear pollution from widely scattered waste material would be even greater and would be long lasting.'

'I don't doubt it.' Max looked as though he'd aged ten years. I could follow his thoughts: he was seeing Windscale and sniffing the pervading odour of ammonia that hung over the denizens in their white coats with radiation-detection badges at the lapels, their trousers tucked into their socks like clipless cyclists, the toecaps of their special footwear painted red. Other workers swathed in sheets of PVC with film detectors and doseometers like pens of shining silver. Max spoke again: 'I'll tell you something, Shaw: *it can be done*. Make no mistake about that.' He thumped his desk, savagely, with a balled fist. 'It's always been my nightmare...that something like this would be threatened before I was turned out to grass! We're paying for past shortsightedness...back in '76 the Atomic Energy Authority decided it would be too bloody expensive and time consuming to develop techniques so that the nuclear reactors could burn up their own waste. Now we're faced with the result! God in heaven, don't we ever learn?'

A rhetorical question. I asked, 'Do you want to know why all this is to take place?'

Max glared. 'Tell me.'

'All right,' I said, and I put it baldly and without emotion. 'A take-over of Britain. Dissolution of parliament, of the whole democratic system. Disarming of the forces, and control of the police to be handed over... and all that goes with all of that. The demand will be for total surrender.'

'God in heaven,' Max said again, and sat staring blankly as though he'd suddenly seen Armageddon. He didn't say any more. Things went racing through my mind. You can't hold up the shipping of a country like Britain, you can't keep every incoming bottom waiting outside while a check is made, the more so when you haven't a clue when the lethal cargo will arrive, nor where, nor where from. Daily a hell of a lot of shipping enters Britain's ports—Southampton, Tilbury and the Thames, the Clyde, Liverpool, the Bristol Channel, the Tyne, the Humber, the Forth and all the smaller ports around a vast coastline from Shoreham by way of Aberdeen to Falmouth. All manner of cargoes from all the world. Imports can't be clogged up, nor exports delayed until inward cargoes are cleared. Naturally the anticipated authorised shiploads of nuclear waste for the temporary storage ponds at Windscale could be checked for strange devices and their crews third degreed. Or better—the first thing to do might be to halt all such known cargoes and prohibit entry until we had dealt with CORPSE. But in my view, and this I put to Max, CORPSE would *not* be sending in their destruction via the authorised cargoes for Windscale. It would come unheralded, in any sort of vessel, the sealed containers loaded anonymously with mundane cargo-parcels as per manifest. From now on out, all and any cargo entering Britain could contain the deadly load and must be suspect.

Max said, 'I'm not ruling out the big loads for Windscale, Shaw. All right, we can prohibit them, refuse entry, and I shall suggest this. What do we do if they enter notwithstanding? Do we send a bobby? Or do we send in frigates to blow the vessels up once they're in the rivers, and do CORPSE'S work for them?'

'Stymied,' I said. 'We can't win. On the face of it anyway, we're left with just the one alternative: comply with the bloody demands of CORPSE.'

'Balls,' Max said briefly. 'Tell me how they mean to go about taking us over, will you?'

I said, 'That, I'll do.' I took a deep breath. 'They have a highly-trained corps of...*gauleiters* I suppose you could call them. People well versed in the theory of government by force and decree. Probably some with practical experience under the colonels in Greece, and under the rightist regime in Chile. A dictatorship, foisted on the country to take over the vacuum, backed by a well-equipped military force that's been in secret training for a number of past years. Some will be domestic, most will come from outside.'

'Where?'

'I don't know,' I said. 'CORPSE was not communicative, just dictatorial. The world's their oyster.'

Max pointed a finger at me. 'You'd better open up that CORPSE oyster, Shaw, and double quick. That's the other alternative, isn't it? This is a backlash of the Right—and it must be broken before it erupts. Before the boil festers to a head.' He blew out his cheeks. 'At the same time, we don't want to over-react—'

'Can one over-react?'

'Yes,' Max snapped. 'One can! Look at it rationally, for God's sake.' He leaned forward, heavy and pugnacious. 'Agreed CORPSE *can* do what they say if they mean to go ahead, but this country—a democracy for centuries—do you really think it's going to give in to the imposition by outside force of a damn dictatorship?'

'The threat's a big one,' I said. 'That can weigh.'

'Nonsense. We're not that pusillanimous.'

'A philosophy.' I pointed out, 'that may appeal more to dwellers inland than on the coasts, where many of us do in fact dwell.' I added, 'In any case, the real point is this: CORPSE genuinely believe it *is* possible, and the threat's for real, never mind the chances of the result.

51

They have it all worked out down to the last detail—what they mean to do when they take over, that is. You don't go to all that trouble over many years if you're not prepared to take the first step that can put you where you want to be.'

I filled Max in further.

★ ★ ★ ★

By the time I left Focal House the wheels were being oiled anti-CORPSE-wise. Max had the ear of government and he called Downing Street direct. The Prime Minister was sceptical, naturally enough: as Max had said, England had been a democracy a long, long time and neither its ministers nor its people were orientated towards anything else. Every now and again the twin bogeys of communism and fascism loomed, but they always vanished like summer rain and left the bloom of England untarnished. Basically, they couldn't happen here. Nevertheless the warning had been passed, and the PM passed it on: Defence Ministry was alerted, so was the Yard and all Chief Constables. The various port authorities, all of them from Thurso in the north of Scotland to Falmouth in Cornwall, would be warned to be on their toes pending detailed instructions from

Whitehall. Trinity House would be brought in via their pilots; HM Customs would be extra vigilant in checking cargoes inwards. The positions at sea of all vessels known at any time to be bound for British ports would be estimated hourly. There would be consultations with the experts from Windscale and the Nuclear Inspectorate, all the brass assembling in the Home Office next morning. After that, further orders nationwide would be issued. In the meantime, the EEC governments and Washington, plus the Commonwealth governments, would be informed and asked to vet the loading of all ships leaving their countries for ports in Britain. At this stage, it was all that could be done. Fast developments were not expected; CORPSE would understand that time would be needed for decisions to be arrived at. A system of government doesn't fold its tents overnight and steal away at dawn. I made this trite remark to Miss Mandrake as we drove away from Focal House in a Mercedes that I'd signed for as a replacement vehicle—bound for Corby, where I had unfinished business.

She said, 'It's the public that's going to be the final arbiter, isn't it?'

I knew what she meant. 'Dead right,' I said. 'Once the news leaks, and it will...that's when the trouble starts.'

'Which is maybe what CORPSE are banking on?'

I nodded, braked hard behind a pantechnicon: I was becoming allergic to being behind pantechnicons. 'Could be. We'll have something like a revolution on our hands even before they come. All the extremists, both sides, making hay. In a sense, doing CORPSE'S job in advance...softening up the ground. They'll hardly need the threat, just the threat of the threat could be enough.'

She sat in silence after that, her face troubled. I sensed the way her thoughts were going, along the same lines as mine. Internally the country would face all manner of strains that would lead to a slowing down of production and a disruption of normal life: everyone would march and demonstrate, and strike, demanding this, that and the other. Striking was today's panacea: you struck because some country over which Britain had no control did something you didn't like, you struck because the police were too efficient and nabbed your mates, you struck because other trades struck and affected your pocket, you struck because you might soon be out of work. Why not strike against CORPSE? CORPSE would come to life with a great big belly-laugh and pass a vote of thanks at the next committee meeting, but at least you would have shown you didn't approve of being scattered piecemeal in a nuclear holocaust...as we came once again to the A1, I pondered on the viability of CORPSE'S plans to take over Britain. It all sounded basically crazy, but it could happen. CORPSE had the whole thing taped from A to Z, as I'd said to Max. That corps of leadership was ready and waiting, with the strongarm squads ready beside them. A number were *in situ* already, according to CORPSE. Many more were on their way in, using all conceivable methods of entry I assumed: it was difficult to watch the whole of Britain's coast-line all the time. Even the official modes of entry... Immigration would be more than ever alert at the ports and airports but it would still be child's play for determined persons to get past them. After the first attack—after the blast had happened—the tame *gauleiters* already here would most likely take over the RSGs, the Regional Seats of Government scattered about the country for use in a nuclear war. Of these, the London area had five: in Bexley, Sutton, Redbridge, Enfield and Hillingdon, the latter being beneath the new civic centre as was the Redbridge one. Naturally, they would be strongly defended but CORPSE could be presumed to have taken care of that. The defence would have been pre-softened by the panic situation.

Massive explosions in the Thames, in Liverpool, in Hull and Southampton, say, would have a pretty poor effect on morale.

★ ★ ★ ★

This time we made the Adger-Corby complex in daylight. An appointment with the brass had been fixed ahead for me. My interest lay in Chartner. Why had he been the target for the attentions of CORPSE? (I'd asked that whilst underground below the warehouse, but the question had remained unanswered.) One of the top men at Corby had known Chartner well. A personal friendship had developed as a result of business meetings. He said Chartner had been a passionate believer in democracy and had deplored the emergence in recent years of extreme groups that were gradually eroding the basis of parliamentary government. He had become almost neurotic about it, in fact, and it was because he had seen the hand of militant extremism emerging for the nth time in the Corby dispute that he had come in person to try to sort it out. My informant made the point himself that someone could have had a vested interest in ensuring that conciliation did not come about, though murder was a pretty extreme measure and could only have a short-term effect in any case.

'*Pour encourager les autres?*' I suggested. 'Mediators might get short on the ground if enough were killed.'

'I doubt the proposition, Commander.'

I didn't myself; but I let the point pass. The assembled management impressed on me the vital importance of maintaining chemical production. Adger-Craby, it seemed, produced just about everything British industry needed in chemicals to keep going at all. They hadn't been in Corby long, but they were the biggest plant in Britain including even BP; and strikes both official and unofficial were turning the Board grey. I asked, why the redundancies?

'Over-manning,' was the brief answer.

'Union inspired in the first place?'

'Yes. Now we need, really need, to shed the fat.'

'Going back on agreements?'

There was a flush. 'Certainly not. We're trying to *reach* agreement, but there's no co-operation—just strikes and walkouts. The rundown of British Steel hasn't helped.'

I could well see that. Most of British industry was in a state of morbidity and every job lost looked like one gone for ever. But those strikes: as the man went on I began to form the impression that CORPSE had already started its work and that the killer organisation could well have been the *agents provocateur* behind any amount of industrial trouble. We tend to blame the communists; that easy blame could have proved a very handy smokescreen for CORPSE. In the meantime it seemed to me that Chartner had been simply the victim of his own antiextreme obsession, a first blow by CORPSE to show Britain that it meant what it was about to say. In a sense, I was more intrigued by the girl's murder. When I left Corby I drove with Miss Mandrake to Peterborough nick and found they had just contacted FH and tried to reach me at Corby, asking me to report. An identification had been made and it was a weird one: the girl's name had been Sandra Shingler, British; but she had lived in Spain the last year or two and had acquired, on account of a liking for sherry, the sobriquet of La Ina. Here came the weird part: sherry drinker or no, she had taken an interest, and more than an interest, in a crazy offshoot of the Protestant religion operating under disadvantages in Catholic Spain—a sect that called themselves the Flood Fearers. Peterborough police, in the person of the Superintendent who was giving me the information personally, knew no more about them than this. Except to tell me that La Ina had been drummed out by the ordinary members of the sect—this being why she'd returned to Britain—because she had become the mistress of the pastor.

I grinned. 'That's what you mean by taking more than an interest?'

'Right. In case it's of use, the name of the pastor is...' The Superintendent ran a finger down the identity report. 'The Reverend, which may or may not mean anything, Clay Petersen.' He looked up. 'Does it help?'

'No,' I said. 'Nationality?'

'US citizen.'

'What else?' I asked rhetorically. I'd once heard coffins advertised, or I think they called them caskets, on US radio at 0600 hours. A glowing tribute to comfort, and it had been followed by a man who called for three radio cheers for the Lord Jesus Christ, whom he'd met in person. I was willing to believe anything of American religion. The Flood Fearers sounded akin to the Flat Earthers. I asked, 'Would you be willing to tell me how you came by this identification and the other information?'

'I was coming to that,' the police chief said. 'A phone call came in...a man's voice that said he had something to impart...a known snout, as a matter of fact, by the name of Flash—a nasty little creep but harmless. Anyway, a meeting was arranged in Kettering, a Wimpy bar. Flash turned up and gave my DS an address where we could find the dead girl's sister. Flash isn't known to the family and he's not involved beyond the fact he had kept his eyes and ears open as usual in the interest of getting a fiver from police funds...my DS went into him deep on this occasion.'

'And the sister? You found her?'

The Superintendent nodded. 'In a way she seemed relieved to talk, according to my DS. Relieved that it was over...initially she hadn't wanted to make the identification—and, of course, didn't.'

'Why not?' I asked. 'Did that emerge?'

'She refused to say,' the Superintendent answered, frowning. 'My DS didn't press it. He had orders to play it cool. Reason: before Flash's call came in, I'd had certain messages from my Chief Constable, who'd had them from London. I dare say you'll understand.'

'Sure.'

'Well, I decided in all the circumstances that you'd prefer it if I left it largely up to you to take further if you wished.'

I said with gratitude, 'Thanks. That's great.' Miss Mandrake and I left the nick with the sister's address and directions as to how to find it. I found a car park on some waste ground and walked through to a street the other side of the public library, leaving Miss Mandrake in the car. I didn't want to scare the sister from the word go by arriving like a posse. When I rang the bell it was a long while before it was answered, and I was aware I was being studied from an upstairs window. Then the door was opened on a chain and a man's voice—the husband, as I'd been told to expect—asked if I was the police again.

'Not police,' I said. 'I'm from London and my name's Shaw.' I handed my identification past the chain.

The chain came off. The man was in his middle twenties, wearing a T-shirt and jeans. 'I was told you might come,' he said diffidently. 'Want the wife, do you?'

'If I may,' I said, and he stepped aside and called 'Denise' loudly up the stairs while I walked along a narrow passage to the kitchen at the back. The husband followed me in.

'I kept telling her,' he said. He looked and sounded thoroughly dejected. 'Wasn't no use, not a bit.'

'Women,' I murmured, smiling, 'can be obstinate.'

There was a flicker of a grin; he had a decent face behind the anxiety. 'Is she going to be in trouble?'

61

'Not from me.' I turned as the wife, Denise, came in: she was a wisp of a girl, around nineteen at a-guess, with big eyes, and dead scared, and I could find no likeness to the body, though to do such would perhaps have been difficult after so long in death. I told her my name and said she had nothing to worry about, and that I was immensely sorry for the tragedy. I added, 'Try not to worry. It's not a crime, not to report a relationship.'

She was on the verge of tears as she said, 'I don't know how the coppers found out, that I don't.' I didn't give her any names; Flash's anonymity had to be respected—the Superintendent, quite unnecessarily really, had insisted on that.

I said, 'Things emerge. Peterborough's not all that big. Many people must have known, or guessed, from the press reports, surely?'

'No,' she said. Tears streamed; her husband went to her and put an arm around the thin shoulders. He answered my question:

'Sandra'd only been here two days. First time she'd been here...Denise used to live in Newcastle.'

'A long way off,' I agreed pacifically. In Newcastle they wouldn't be that interested, and of course no photographs had been published any more than the branded CORPSE had been mentioned until Chartner's wife had been found. 'I'm wondering *why* you didn't report, that's all.' Clearly, there was a reason.

'I kept telling her,' the husband said again. 'I didn't like it all along, honest I didn't. Blood's thicker'n water, whatever...'

'Whatever what?' I asked. I was wondering if there was some misplaced sense of shame, if, for instance, the late Sandra had been on the game or something up in Newcastle. People do value their reputations, and those of their families rub off. But it was very far from that when, after much patient probing and re-assurance, the truth emerged and when it did so it hit me like a bomb. Or a shipload of nuclear waste. And this was it: Sandra had got mixed up in something: they genuinely, I believe, did not know what; but it was nasty and she had been killed because of it. On arrival in Peterborough she'd said she had left Spain because 'they' were out to get her. No clues as to who 'they' might be. She had felt sort of secure in Peterborough, but the security had been more apparent than real as it turned out. The night she reached her sister's home she had been in a very bad state, nervy and crying, and she had said that her sister and brother-in-law must never admit she'd been there, or that she'd told them anything about

Spain, because if they did, then 'they' would get them too. Or anyway, one man in particular would. She had come out with the name before she'd realised, and the name was Polecat Brennan, and the name of Polecat Brennan, so called because he had a vicious nature and a foul temper, was one that came back to me from years past amid best forgotten memories of spilled blood and violent upheaval and threat to world peace and stability. Polecat Brennan, it seemed, had come from Spain in pursuit of La Ina. It was a fair bet he'd gone back to Spain again by now, that in the interval he'd done his dirty deed on the girl.

There was one thing that didn't check in my mind: Polecat Brennan had been a member of WUSWIPP, one of the strong-arm mob that largely saw to WUSWIPP's killing duties. I wondered how it came about that he'd used the CORPSE brand mark.

I left that sad little house, found a call-box and rang the nick, suggesting they put a watch on the sister and her husband, partly to see what turned up and partly for the couple's protection in case my visit had been noted. I said nothing about Polecat Brennan or about what I'd been told of the murdered girl. I hadn't promised not to, but I knew that was what that couple would have wanted. Also, I meant to get on the Brennan trail myself, untrammelled by the police. Therefore I cut the call when the questions got close. Of course, the killer didn't have to be Brennan, but those two people had managed to convince me that it had been despite the use of the brand mark. Going back to the car park, I orientated myself mentally towards Spain: I saw a connection with the Flood Fearers, however vague—or maybe not a connection exactly, but a link that could put me headed in the right direction. Sandra Shingler had been my lead-in to all this and I felt strongly that she was going to provide a lead-on for the future, especially, of course, since Polecat Brennan had entered the canvas.

It was dark by now, and some rain was falling, a miserable night. There were few cars parked, but a Dormobile with drawn curtains had come up near the Mercedes. I approached from the back of the Merc and saw the headrests of the front seat silhouetted against street lamps and hiding the outlines of Miss Mandrake's head. So I thought. When I got alongside and bent to open the door I saw she wasn't there. Gone to spend a penny most likely. I started to get behind the wheel and something took me hard on the back of the head though I hadn't heard or seen anything moving. I knew nothing more for a while and when I came round, which must have been in a matter of minutes, I was in the back of a moving vehicle, the Dormobile I'd seen on entering the car park, Miss Mandrake was sitting white-faced and bleeding on one of the seats, and beyond the curtains was a fiery glow. A man holding a gun jerked a corner of one of the curtains aside briefly and I saw the source of the fire: the Mercedes, no doubt with a petrol can upended over the cushions. The effing firm had lost another car…and I was making a habit, it seemed, of being hooked away in alien vehicles. But this time it wasn't CORPSE: as my head began to clear I recognised the man with the gun. He'd aged, but he was Polecat Brennan.

CHAPTER 4

No one spoke: questions met with a nudge from Brennan's gun, and an order to shut up. There were two other men aboard besides Brennan and the driver, and they all had automatics handy. Nothing that tallied with the Hammerli that was believed to have killed La Ina. We drove out of Peterborough heading north then east: through the windscreen I picked up the road signs for Wisbech. Flat fen country interspersed with dykes came up in the headlights: it looked unbelievably dreary and menacing beneath the drizzle. We passed through Thorney, Guyhirn, Wisbech and I guessed we were heading for King's Lynn and a boat out of the country. But we by-passed King's Lynn and headed north up the A149 alongside the Wash and all the sandburied golden treasure left behind by King John when the racing tide had swept in centuries before. Not far from the royal retreat at Sandringham we turned off left, and after driving a little farther towards the water, the Dormobile stopped. Miss Mandrake and I were told to get out, which we did, and Brennan and the other two men accompanied us. The Dormobile drove away and we walked, coming down to wide sands as we left the metalled road. The rain continued, and there was some wind that blew it into our faces. It was a depressing progress. Soon I saw a rowing boat drawn up on the sand, just clear of the sea: it was, by the look of it, high water and soon, when the stage of slack water passed, the tide would be ripping out to sea. Two men waited by the boat with wet-weather gear drawn tight all round them. Brennan went ahead and made contact, then we all joined forces, still no word said. The boat was pushed off the sand and we piled in under the guns. I was watching for the right moment and I knew Felicity would be too, but it didn't come: the guard was much too tightly kept. We sat on the centre thwart with Brennan and one man behind us, the other man in front, while the crew pulled away from the shore. They had a heavy passenger load to haul but it was not difficult as the tide began its rush for the open sea and bore us along swiftly. It was really incredible just how fast that tide moved, how quickly the whole Wash began to empty. It was not long before we were beyond its confines, past a line drawn from Gore Point to Skegness, and beginning to come up towards the Burnham Flats. Seaward of the Flats a ship was sighted, making way through the water slowly. Up in the bows of our boat one of the Brennan gang briefly showed a torch towards the ship. There was no visual response, but the vessel's silhouette changed shape as she altered course for us. The rowers carried on rowing: obviously, the sooner the transfer could be made, the safer Brennan's mob would be. They wouldn't be wanting any interference from the shore if anything untoward should be noticed— which I had to admit was unlikely if all went smoothly.

But it didn't. God was on our side.

Suddenly, the boat lurched and the way came off: for my money, we'd hit the Burnham Flats themselves or some shifting sand that had formed a bank beneath the water, extending from the Flats in the same way as the notorious Goodwins shift with every tide. Whatever it was, it upset Brennan. Literally. As I felt him cannon against my back, and as the men in front of me lurched about as well, I brought up a knee and got one of them in a tender spot. He howled with pain, and as he doubled up I took him on the point of the jaw and undoubled him again. He crashed across his mate and went overboard. Felicity came in right on cue: she leaned backwards, her body almost flat, and got her hands tight around Brennan's neck and held him. The confusion was utter; from our starboard side came a cry of sheer terror and pleading. The man who'd gone overboard had been gripped by quicksands and was being sucked down. I saw an oar being upraised in the bows and before it could come down on my head I grabbed the blade and gave it a very hard shove, and its holder lost his balance and went the same way as his mate. Meanwhile Brennan was in danger of being throttled and one of the other men was wrenching at Felicity's arms. She had a grip of steel and he wasn't getting far but he was well occupied and I brought the heavy oar down on his head and he didn't know a thing. All this time, the larger vessel, a coaster of around two thousand tons at a guess, had been lowering a boat, having prudently stood clear herself of the shallows, and this boat was now approaching. I yelled at Felicity to leave Brennan and make herself scarce in the water but to take care to remain waterborne and not touch bottom if she wished to live. She obeyed; I went over with her, going in gently and floating. We urged our bodies away from the treacherous sands, in the direction of Gore Head, while Brennan and his mate, remaining in the boat's safety, used their guns to try to shoot us out. Lead pinged and zipped round us but we were becoming more invisible in the darkness and nothing found its mark. The sound of gunfire, however, spread. Something, some unknown vessel passing north to seaward of the Wash, put on a searchlight and began sending exploratory signals by lamp.

Brennan stopped shooting, and we kept going on our backs until I put a leg down and failed to find bottom, after which we rolled over and moved faster for Gore Head. By this time the sweeping searchlight must have been spotted from the opposite shore, for we heard a power boat coming out from the direction of

Skegness. The ship that had come in to pick us up was sheering off now; I wondered if it had picked up Polecat Brennan.

* * * *

It felt good to be aboard the Skegness lifeboat. We cruised around the perimeter of the Flats, seeking Brennan. There was no sign of him. The rowing boat was there, high and dry as the tide raced on out...probably he'd been taken off in safety. He'd always had a charmed life in former days.

'The coaster,' the lifeboat coxswain said. 'We'll have the legs of her.' The ship was out to sea again now, her engines no doubt set at Full Ahead, on a northerly course.

I said, 'We leave him. With any luck he'll think I went the way of those two mates of his.'

'But surely—'

'No. It may sound crazy, but it's not. I've a shrewd idea where I'll pick him up again, and he's infinitely more valuable on the loose, believe me.' Already I had made my identity known to the lifeboatman, though I'd gone into no details as to Brennan's background and likely associations. In the meantime I was squeezing water out of myself, and Felicity's teeth were chattering. Brennan would keep, and

71

what I'd said had been the dead truth: Brennan would lead me, if not all the way, then
nicely along the line that might put me in touch
with CORPSE—even if only indirectly by way
of WUSWIPP—and that was the vital thing.
I got the lifeboat to put us ashore in Cromer,
and from there I telephoned the Coastguard station in Gorleston. From information on the
plot, they believed the pick-up vessel to be the
Camilo Ruiz, registered in Barcelona and
bound from Leith in Scotland to Almeria in
Andalusia. That fitted. Maybe the *Camilo Ruiz*
had now shifted target from Almeria to, say,
somewhere in Scandinavia—but it fitted.

★ ★ ★ ★

Focal House made all the arrangements as
to bookings and passports and next day Miss
Mandrake and I were in the Gatwick air ter-
minal. We were to travel to Malaga, and thence
by self-drive hired car to Torremolinos, as
tourists: Mr and Mrs Groves, independent of
the package tour operators, though we couldn't
help but be surrounded by their clients once
we reached the Costa del Sol.
We sat in an exclusive lounge bar overlooking
part of the runway pattern, and drank expensive drinks, sitting on our own by a window.

Felicity gave a sudden shiver. I looked at her. 'Not getting a cold, I hope?'

'No. It's just that I can't get those two men out of my mind. The quicksands.'

'Horrible,' I said. 'Down and down, till the sand fills your mouth and lungs. It could have been us. Brennan may be there yet for all we know.'

'If he is—'

'It'll take longer without him, true, but we'll pick up a lead. I've a feeling Spain holds the box of secrets, as it were...and Brennan won't be the only key to it.'

'I think we made a wrong move yesterday. If we'd taken Brennan in and put him under the grill—'

'No,' I said flatly. I finished the remains of my Scotch and took my glass and Felicity's to the bar and had them refilled. My thoughts roved gloomily over the possible future: frankly, I didn't see how I or anyone else could possibly, short of total world co-operation and just try that on the array of power blocs into which the said world was split, prevent the sailing and arrival of ships unknown with cargoes that would in all probability not appear on their manifests. I was becoming more and more convinced that the threat would not materialise by way of the official Windscale deliveries, though

73

Max, I knew, was still pressing for government action to halt all such deliveries until the situation clarified. There would be difficulties even in this since it would give rise to massive speculation and all manner of theorising in the press that would start to set the public on edge. And the counter-action was pathetic, really: Customs and Excise were fully stretched as it was, and the inward shipping would in time be queuing up from the Downs and the Bishop Rock to all ports in the British Isles. Strangulation would set in. And the extended defence— the Royal Navy—scarcely existed any more. The odd through-deck cruiser, a handful of frigates, a collection of fibreglass minehunters and whatnot, submarines, fishery protection vessels...sure, a small number of merchant vessels could be checked at sea but it would only be a drop in the ocean. Set against CORPSE, it all began to look pretty small and insignificant. I thought, as I went back with the drinks, about the incoming crowds we'd seen in the arrival area: all nationalities, all colours, all ages. Any of them could be freshly infiltrating arteries of CORPSE, all set for the off. One thing would be pretty certain: they would all head well inland! When the explosive devices blew and the death-ships fragmented to scatter the nuclear debris wholesale, many miles around the coasts would wither.

Our call came through on the wings of one of Gatwick's cultured voices and we drifted towards the departure gate. I kept an eye lifting on our flight companions. An unremarkable bunch, all heading for sun and holiday and well prepared in advance with dark glasses through which Gatwick must have been all but invisible. Shoulder bags, jeans, funny sunhats, suntan lotion, cameras, giggles from a bevy of maidens casting anticipatory eyes towards some youths who might relieve them in due course of their maidenly state...some matrons with sportily clad old husbands, flowery shirts and all...Gatwick, anyway, was normal. I spotted no villainously familiar faces, no tails, nothing of that kind of interest. The flight was mundane too, though after departure I looked down upon disappearing England with some nostalgia, hoping I would find it as I left it, all happy transistor din, petrol fumes, and A23. Alongside Felicity and I sat a couple who lost no time in identifying themselves as Chester and Edie Ogmanfiller from Lewiston, Idaho.

'Real glad to make your acquaintance, sir...'

They were on the wrong side of middle age, they were all smiles, and they talked the whole way to Malaga. They'd already done Paris, France and had come back to Britain before going on to Spain because they liked London so much; I dare say the chewing-gum walked into the pavements of Piccadilly made them feel at home. They, too were going to Torremolinos, so we would meet again. As a matter of fact we had them with us all the way to Torremolinos: decanted at Malaga's airport, they found their booking had got all snarled up and there was no self-drive hire car waiting for them, and at that stage another could not be got but one would be delivered as soon as possible at Torremolinos, so what could I do but offer them a lift in ours?

'That's very kind of you.'

'Not at all.'

Edie Ogmanfiller was too fat and generally cumbersome to squeeze into the back of our two-door model, so Felicity went in the back with Chester and I had Edie in front. I had to put a good face on it, and I saw the funny side: world salvation arrives at the hot spot with the fat lady of Idaho.

★ ★ ★ ★

Torremolinos was bursting its seams and sweat seemed to run in rivers from lobstered flesh. What wasn't a tourist was a waiter, or a shopkeeper flogging trinkets made in Japan

76

but Torremolinos orientated, or a tour official looking like death as his charges battered him verbally about double bookings, overused sanitation, or bugs in the bedclothes. It was all an expensive way of not enjoying oneself, but we were here on business and I got down to it as soon as we had checked into our accommodation. It was a nice room, with a balcony and an outlook over the blue and polluted Mediterranean and a lingering smell of garlic. We left it after unpacking our bags and checking for bugs, just in case, and this time I meant metal bugs, and we went out into the heave and tumult to see what might be seen. I was upon religion bent: the police superintendent in Peterborough had told me the Flood Fearers' base was in Andalusia, hence our destination. Andalusia was a big place, of course, but one had to start somewhere. Currently there was not a parson in sight, at least not one in a dog collar, and very possibly the Flood Fearers didn't wear such anyway. I spotted a scurry of Catholic priests from time to time, averting their faces from sin, but there would be no help there. In Spain adherents even of the established Church of England were written down officially as heretics.

Sweltering, we found a bar with small sun-shaded tables. Felicity drank some local vino and I drank Fundador, a very nice Spanish brandy that went well with sun and heat. In point of fact the sun didn't really penetrate the street canyons of Torremolinos. In some ways one might as well have been in New York or Chicago, though the *guardia civil*, well in evidence in their leather head-dress with the flat back, didn't look like the average American cop, all gun and gum. I was thinking of New York when a tired voice by my side said, 'Well, gee whiz,' and I looked up at the Ogmanfillers.

'Heat affecting you?' I asked, waving them to a chair.

'I'll say!'

They sank down with relief and started smiling again, and talking. They insisted on buying us drinks when the waiter came up. I was hardly listening to their chatter and nearly missed something interesting—would have done if Felicity hadn't given me a nudge under the table. I said, 'I'm sorry, I didn't catch that?'

'Churches,' Ogmanfiller said. 'God—you know?'

I knew, I said. I waved a hand around. 'Spain's full of them.'

'Catholics, sure.'

There was a tinge of disparagement in his tone: I gathered the Ogmanfillers were Protestants. They said that whilst in France and

Britain they'd done a number of churches. Just for the architectural interest, of course, the buildings themselves; they hadn't liked a lot of what they'd seen in France—too much darned show, Ogmanfiller said. Give him the simplicity of, say, the Scottish kirk which his folks way back had been members of. He said it with nostalgia and in my mind's eye I saw him in the tartan of the Clan MacOgmanfiller and wondered in what form he would wear it: once, in a bar in York, old not New, I'd seen an American backside wearing Bermuda shorts in the honoured tartan of the Black Watch. Anyway, it turned out that Ogmanfiller had been referring to his maternal ancestors. He didn't say what the paternal ones had been. As the Ogmanfillers yacked away, veering off religion now, I brought them back to it. I had had an idea: to go on a Flood Fearer hunt in company with Mr and Mrs Ogmanfiller from Idaho might be good cover. We would look kind of genuine...the Ogmanfillers were genuine tourists all right and no more to be wondered at than any other American tourist doing religion in Spain. And their interest would be for real too: they could be relied upon to make all the right noises of enquiry. It just might be an aid to my investigations, so I began to lead them towards the sly notion. But I scarcely needed to. They knew all about the Flood Fearers, and of course this wasn't really surprising since, as it turned out, the sect, like the local pastor himself, had had its origins in the U.S.A.

'They're still there,' Ogmanfiller said.

'You don't say.' I caught Felicity's wink: don't overdo it, the wink said.

'He's right,' Mrs Ogmanfiller said earnestly.

'Built an Ark,' her husband went on. 'Made an Ark on dry land. No animals. Just the congregation, get it? When the rains start, the Flood Fearers get aboard the Ark and ride the Flood in safety. There's electronic warning devices from the pastor's residence to all the congregation, and when the pastor gets God's warning, well, he alerts the rest and they all climb aboard.' Ogmanfiller made a joke: 'Guess that pastor's even got heaven bugged.' He roared with laughter and slapped a colourful thigh. 'Didn't know they'd come out here to Spain?'

I said, 'I'm told they have. I don't know about the Ark. I had another vision: the Ark, navigating into a British port loaded to the gunwales with nuclear waste and a latter-day Noah high-tailing it ashore after setting the explosive device. It wasn't really very funny. Anyway, I suggested to Ogmanfiller that we might all join forces and go for a look around. He wasn't keen at first. The sect in the States, he said, didn't welcome outsiders. You couldn't blame them. I knew he could be right, which was precisely why I wanted him along. The Ogmanfillers of this world get places by sheer persistent inquisitiveness, and their open-eyed wonder of itself puts them beyond suspicion. I could sense his inquisitiveness already starting to rise to the surface and overcome his hesitation. It would make a good story for the folks back home in Idaho, and he might get some good movie shots. I gave him another spiel.

He glanced at his wife. 'What d'ya think, Edie?'

She said, 'Well...'

Ogmanfiller turned to me. 'Okay, we'll come. Know where these Flood Fearers are?'

'No,' I answered, 'but we can always ask around.'

Next morning I did just that and to my surprise it wasn't easy to get a line on the Flood Fearers. I would have thought they'd stand out a mile in Andalusia, but no. They evidently kept themselves to themselves, with notable success. In the end it was a priest, all black like a crow except for a touch of white at the adam's-apple, who gave Felicity the word outside a bar. She spoke Spanish, and she used it to good effect. The priest was almost blushing beneath his wide-brimmed black hat, probably imagining all manner of things beneath Felicity's T-shirt and jeans. Later, there would be many Hail Marys to be said. When Felicity spoke of the Flood Fearers he crossed himself and uttered many words, then went away fast, beetling off into the skyscraper hinterland that sat so oddly on the coast of Spain. Felicity interpreted and we went along to the hotel where the Ogmanfillers were staying. We found them drinking mint juleps on the terrace, under an umbrella of many colours, like Ogmanfiller's shirt.

'A little way beyond a village called Carena,' I said. 'Around fifty miles north-east by the road map. I suggest we take my car.'

This suggestion was agreeable. Driving out of Torremolinos, I felt a weird prickling in my spine, some sort of premonition coming to me very suddenly. It was a lovely day if you didn't mind the tremendous heat, with a cloudless blue sky beating the sun down on to the equally blue Mediterranean, and here were we, going off to snoop at a bunch of people anticipating the Flood. And in my book something else, something much nastier even if on a less world-wide scale. I glanced over my shoulder at

Ogmanfiller, chatting easily to Felicity. He certainly wasn't worried, and no reason why he should be. He was getting his movie camera all set up for the shots of a lifetime.

CHAPTER 5

It was, I believe, the analogy of the Ark that had cast a shadow on my premonitive mind. Somehow, the Ark had always had a doomful ring to me—it shouldn't, of course, since it was a message of hope, really, that the good would survive so long as they took prudent precautions after receiving the warning from above. I think maybe it's largely because of my basic naval training: the Ark didn't appear in retrospect all that seaworthy and must in fact have been remarkably unstable. However, when we had covered the fifty miles of dusty, rutted track that passed for a first-class road, there was no Ark visible although, from the village of Carena, which was perched upon a peak, we had a tremendous and awe-inspiring view all round. We saw the great ranges of the Sierra Nevada, we could even see the ancient city of Granada around the climbing towers of the Alhambra in the far distance. The countryside was all aridity, burned brown except for occasional patches of green cultivation. It would have to be some flood to make any impression here, I thought.

I had stopped the car, and I turned round to Ogmanfiller. 'No Ark,' I said. 'Not unless it's being built under cover.'

'Well, gee.'

'Anyway, we'll go on, see what we find. Want to take any film shots from here?'

'I guess not,' Ogmanfiller said. 'It's all too distant to make good film.'

I shrugged: it was his business, but I would have thought a touring American would have come with the very best there is in film equipment. Maybe the Scottish ancestry had bred a frugal streak...I drove on, down from the heights into the broad sweep of the valley below. We met two trudging priests ahead, and I halted, and they gabbled at Felicity, and crossed themselves, and carried on towards the small cluster of dwellings behind us that formed Carena. Felicity said the heretic settlement was two miles ahead, just off the road to the left. We were on track all right. The sense of doom increased: this was wild country that almost certainly would hold bandits, and was well off the tourist routes. We were out on a limb and

I thanked God for the Ogmanfillers: without them, we would stand out a mile as intruders rather than simple tourists bent on getting away from the package operation. Driving on, we found no more human life. Just donkeys and the odd mangy dog padding back, like the priests, towards Carena and giving us a wolfish grin in passing.

'Oh, the poor thing,' Mrs Ogmanfiller said in regard to the first dog.

'Poor thing my fanny, Edie,' Ogmanfiller said. 'Guess it'll have rabies,' and at once his wife withdrew a flapping white hand into the car's safety. Humanity loomed, however, a little farther along: a *hombre* in a dirty black beret with filled cartridge belts over his shoulders and a derelict-looking rifle in his hand. He grinned at us, not appearing to be dangerous, and waved, and we went onward.

'What's he doing?' Ogmanfiller asked. I was glad he hadn't used his movie camera.

I said, 'Could be a bandit, I suppose. Or he could be an extended guard on the Flood Fearers.'

'Guard, gee!'

'Well, I doubt if they're popular with the priesthood, and what the priesthood doesn't like, neither do the parishoners. If they didn't take precautions against things closer than the

Flood, they might end up with slit throats.'

Mrs Ogmanfiller gave a little scream, but I think really she was enjoying it and so was her husband. Back in the States, he told me, they didn't need to guard religion, they were broadminded, all were tolerated.

'Just the same,' he said, 'I guess these people aren't quite the same as ours.'

'No Ark?'

'Not just that, I guess. I don't know…just a hunch that they're a breakaway sect, another fractionising. It happens. Why come to Spain, though?'

'Why indeed?' I murmured. At that moment we came round a large overhanging bluff like a cliff and seemed to reach journey's end, or near enough for the car. Off the track another track ran to the left in the shadow of the bluff. Lines of ruts would be more accurate than track, and these un-negotiable ruts ran towards a long, low, white-washed building with a very tall steeple surmounted by a cross. To the right of this building, this church as it obviously was, rose another structure, square and high. Something big. I pondered on it as I stopped the car: a power unit to produce electricity for the organ and lights, or a landbound slipway for an Ark under construction? Maybe we would find out, maybe we wouldn't.

I said, 'Right! All out.'

We got out. Ogmanfiller stood looking all around and shaking his head in apparent amazement. 'Nobody about,' he said. 'Nobody at all.'

'It's not Sunday, Chester.' Edie looked hot and thirsty.

'Why no, it's not, but still.'

I said, 'Come on, we'll go and take a look. Got your camera ready?'

Ogmanfiller nodded. We trudged along the track, with me in the lead and Ogmanfiller behind me, then Felicity, then Mrs Ogman-filler bringing up the rear and making heavy weather of the ruts. The Flood Fearers' church looked as though it had been built simply of breeze blocks, but even so, it must have taken the volunteers a long while to construct. The steeple, I fancied, was of steel and seemed to be at the wrong end. It was a curious set-up, what with its outbuilding, and inside it was even curiouser. The door was only on a latch, and I pushed it open and we went in. As I'd seen from the outside, there were few windows. What glass there was had a greenish tinge and there was a feeling of being under the sea, as in a bathysphere, with all that green light. The Flood idea again, I supposed. The floor was of plain wood planks. At the far end—beneath the steeple, unlike the Church of England or any other religion I knew of—was an altar. Over it loomed, not Christ, but Noah. It was fairly obviously Noah, though beards were pretty anonymous and fashionable then as now, because he was rising with accompanying angels from a miniature plastic Ark, which was surrounded by rough waters constructed, at a guess, from some sort of plastic foam painted green. Chips of it had dropped away and lay around the altar like confetti. Beside Noah was a woman, naked and well formed. There was no sign of an animal, thus it was not an accurate historical representation of the facts. There were no pews, as such, for the congregation: seating was arranged in a number of separate boat-shaped wooden structures complete with thwarts. Each 'boat' had one rowlock fashioned as a candlestick with electric candle. And suddenly I jumped a mile as tinned organ music clicked into *Fierce Raged the Tempest O'er the Deep*. As this happened, a figure came through the door. He was a tall man in a white cassock with a green cord around the middle and he had very long, dark hair. The cassock was really more like a monk's garment, with wide sleeves in which the man's hands were invisible as he held them clasped before his body. I hoped Ogmanfiller would start being a tourist, and up to a point he did.

He aimed his camera at me and said, 'Reach.'

'What?' It didn't strike me as funny.

'Reach,' Ogmanfiller said, and there was a difference in his voice, 'This is no camera, buddy, it's a gun. Reach.'

I didn't reach. I had seen Edie Ogmanfiller come up behind Felicity, and I went to help her, but too late. A fist like a ham with a revolver in it came down on Felicity's neck and she went out like a light, not uttering a sound. I made a dive for Ogmanfiller, wrapped my arms round his legs and brought the back of his head down with a crash that must have dented the wood planking, but it failed to damage Ogmanfiller. Up came the camera before I could get my hands on it, and a bullet zipped past my face so close I could feel the burn. It sped on and broke away a good deal of Noah's beard and a window pane. A moment later the monklike figure, uttering oaths, took off and landed on my chest like an all-in wrestler and before I could start to dislodge him Ogmanfiller, squirming clear, had me just where he wanted me.

He was grinning widely. 'Stupid bastard,' he said, breathing hard. 'You got yourself right into this situation, didn't you, came looking for it like a real goddam sucker!'

* * * *

I felt that my lungs had burst. Under
Ogmanfiller's camera gun, I was hoisted to my
feet by that athletic monk, who also now produced a weapon: a knife, very sharp, which he
laid against the back of my neck and said it
would go right through the first time I made
a move he didn't like. Felicity was lifted like
a feather by Edie Ogmanfiller and held mother-
and-babylike in the fat arms. I was shoved out
through the door by knife action and felt blood
run. Ogmanfiller moved alongside me with his
camera. Once outside, another man showed up,
also with gun, this time a sub-machine standing out oddly against the clothing of his
religion. His cassock or whatever was similar
to the first man's but his girdle was plain white.
Green, the colour of flood, probably distin-
guished the pastor, or boss. The Reverend Clay
Petersen, seducer of La Ina? I was herded along
towards the square building and the man with
the sub-machine gun brought keys out from
below his robe and unlocked a door, a wooden
one and heavy, backed by steel.

In we went.

At the far end were vast double doors,
currently shut and doubtless locked, and in

between were the makings of an Ark. Wood lay everywhere and there were piles of shavings, but no one was at work, and somehow the construction had the air of abandonment: it was probably just cover, in fact, and never mind the huge blueprint that hung on one wall with all the cubits and whatnot converted to metric. An irreverent hand had painted across the bottom in aerosol spray, *Real Madrid olé*. That brought a touch of normality, but the feeling didn't last. The whole ambience of the Ark was against it. So was the fact that we were pushed into the bow section of the Ark and I almost fell over a lavatory pan, unconnected and lying on its side near a carton of tubes of Bostick. The cleric with the green robe, who was ahead of the procession, had obscured the thing from my sight with his flowing robe. He led the way for'ard, nearer to the bows, and stopped by a sort of hatch that in a normal vessel might possibly have given access to the double-bottoms. Lifting the hatch-cover, he revealed electric light that showed up a concrete base about a couple of feet below: the Ark was evidently resting in a hard bed in which, pending completion, it would await the Flood. At least, I supposed that was what the faithful, if there were any genuine faithful, would be told.

We all dropped down the hatch, one by one.

The pastor went down first and was waiting, with gun, to shepherd Felicity and me once we were through. The space was a little more than I had estimated from above, between three and four feet in fact, but progress was extremely difficult. It was worse than the orlop deck of Nelson's *Victory*, but after a while the going grew easier, the headroom increasing as we entered a downward-sloping passage. It didn't go far before it widened out into what looked to me like a natural cave. I had heard of the cave-dwellers of Andalusia, but so far as I knew they lived, not in totally underground chambers, but in caves opening to the fresh air from the sides of the mountains. And they were gypsies, mellow-hearted players of Flamenco music, plus of course a few bandits...not like this mob, CORPSE as I was now convinced they were, dedicated to power seizure on a grand scale. When we entered, the cave was empty but for its simple furnishings: two desks, one of them covered with what looked like radio equipment, and a big wall map showing the world's seas and continents and with a number of tiny and currently unlit light bulbs dotted around the coasts, the vulnerable coasts, of Britain. It was not dissimilar from, though much larger than, those find-it-yourself town guides that show a light saying 'You Are Here' and when you want to find the library, the police station or whatever you press a button and the relevant light comes on and tells you where it is.

I was looking at this when from an area of shadow at the far end of the cave something familiar emerged: the man in purple, the chairman of CORPSE all the way from London, still hooded.

'Ah, Commander Shaw,' he said. 'You came to look for us. That was foolish, was it not?'

I shrugged. 'Apparently it was.'

'Yet it was natural, and to be expected.'

'So you arranged for the Ogmanfillers to be around.'

There seemed to be a smile in the eyes behind the slits. 'Quite so. It was better to have you safely where we wanted you, rather than chance you snooping around. We knew all your movements, you see—'

'And I walked right into the Ogmanfiller trap,' I said bitterly, to save him the trouble. 'They didn't need to play their hand at all, did they? What about Polecat Brennan, may I ask? Do I take it he defected from WUSWIPP?'

'Correct. He saw CORPSE as a more profitable enterprise, Commander. He was right to do so. The force of the political left is running down—'

'The signs haven't yet reached me.'

'They will do so. There is a turning in the tide.' The purple man seemed utterly confident and easy. 'There is a turning in the tide also of all the official forms of government, all the establishments. The power base is shifting to the people, as a result of pressures from both Left and Right I admit, but the Left is beginning to be unsure of itself now. There has been a backlash, and the backlash will grow and grow until it is irresistible. You will see.' I recalled Max's remark: that this was a backlash of the Right. Max had been spot on, and in fact I hadn't doubted it when he'd said it. All the same, I knew the purple man had got it all wrong: the pressures he'd referred to had *all* been from the Left rather than the Right. His confidence was for show only: the power-emergence of the Right hadn't started yet. It would do so when CORPSE went into action, and not before. That was what CORPSE was all about. The fact that Polecat Brennan had defected didn't mean WUSWIPP had the skids under it—far from it.

The CORPSE chairman was continuing. He said, 'The moment you began to grow inquisitive, Commander, you had to be brought in. I'm sorry...but your job for us was done once you'd communicated our message—which

94

you did very successfully. Whitehall has taken the point—'

'You mean they've started the strike-back.'

'There is no strike back, there can't be.' The hand emerged whitely from the purple, and waved in the air. 'What we plan to do is irresistible. The British may build booms across all their harbours yet our ships can still be fully effective when laid alongside the booms. If you open fire on the ships as they enter, you will only destroy yourselves the quicker. Our crews are dedicated men prepared to take the risks, those few of them that know the facts about their cargoes. To destroy all inward shipping out at sea would be a task far too great and too politically dangerous for any government to contemplate, as I know you will agree. There is, quite simply, no defence of any kind.' The man paused, weightily. 'There is only surrender, after which Britain will be governed in the best interests of her people.'

'By you?'

'By a Directorate.'

'CORPSE!'

'The term CORPSE will disappear when the take-over is complete, and when all selective eradication has been done. If you wish a few names of persons to be eradicated, I

95

will tell you.'

He did so: his list was very comprehensive, and I dare say some of the politicians and union bosses back in Britain would have been surprised how highly they were rated, eradicationwise, by CORPSE. They were just the tip of the iceberg, too, the man said; total elimination of elements considered undesirable would take some time, for nominal rolls of persons as submitted to the Directorate would have to be examined carefully to ensure justice for all. These nominal rolls would cover the whole range of the British Establishment: after the politicians and union leaders would come the law officers of the Crown, the Civil Service, police, armed services, education—the universities in particular—the Church, local government, medicine, writers, artists and broadcasters, the industrialists and the City. The mass of the people were expected to be docile, cowed in advance by the immensity of the threat, ready to be led by the iron will of the newcomers. I decided that I'd been right in my initial belief that the man in purple was a German: few other races would make the crazy and dangerous assumption that the British people would sit down meekly under threat. The breed hadn't changed all that much. Nevertheless, I took his point about the virtual impossibility of any defence against the threat itself.

I gestured towards the wall map. 'Your action chart?' I asked.

'Quite so. It will not show the dispersals at this stage, but some of the ships are already at sea and moving towards your ports and estuaries.'

'Largely from Japan, I suppose?'

The hood nodded. 'Largely, yes. Also from America, and other places.'

'And the Ark? Is that involved?' I asked with heavy sarcasm. The man laughed indulgently; he explained that the Reverend Clay Petersen had a genuine congregation of expatriate Britons plus a handful of Americans, good Protestants now reached by the pastor's words, for whom the Ark was a symbol and a hope for the future. They regarded Britain as a land of wickedness, rotten with strikes and layabouts and aborted teenage schoolgirls and vandals and muggers and Socialists, a land that God must surely hit back at soon while they were okay aboard Petersen's Ark. They had opted out of sin on their retirement pensions, be they DHSS, Paymaster General or Deferred Annuities for the self-employed, and they came from all over southern Spain, every Sunday, to worship. They knew nothing of the cave that was to be the operational HQ for CORPSE, they just loved their Ark and the impassioned fervour of Petersen, and they provided excellent cover for the comings and goings of the CORPSE executive. The parishioners didn't come just on Sundays: there were flowers to arrange, odd jobs to do, and there were Bible readings, quite well attended. The local populace had got used to them, whilst any faces, strange to the parishioners, seen going into the big out-building could be explained to the faithful dodderers as those of Ark builders; and the steeple was a very fine transmitting and receiving aerial. The operational base of CORPSE was much more secure here than it would be in any big city, just so long, of course, as no one outside ever got to know about it till afterwards, afterwards being the big blow-up series in Britain. Of course, Sandra Shingler had been an embarrassment...Sandra Shingler, alias La Ina, had been hounded out by the righteous members of the sect, led by the wife of a retired brigadier, a forceful lady who had come upon sacrilege beneath the plastic beard of Noah. Miss Shingler had become a threat to security and so Polecat Brennan had been despatched on his killing errand. Petersen, reprimanded by CORPSE, had squared matters for himself with his congregation by saying that La Ina had been infiltrated by the

Devil to sow seeds of discord within the sect, that he was himself blameless, and that to allow bad feelings to fester would be to play straight into the wicked hands of Lucifer. It was a matter of sheer luck that the brigadier, when a captain during the war, had been surprised in a similar situation with an ATS corporal in the back of an army truck and got away with it; also that he was a fair-minded old codger. He'd spoken up for the pastor and quelled rebellion in the ranks, thus doing unto others as he'd been done by himself.

So there we were, Miss Mandrake and I, deep in the heart of CORPSE, and very full precautions would naturally be taken to ensure that we didn't get out again. And as the man in purple reached the limit of what he was going to say for now and gave a gesture, the precautions were set in train. The cleric with the sub-machine gun prodded me in the spine and told me to walk forward, which I did. I was propelled into the shadowy part at the cave's end and I saw, dimly, two heavy doors, both of them appearing to be of new construction. Felicity was being brought along behind me by Ogmanfiller, who had his lethal camera in her back—I saw that when I looked round in hopes of being able to achieve a strike-back before we were pushed into whatever lay behind those doors. It was, of course, useless; I wasn't willing to see Ogmanfiller's wretched camera blast Felicity's spine through her stomach, so I had to settle for an imprisonment that I could only hope would be temporary. As we neared the doors, the man with the sub-machine gun pushed past me and pulled one of them open and I looked into total blackness like the tomb. Once again I was pushed forward, through the door, and the gun-bearer flashed a torch within. I saw a space about four feet square, most of which was taken up by what seemed to be a pit. There was a ledge running all around the pit, a ledge no more than a foot wide. I didn't like it: the torch was reflecting off polished sides and from down the pit as I entered came a gleam of water. It was like a well...maybe fed by some underground spring or river. Rain, should it come, might lift the level. Or I could slide into it as a result of some involuntary movement when I grew tired. I thought of Noah: I could do with an Ark now. The door was banged shut behind me and I heard bolts going home at top and bottom. No Felicity: then sounds indicated that she was being shoved through the door into the adjacent compartment. After that there was brooding silence, the awful and utter silence of the grave. I kept very still and began to sweat, though it was oddly cold in that dark pit-head. I didn't fool myself I could keep still for long: it was just a question of time before I fell in. It was difficult to keep my balance, I found, and found very quickly; the darkness seemed to be doing something to my ability to maintain straightness, and I kept swaying forward. After a while I did the sensible thing and lowered myself till my rump was on the ledge and my legs dangling into the pit. That was safer, I thought, though the hard edge of the pit dug into my thighs and in time would grow bloody uncomfortable. I tried to forget my woes and think about Felicity, who was probably in a similar situation...but that was just as depressing. I forced my thoughts ahead, tried to be constructive and project towards escape, but only to see the total impossibility. We were probably expendable and would be left to die, unless the man in purple fancied he could find a use for us in the construction of his New Britain...

In point of fact I don't believe I'd been long in my prison before I heard muffled gunfire: two shots, fired inside the cave, then the silence came back until I heard the bolts on my door being withdrawn, and light filtered in, and once again I was at the wrong end of the sub-machine gun. There were four more men

101

present now, a species of phony acolyte judging from their robes, now bloody. They were carrying dead Ogmanfiller, and as I watched the flowery-shirted American was thrown forward and his body plopped with a big splash into the water of the pit. Then dead Mrs Ogmanfiller went in, making a much bigger splash. No doubt they'd served their purpose...Edie and Chester, prime and primed tourists on a mission of evil, who wouldn't be seeing the folks in Lewiston, Idaho again; not in this world.

As a matter of fact, their sad ending gave me hope: I was as yet alive and could have been dead as the Ogmanfillers, *ergo*, I was as yet required by CORPSE and so was Miss Mandrake. My heart lightened as my legs dangled down towards the floating bodies, but it didn't lighten all that much. I thought about Britain, and what awaited it, what was even then ploughing across the seas for British shores. Just at the start of their death voyages, those hulls would be forging through the clean seas, every turn of the screws shortening the time available to put some sort of spanner in the works of CORPSE, while I was incarcerated in impotence, willy-nilly, underneath that stupid Ark and right alongside the nerve centre of the operation, the place from which via church steeple the final strike orders would go.

CHAPTER 6

I was still there next day, and still alive. In the meantime the Reverend Clay Petersen had personally and with attendant armed guard brought food and drink. Some of the local vino, very rough stuff, and a hunk of bread. It sustained life, though.

I asked about Miss Mandrake.

'She's okay,' Petersen said briefly. He didn't want to talk, so much was clear. He was halfway out of the door already, having taken back the now empty cup made of cheap china that had held the wine. No chalices for me.

I asked, 'What's the hurry?'

'It's Sunday,' he said.

'Ah, yes. And you have a service to take. Tell me, are you genuinely a clerk in Holy Orders, Mr Petersen?'

'Get stuffed,' he said. He went out and banged the door. I took his answer to be a negative. I thought, as I had thought many times over the silent hours, about Chester and Edie Ogmanfiller floating and bloating there below. Now and again, I don't know why, the unseen

103

waters had surged and gurgled. In answer to the spring's pressure, or the river's ripples—even an underground waterfall somewhere? Or it could have been subterranean fish, perhaps, a-nibble at dead flesh. Whatever the reason, it had been gruesome. I hoped Felicity had no water-pit to contend with. Time went on passing and Sunday got into its stride: distantly, I heard the church bell summoning all those retired expatriates. On arrival with the Ogmanfillers, I had seen no belfry, only the thin steeple with no bulk to hold even one bell. Either the sound was tinned like the organ music, or one of the acolytes wielded a handbell, though it sounded heavier than that. Whatever it was, it had a most curious effect: somehow or other it appeared to affect the water in the pit, to ripple it perhaps. At least, that was the only interpretation I could put on the fact that with every ding and dong of the bell, the Ogmanfillers squelched slightly, as though emitting wind. Trying to disregard the horrid sounds, I thought about the congregation, now arriving in the good light of day above. Their most senior member would probably be the brigadier who had caught the rector at it; there could be other military men as well, I supposed, and even if there were not, they would all be patriotic Britons as Britons who have escaped the restriction of actually living in Britain always tend to be. Good, solid citizens—former self-employed fishmongers and tailors, bank managers, audit clerks, legal executives, tax inspectors taking cover from their former comrades. They would all be aghast if they knew what was below their place of worship. If only I could dig my way out during matins, I would find myself among friends—if only I could make them believe fast enough, which I probably could not. The Reverend Clay Petersen must have a persuasive tongue and a grip of iron upon his congregation. The answers would be ready and the good Flood Fearers would leap from their ridiculous rowing boat pews and tear asunder the emissary of the Devil emerging from below the earth.

In any case there was no possible way out.

The bell stopped and so did the Ogmanfillers, and silence reigned again. But not for long. The gurgling started and this time it didn't stop and after it had been going on for quite a while, a good fifteen minutes by the luminous dial of my watch, I began to feel water lapping my shoes and I withdrew my legs and lay flat and dangerously along the narrow ledge. The gurgling grew slowly closer: for me, the Flood had come. Up came the water until it lapped my body and a moment later I felt soggy flesh impinge against my arm. It was a bad moment; in the intense blackness of the pit-head the luminosity of my watch was just enough to reveal, in greenish and unearthly light, Mrs Ogmanfiller's breasts. I had to grit my teeth against an unmanly scream as slowly but inexorably Mrs Ogmanfiller crushed me into the solid wall, no doubt thrust in her turn by her husband as he rose whale-like to the brim. Then, very suddenly, the pressure eased. There was a very long-drawn gurgle and a loud sucking sound as, way down below somewhere, the plug was pulled out of the bath. It must have gone down at whirlwind speed, faster I believe than the Ogmanfillers could catch up, for it was a good many seconds after they had gone back down the hole that I heard the double plop. I was glad they'd gone, but the fact of their rise and fall gave me pause for much thought and conjecture.

The plop, for a start, had positively been double: by deduction, the pit widened out farther down, or the second Ogmanfiller would have followed a split-second later into the exact spot penetrated by the first, channelled as it were by the pit walls, and there would only have been one plop. I don't know what that proved. More interesting was the movement

106

itself, the movement of the water. I went back to my theory of a subterranean spring, one of fluctuating intensity. It had to be that—anyway, I could find no other explanation; I didn't think the waterfall idea could be on. True enough, there are underground waterfalls in various parts of the world, Yorkshire being one. But Spain? I simply didn't know. Spain's a dryish land in summer, it's hard enough to grow anything in the burned-up ground, and I would have thought someone would by now have tapped any underground supply of any real size. But maybe they had, of course, somewhere along the waterline...unless it was salt in origin? It's not impossible to get a sea surge, if sea caves happen to interlink along the way with the land cave systems, but I reckoned fifty-odd miles was in fact much too far to be viable.

What did seem certain was that my pit was connected to some kind of underground cave system and it could be a way out. That was, if one had the right survival equipment including breathing apparatus to tackle the water. Without that...well, it all depended, of course. The way just might not be long, though it could be blocked by the Ogmanfillers currently. They could be jammed up against the plug hole...

Something moved against my right ear: by

this time I had resumed my sitting position, legs down the pit and bottom on the ledge. My ear tickled it; it was like a fly, or a wriggly worm. Little bits of rock—it was soft rock, sandstone I fancy—added to the tickle and I heard a small sound, then another. It became a kind of sawing and more material flew around. I felt the wall by my ear and something moved against my hand, in and out, round and round: Miss Mandrake up to something and it sounded useful. I grabbed the thing that moved and held it fast, thereby giving the signal that I'd cottoned on.

Whatever it was, was withdrawn.

I put my mouth to the hole, which I judged to be less than inch across. I called through to Felicity, removed my mouth and put my ear in its place.

'I found a bone,' she said.

'Are you expecting to join me?'

'That's hoping for too much,' she said. 'But it's nice just to hear you. The rock's pretty easy to work, as a matter of fact,' she added.

'Yes. Have you got a water-filled pit?'

'A *what?*'

I said, 'Never mind, if you haven't you haven't, but I have.' I told her the facts, briefly, leaving out the Ogmanfillers. She didn't comment, but started work again on the hole, wielding her bone. I wondered whose it had been and how old it was. I knew that in Spain they put their dead in things like shelves slotted into the mountainsides; maybe in some cases they had put them underground, like in the catacombs below Valletta in Malta, and under Rome. It wasn't important; the bone, some of which was broken away, had a sharp end, which *was* important, and had given Felicity her start. It was a long bone, thigh probably, and I took one end and we pulled and pushed like two men hand-sawing through an oak. After a while we had a hole nearly six inches in diameter, for once we could get our hands in we speeded up the excavatory process. I still couldn't see Felicity through the blackness, but I could touch her and we could converse almost normally. That was a help. I told her then about the Ogmanfillers.

'Ghastly,' she said. 'Poor you. I don't feel very sad about Chester and Edie, the bastards.'

'Quite. But they've given me an idea.' I explained my theories, making the dangers sound somewhat less than I feared they might be, for I was fast coming to a decision. 'I've half a mind to try it out. Win or lose it all. If the worst comes to the worst, there'll be a surface to float on.'

'With the Ogmanfillers.'

'Yes.'

I could almost feel her shudder through the hole in the wall. I talked on persuasively; I didn't want her to feel she was being left to face Petersen and the man in purple on her own while I drowned in the murky subterranean depths. I said if I got out I would be back with a posse and the Flood Fearers would find they had other worries. She countered that by saying there was nothing very elaborate about this set-up and if the pastor and his purple mate got away, they could always re-open the shop elsewhere, no difficulty. With that I had to agree; but emphasised that the villains would not get away once I had the place ringed with the *guardia civil* plus the military. After that, Focal House and the hot grill. Talking would take place.

'Think of what's at stake,' I said.

'I am.'

'And us sitting here helpless.'

She said, 'Right, but I reckon we're all going to be helpless, out or in, us and Max and the British Government. What's going to happen *will* happen. You've almost said as much yourself, if not quite in those words.'

'Yes, I have. But we have to do what we can. And don't forget WUSWIPP. This time, they're allies—For as long as it suits them, anyway. WUSWIPP's widespread enough to stop CORPSE in its tracks at the drop of a hat.'

A disagreeable sound came through the hole. 'Why haven't they already, then?'

I said, 'I don't know, unless they want a *quid pro quo*. WUSWIPP is, as ever, WUSWIPP. Or maybe they don't know enough yet. There, I can help. If I get out.'

'You've made your mind up, haven't you?' she asked. She sounded scared, and sad too. We'd had some good times together, after all, and I just might not find a surface. Below ground, people can get stuck. For my part, I hated the thought of plunging down towards the Ogmanfillers and I hated leaving my Miss Mandrake up top. At that point she said that a little more work would enlarge the hole and she could come through and take her chances with me. That, I was not having, and it was not to do with the fact she was a woman, except that she was a woman named Felicity Mandrake for whom I had a very high regard and more. He travels the fastest who travels alone, and had my companion been someone for whom I had no emotional feeling, then I could and would have left him, if he got himself stuck, in the wider interest of one of us getting out and away to spread the gospel about

the Flood Fearers. That's how we're condition-
ed in 6D2. But Felicity I would not leave to
drown and her presence would be an inhibi-
tion. To that extent, the teachings of 6D2 had
failed to stick, and to that extent I was a rotten agent. However, there it was. I reckoned
Felicity would be a damn sight safer left imprisoned, that Petersen wouldn't kill her or
anything like that while she had a possible use,
for instance as a bargaining counter. That, I
had to concede might hold dangers for her, but
my intent was to lose no time in cordoning the
church and grounds and extracting Felicity as
a first priority.

Tritely I said, 'No time like the present. Try
not to worry. I could be back by evensong.'

* * * *

I had to screw myself up to it. I had no idea,
no way of estimating, how far down the waters
had gone. For all I knew I might hit rock, and
even if the Ogmanfillers broke my fall I could
still do myself a lot of irreparable damage.
Screwed up, I took a step forward and dropped. It could not, in fact, have taken me long
but the journey seemed immense and gave me
time for all manner of morbid thought. Blood
pounded in my ears, my body scraped and
112

bounced off the pit walls and I saw those ships a-sailing in a blood-red sunset for the British coasts, crammed to the gunwales with radioactive substances all ready to emit their betas. Plutonium, uranium, tritium...very nasty muck, especially plutonium. Three millionths of a plutonium gramme could cause cancer in dogs. In aerosol form it's five million times more lethal than lead. Very, very toxic. And long lasting: I'd read that plutonium 'wasted' today would still retain half its initial radioactive death dose after a span of years equivalent to ten times the time-lapse since the birth of Christ, which carried one back retrospectively to pre Noah at a guess. All that flashed before me in about half a second.

I entered the water.

Safety! Had I not been submerged I would have taken an enormous breath of relief. I went deep; it was very cold. I came up again and took in air, shivering like a leaf in a gale. To my surprise the Ogmanfillers had gone. Sucked down further? I could feel no suction. Possibly they had at last sunk under their own waterlogged weight. I recalled Edie Ogmanfiller's breasts up top; in my green luminous glow they had looked more bloated even than in life.

Resting a while, I listened for any sound from

113

overhead: nothing. I thought of something I hadn't thought of earlier: when the Flood Fearer bosses found the hole we'd made, and didn't find me, they would know Felicity knew my plans. True, I could only have gone down into the pit, no mystery about that, and my object had to be escape, but they might take it out on Felicity and try to wring from her a statement as to my precise movements and intentions if I made it. Too late now, of course; and she might be able to persuade them I'd fallen in, tripped over my big feet, uttered one last despairing scream and vanished for ever towards hell. She just might. I certainly wouldn't bank on it. One more series of deep, chest-expanding breaths and I went down again, somersaulting in the freezing water—which, by the way, was fresh not salt or even brackish—and thrusting powerfully with my feet. There was a good deal of pressure and I hoped I wouldn't get the bends or something. Down and down and down and every thrust more of an effort than the one before. When I thought the end of life had come the waters began to narrow in and the walls' contours forced me round something like the U-bend in a lavatory pan. Here I found trapped air. It was horribly stale and smelly, but it was air, and it helped. Having breathed, I plunged on and all of a sudden I came to the tunnel's end. My head sped out into quite fresh air and my groping fingers found a ledge of slimy, slippery rock.

Wonderful, I thought, bloody wonderful, at least I was alive yet and able to breath. I felt around and found the ledge was quite a wide one. Walkable, if there was anywhere to walk to.

I heaved myself out and for a while lay flat and gasping like a salmon. When I was rested I began walking, taking it with immense care, arms outstretched ahead. I took the wrong direction first time, and touched solid, blocking rock. I turned round. After more walking I touched rock again but this time I was able to outflank it, following my feet around the ledge.

I moved on, slow but sure. It was very slow, in fact. On and on again, with rests. Time passed. The tension didn't. I had to drag myself along; I was wearing crêpe-soled shoes and they gave me a good grip but they didn't prevent aching feet. On and on. At last I virtually collapsed and put my head in my hands, aghast at the time I'd been down under the earth as revealed by my waterproof wrist-watch: something like five hours. I was bloody well lost and there was no blinking that hard fact. I was no doubt in a maze of underground passages, of lakes, of rivers formed by rainwater millions of years old that through the ages had seeped and dripped down to this God-forsaken place in earth's heart. It was all too possible I would never again see the light of day. After a long rest I got up and moved on notwithstanding; it was all I could do. More time passed. About a couple of hours later I banged smack into a stalagmite and cursed it viciously, and my voice echoed back at me a hundred times, from which I estimated myself to be in a cavern of very vast proportions. And then, as the echoes died away, I caught another sound and wished I hadn't sworn at that bloody stalagmite: footsteps, faint and distant as yet, but beginning to echo. I was not alone. The hunt was up. I might never be able to get out, but the Flood Fearers were taking no chances on it, and that meant that a way out existed somewhere. If I could find it before they found me; and only luck would tell.

I stopped moving, and thereafter kept very still and silent, on my feet with my back against cold rock. Then I remembered: I had only recently rounded a corner, had in fact almost gone over an edge into God knew what—water, or a precipice. Cautiously I moved back closer to this corner, stopped again, kept quiet, pressed myself against the rock and waited for what was approaching from behind. I could still hear the footsteps, but spasmodically now, as though the pursuit was uncertain of its own sense of direction. From the sound-pattern of the footsteps when they got on the move, I judged there to be two men after me, but I couldn't be sure because the echoes might be confusing the pattern. Sensibly enough, considering I was unarmed, they were using torches: I could see the ends of the beams after a while, losing themselves in an immensity of space overhead. They flickered everywhere, searching and probing. The men probably expected to find me a corpse in the water.

They were on track, anyway: they were coming closer, though they still had a long way to go. Time passed; the torch beams swept nearer ahead of their holders. Soon I heard voices— tired, angry, thoroughly fed-up. There was a quarrel in the air, and the term bastard was used frequently, more often than not adorned with eff. I wondered if one of them was the Reverend Clay Petersen in person or whether he was closeted with his congregation in evensong, for which it was now just about time if the Flood Fearers followed the precepts of the Church of England, which they probably did considering the conservative nature of the clientele. Petersen or no, on they came, and began to approach my corner. In the light of the torches as they dipped from time to time, I was able to see what I had nearly fallen into: a long way down there was hard and jagged rock, or perhaps the jags were stalagmites. Anyway, they were sharp.

On came the Flood Fearers, plod plod. I braced myself; someone was going to go over that sheer drop and it wasn't going to be me. Now I could hear the heavy breathing of weary, disconsolate men. They were only feet away. One said, 'Jesus'. I didn't recognise the voice. They came round that corner very circumspectly indeed, watching where they put their feet. One slip and they would have had it. This, they would know. One of them, the leading one, was not in fact conscious of it for very long, because as he came round the corner he caught a glimpse of something—me—and the sudden start on an unpropitious piece of ground threw him literally off balance and over he went, screaming, to death by impalement. In the meantime the other man had opened fire. Bullets zinged off the rock face and chips flew; the firing was far from accurate. The man was badly rattled and the screams from below didn't help; his mate hadn't died yet and was busily sending out a propagandic warning note. I had to get the man, get him alive and make him lead me out, always assuming there was a way out to freedom. I didn't wait to think too long. Thanks to the torch I could see the way, and I saw that just here the ledge was reasonably wide. I kept close to the rock and I charged, like the Light Brigade, straight into the gun. Explosions echoed like an artillery barrage and more rock flew, but I still didn't get hit, it was all much too wild. As the man turned away to get the corner between himself and me, I crammed on more speed and then jumped him and brought him flat and winded to the rock ledge, with me laid along his back. The rubber-protected torch flew and fetched up between the rock face and the villain, still switched on.

The man was snarling like a wounded tiger and was obviously just as dangerous. I lifted his head by the ears and slammed it into the rock, hard, face first. I said, 'The gun, friend. Bring it out and pass it over.'

He had it in his hand still, and the hand was twisted up beneath his weight and mine. I eased up enough for him to bring out his hand, then I seized the automatic from it. The slide was empty, which was no doubt why he'd turned to run. I ferreted about in his pockets and found his ammo store and reloaded, then I got up, grabbing the torch on the way.

'On your feet,' I said.

He clambered up and I kept both gun and torch on him. He looked Spanish, probably a disorientated Franco man who didn't like the way things had gone since the death of El Caudillo. Sartorially, he was simplicity itself: dark-coloured shorts, bare and hairy chest, with the cord of his religion tied about his waist and the ends dangling down his flies. The face was as dark as the shorts and was contorted with rage and anxiety. I stared at him in silence; the screams from the rock jags had stopped now. I asked, 'You speak English?'

'*Si*...yes.'

'Good,' I said. 'Now listen well, friend. You're going to lead me out of here and you're not going to make any mistakes on purpose, right? Because I'm going to kill you the very first time you do anything, repeat anything, I don't much like. So watch it. For a start, take off that cord and hand it over.'

He obeyed. I took the cord and told him to turn round with his wrists crossed behind him. I lodged the torch on a recess in the rock wall and, one-handed, looped the cord round his wrists and hauled taut. I put the automatic between my thighs and held it safe while I finished the roping in good seamanlike fashion, and when we were ready I gave the order to

120

move out and repeated my warning once again. Back we went towards my ambush corner with me holding the end of the cord and I saw my guide turn and look down briefly then jerk his head away. He kept very close to the wall. We plunged on into the torch-lit gloom. We hadn't gone more than, at a guess, a hundred yards when rising sound was heard from the distance ahead of us. At first I couldn't make it out, then I realised it was water, rushing fast from God knew where with its destination equally uncertain, though for my money it would be ultimately to fill the pit down which I'd come originally. I could only hope it wouldn't rise too far: we were high up currently on our ledge and in that, perhaps, lay safety. I shone the torch down into the valley that had become a watercourse already, the underground river that I had suspected, and I shone it at a very particular moment: past me at a rapid speed went both Ogmanfillers, much worn now but still close together in death as they had been in life.

CHAPTER 7

I couldn't make it out, and my guide was no help. I believe the awful sight of the Ogman-fillers had been the last straw. Even if he'd changed his religion for political purposes to Flood Fearer, he must have been a Catholic at heart and there was something about the journeys of the Ogmanfillers that shook even me. But now the Flood seemed to be upon us and we had no Noah. I made a few assumptions, based upon a sketchy knowledge of cave systems and the weird vagaries of underground water channels. Since that rushing river was scarcely likely to have its origins in the fresh air, at any rate not at this time of year in parched Spain—though it would need to have a high water-table—I decided its origins were perhaps in some local mountain where there was some vast age-old pool in which the millions of years' worth of drippings had collected. From that pool its course ran towards my erstwhile pit, possibly backed by subterranean springs which could help to push it willy-nilly along the tunnel. Why it alternately rose and

122

fell away again I knew not, nor did I know if there was any discernible pattern in that rise and fall. Perhaps there were underground upheavals from time to time, movements and surges that didn't reach the surface; perhaps there *was* a spasmodic waterfall somewhere around that responded to overfill and exerted pressures when it was in action, and when it was not the tide receded again. Meanwhile it was still rising, as my torch showed. An hour later it was only a matter of inches below the ledge, though, since we were now going very slightly down hill, this could be due to the dip of the ledge itself rather than to a rise in the water-level; I hoped so. I was thankful when we veered away, going sharp left into a narrow and climbing tunnel where the waters were not. In the tunnel it was very dry, as though there had never been water at all, and after another half-hour's progress I saw the loom of something lighter in the distance, a round patch of moonlight, and I knew we had all but made it.

★ ★ ★ ★

We stumbled out, dead weary now. I switched off the torch; we were in bright moonlight, with the terrain standing out sharply.

123

There was no sign of the Flood Fearers' establishment, not even the radio steeple. Away westward there were mountains, closer to us there were hills, and all was peace and quiet. Distantly I picked out a white ribbon of roadway, or track.

I asked, 'Where does the road lead, *amigo?*'

'From Seville to Granada.'

'And in between?'

'Estepa, Antequera, Loja.'

'And the nearest?'

'Estepa.' The man was very monosyllabic: he couldn't be sure of his future, but if ever he rejoined the Flood Fearers he wouldn't want to be accused of volunteering anything. I pondered on Estepa; there would be a presence of the *guardia civil*, but in Spain there's a touch of the yokels in the backwoods, and anyway, the Flood Fearers, if they didn't assume I had died back in the cave system, might opt for the nearest town as being my destination. On balance, I fancied either Seville or Granada and, making a fast estimate that took vaguely into account our underground travels in a frankly unknown direction, I decided that, whichever direction we'd gone in, Granada was most likely the nearer. Even so, it could be all of eighty to a hundred miles. But with luck we could pick up some transport, even if it was only donkeys nicked during the night from some handy field.

I shoved the automatic into my Spaniard's backbone. 'Walk,' I said. 'Where I tell you, and keep quiet, like a mouse.'

'You do not need me now, *senor!* I have brought you from the cave—'

'Don't teach me my job,' I said, and pressed the gun in again. The man shrugged, waved his arms—I'd untied him now since I didn't want too many raised eyebrows if we were spotted—started another protest, saw it was useless and shut his mouth. We headed towards the roadway. The going was pretty rough, but the moon and stars, the latter hanging like lanterns and seeming extraordinarily close, gave good light. There was no pursuit, no wild bandits on the watch so far as I could see. In fact it was a fair bet that we had all been written off as caught by the inrush of the waters, and if they checked they would find one dead body at any rate on the jags, and that might help them to mould their views. I reckoned that at the very least we would have a nice start. When we hit the road I propelled the *hombre* on fast: Miss Mandrake would be depending on my speed. I didn't care to speculate on what she might be going through. The Reverend Clay Petersen had had a mean and vicious look about him. In the event we reached the old city of Granada in good time, because we came upon a farm lorry outside a small white-washed cottage with another *hombre* in the cab, preparing to set off before the dawn for market. The automatic persuaded him to head with us at once for Granada, and, keeping my *hombre* between myself and the driver, and the gun on them both, we drove off with a mountainous load of melons.

★ ★ ★ ★

Granada's chief of police, called out from bed, was co-operative after I'd established my identity and connections, or rather after he had satisfied himself that I was Commander Shaw by a batch of time consuming telephone calls that he insisted upon making between himself, the British Embassy in Madrid, and Focal House in London, plus another call, this time made by myself, to 6D2 Spain in Madrid. I knew Senor de Panata, Spain's Max, personally; he promised all assistance and said he'd already been contacted by London. All this done, I set out with a posse, back again to the village of Carena and beyond to the church premises. It was all very well planned and the *guardia civil*, backed by a company of infantry, went in as tourists with guns concealed beneath luridly patterned shirts and linen jackets, and they even travelled in a coach—four coaches indeed—commandeered for the purpose from a British touring company that happened to be doing Granada and the Alhambra. We went into action under the divisional insignia and standards of Wallace Arnold and very comfortable it was. The police and troops disembarked in as disorderly a tourist rabble as was possible for disciplined men, and I, for obvious reasons, remained in the background. A casual sort of advance was made upon the church and the building that housed the Ark. The result was anti-climax and a nasty sick feeling in the pit of my stomach. All was in first-class order in the church and Noah was still there, overseeing the plastic Ark and the nautical pews, but no one else was. At the seagoing Ark's slipway, all was equally in order, but still there was no one about and I knew, now, that when the prison was opened up there would be no Miss Mandrake. Of course I was right: the cell stood empty. An exhaustive search was made and in a sector of the slipway building, separate from the ship-yard, was found the domestic quarter of the Flood Fearer pastorate, kitchen, bedrooms, vestry and all; and all deserted, totally. The control-room that I'd been in with the man in purple stood in purest innocence, stripped of radio desk and wall map. I could have imagined the whole thing, and the police chief looked as though he believed I had. What had been CORPSE'S control chamber for the demise of democratic Britain now showed evidence of being a do-it-yourself brewery. Wort was fermenting away in plastic containers bearing the stamp of Boots and there were tins, some empty, some still unused, of Tom Caxton's Best Bitter extract, hopped and all ready to be mixed with the boiled water and then pitched with the yeast. There were containers of finings and citric acid. The very smell said it had all been there for years. Upon examination, the church steeple could have been an aerial, or could not: all connections gone. We went back to Granada; we hadn't even seen a bandit to question. Four 'tourists' were left behind incognito in Carena, to pick up what they could. I couldn't wait to get at a telephone.

★ ★ ★ ★

Back in Granada, Madrid called me before I made any outward call: I was wanted at 6D2 HQ, Spain not Britain in the first instance. I passed urgent messages for onward transmission to Max, then the police chief made a helicopter available for the flight to the capital. By mid morning I was closeted with de Panata. Like Max, he smoked cigars, but blacker and nastier ones. He heard my full report in attentive silence, then said all stops had already been pulled out to find Miss Mandrake. He was confident that at least she couldn't be got out of the country, but I was far from certain on that: like Britain, Spain has a long coast-line and not every foot can be watched, and Polecat Brennan had very nearly got me out from the Wash a matter of days earlier. However, there seemed nothing else for it but to hope and pray until a lead emerged from somewhere, and in the meantime there was the reason I'd been wanted and that reason was most ugent. Max had been in touch personally with Senor de Panata. I was to return forthwith to London unless there were vital operational reasons to keep me in Spain.

'Any change in those orders since Max got word about Miss Mandrake?' I asked.

'No change, none. You are required, and must go.'

'Miss Mandrake's disappearance in dangerous circumstances is not an operational reason?'

De Panata gave me a sympathetic look, and shrugged. 'You have been long enough in 6D2,

I think, to understand that a man's emotions are not—'

'Okay,' I snapped. 'Point taken and I don't need the standard lecture. What's biting Max?'

Quite a lot was. A coaster had entered the Thames from Cherbourg, taking a mud pilot off Gravesend. This vessel had proceeded up river, beneath Tower Bridge with her mast laid flat so the bridge hadn't to be lifted. She had been in the Thames often enough previously and was now moored in mid-stream off the Houses of Parliament, just up river from Westminster Bridge. At low water she rested on the mud. She would answer no signals and she was believed to be deserted; a boat had gone inshore before anyone had ticked over. A few hours after she had berthed the body of the mud pilot had been found floating down on the outgoing tide, and CORPSE had been branded below the right nipple. The river police were under orders to keep well clear until further notice, and the government was considering the viability of a local evacuation.

CHAPTER 8

It was VIP treatment now: a special aircraft had been laid on to fly me into Gatwick, whence I was helicoptered to the landing pad on the roof of Focal House. For a moment after disembarkation, I looked around at London: I had a broad view. In amongst the skyscraper office blocks and things like the Post Office Tower old London could be seen yet. St Paul's, diminished by new neighbours; the Tower of London; the Monument; Westminster Abbey and the Houses of Parliament. How much longer? In the vicinity of the blow-out the effects would be devastating and the damage might well spread way beyond—we would have no means of assessing the potential explosive power unless CORPSE gave tongue on the point. But when the nuclear waste was broadcast on the wings of the bang, all London would become untenable. Was that what CORPSE wanted, to come to power over a useless capital? In the meantime, London looked as though it was carrying on as normal. Buses crawled like fat boiled lobsters, assailed

131

by the black flies of taxis.

I went down to the suite.

Max looked grey-faced. With him was the Metropolitan Police Commissioner, Sir Stephen Carey, a tough copper from Northumberland who hadn't quite lost the Geordie accent, which came across when I asked him if the coaster's owners had been of any assistance and he said they'd flown the nest and taken all their files with them. The premises were blank. Carey's face was deadpan, but I noticed a slight shake in his fingers: Scotland Yard was well inside the first danger circle, and the Met would be on duty to the end, come what might. If there was to be evacuation, they would be the ones to organise it along with the Home Office.

I made my report. I added, 'With Miss Mandrake in their hands, they have a hostage. Not that it adds anything, really, to their bargaining position...not now.'

Max said heavily, 'Agreed. But they're trying it.'

'You've heard from CORPSE?'

'Yes.' Max caught the Commissioner's eye. 'That's to say, the Yard has. A telephone call, very brief, no chance to intercept. The British Government has forty-eight hours as of one hour ago to concede. If they don't, Miss Mandrake dies and proof of her death will be

132

delivered. In the meantime, if anyone boards the coaster in the river, CORPSE sends a signal immediately to blow the nuclear device.'

'Which means they must have the vessel under surveillance. If so, it needn't be close. There are any amount of vantage points where a man could watch through binoculars,' Carey said. 'I have that in hand.'

Has he, I thought sardonically, visualising London's beat men and CID stalking bird-watchers and Peeping Toms day and night for forty-eight hours...but I took one point: anyone glued to binoculars from an aloft position at this point in history might well stand out a mile. It was too crude, too unsophisticated. I suggested, 'Electronic devices, a robot watch?'

'Much more likely,' Max said.

Carey asked. 'Can't they be jammed?'

'It's being considered, but the current view of the experts—yours, ours, and Defence Ministry—is that the whole show could be triggered by any interference such as jamming.'

'Could be,' I said, and spread my hands wide. 'So what do we do? Sit and wait? Has no one any ideas?'

Sir Stephen Carey came in again on that. 'At this moment, there's nothing anyone can do. We've thought of many things...towing out to sea's one. That's not on and we didn't spend

long thinking it might be. Putting a bomb
disposal squad aboard's another, hoping we can
defuse before CORPSE gets the word. That
might still be tried as a last resort, but we don't
pin many hopes on that either. We've thought
of trying to scuttle her at high water, or
flooding with fire hoses, but CORPSE will have
taken precautions against that. Over-ridingly,
we don't want to precipitate the blow-out.' He
paused. 'It's a hard thing to say, but I repeat,
there's nothing anyone can do right now, except perhaps to hope the whole thing's bluff.'

I said, 'I don't think it is.'

'But what use is London going to be afterwards?'

'Quite. I've pondered that one too. I suppose
London could always be written off. London's
not essential to government. Once, we managed
with Winchester. In any case, I don't believe
they're bluffing. Remember, I've met the boss.
He may be mad, but he means what he says.'

There was a silence, while they took that lot
in. I knew Max had realised it, but I had an
idea Carey had been banking on a high degree
of bluff, had possibly fancied the coaster in fact
carried a cargo no more lethal than coal or cur-
tain rods. There wasn't much humour in the
situation, but I could imagine CORPSE laugh-
ing their guts up if the government caved in

134

and then that coaster went alongside to discharge tin trays made in Hong Kong. (As a matter of fact, Carey released the information that Cherbourg, contacted via Interpol in the Rue St Valery in Paris, had indicated her manifest: drums of oil.) I could imagine many people in high places wanting to believe the bluff theory, but they wouldn't find me supporting them...I broke the silence by asking, in a general sort of way, what the chances were of the government conceding.

'Unthinkable!' Max snapped.

Carey said, 'They'd never do that.'

'Has anybody asked the Prime Minister?'

Silence again; evidently no one had done that. I thought it might be worth trying, and said so. Max didn't like me for that, I could see. It would be an impertinence. I let the matter drop; it would be raised again for certain, and by higher persons than me or Max or Carey, once the truth emerged into the light of public day. I did mention that aspect, and Max said what I knew he would say, and that was, the press would hereinafter be muzzled like a rabid dog and, indeed, already had been.

'The public won't know anything,' he said flatly.

'Until CORPSE tells them, and don't say you hadn't thought of that too. *That's* when the

135

Prime Minister will have to make up his mind. A lot of pressure will come from our domestic non-democrats to cave in, and it won't all be from the Right. As I may have said before, it'll be a bloody fluid situation and all sorts of groups will see what they'll think of as their chance to capitalise. And a lot of them,' I added, 'will believe the threat itself, the blow-up, *is* bluff. They'll take a chance.' I glanced at the Commissioner. 'I'd hate to have your job, Sir Stephen, you and all the provincial Chief Constables…you're going to need something not far short of general mobilisation of the forces plus NATO to help you keep order.'

The Commissioner threw up his hands. The shake was worse than ever. Even the Tyneside dockers hadn't prepared him for this situation. He said, and there was a note of near despair in his voice, 'Never mind what I said earlier… there has to be some way out.'

I said, 'There is, or may be. I'm going to try it.' I turned to Max. 'I'm going to contact WUSWIPP.'

★ ★ ★ ★

When I left Focal House, I didn't go with the whole-hearted blessing of Max or of Carey either. WUSWIPP were the enemy just as

136

much as CORPSE and I was to remember this. I had no authority to deal or bargain and I was on no account to commit or compromise the British Government. To myself I said ha, ha to that one. Quite often in life, people are better for being committed without prior consultation, and right now so could governments be. In my view, we were facing life or death for a whole nation. In such a situation, anything went, anything that could help. I left Focal House with two determinations: one, to get in contact with the bastards of WUSWIPP just as soon as I could have the feelers out, and two, to prise Miss Mandrake away from CORPSE. I knew that CORPSE's announced intentions re Miss Mandrake were strictly for my personal benefit. Partly an act of pure revenge, partly an attempt to get me to use my persuasive powers, as the man who'd met them, to bring about the cave-in and the hand-over. There was logic in that. But Miss Mandrake apart, I saw no advantage in my trying to re-establish contact with CORPSE and the Flood Fearers. It was obvious now that they could shift base at the drop of a hat and they could operate from almost anywhere. All they had to do was transmit the signal that would blow the coaster and shatter parliament and with it the heart of Britain and then the domestic *gauleiters* would commute busily in from Ponders End and Knockholt Pound, Bishop's Stortford and wherever, and take up the reins, and take up the gun and the whip at the same time. All the ground work had been done from under the noses of the Flood Fearers and that silly Ark, long, long since and from now on out CORPSE was highly mobile.

En route for my WUSWIPP contact, I proceeded towards Lambeth: old friends had their uses. I walked, because I wanted to take a look at the coaster—her name, Max had said, was *Garsdale Head*, British, registered in the port of Barrow-in-Furness. Her normal duties involved the carrying of general cargoes from the Continent to almost any British port as required. It could well be true that there were drums of oil aboard, but there would be drums of a very different sort somewhere in that cargo below hatches. 'Flasks' sealed in lead, stainless steel and concrete to hold the nuclear waste, so-called safe containers that would not withstand the force of a nuclear explosion when CORPSE pressed the button. Where had they come from? Cargoes can be transferred at sea, and it was highly significant that the *Garsdale Head* had taken an unduly long time from Cherbourg to the Downs. Back in FH, I'd suggested to Max that he might check the movement in the Western Approaches of any ships inward bound from Japan, which was Windscale's best customer.

From Westminster Bridge I paused and looked up river. The coaster was not so far from the bridge: a copper could have chucked his helmet down her funnel if he'd had a strong arm. She looked at peace, though it was the peace of death. Utterly deserted...and I remembered something else about nuclear waste: the containers needed to be kept cool by a constant flow of water or they would boil. Then they might go up under their own steam as it were. CORPSE would have covered that one, though. The *Garsdale Head* would have been specially prepared for her last voyage, and her pumps would still be working—she would have enough power from her generators to last till the deadline and no doubt beyond. For a moment longer I stared down on Nemesis as the crowds hurried by. They didn't know, so they didn't care, possibly wondered idly why I was so interested in one of London's common or garden sights. I looked across at St Thomas's Hospital, filled with the sick and their attendant nurses. They would reap the full benefit; someone must soon make the decision whether or not to evacuate, and they hadn't got long if Matron wasn't to be caught with her pants down.

I moved on.

★ ★ ★ ★

The man I wanted was a dirty little rat, a Senior Citizen who had once worked for the Central Electricity Generating Board as a machine minder or something. He'd been vaguely technical and he was, I happened to know from past days, still on the fringes of WUSWIPP. Low down in the hierarchy, but that didn't matter, he was only to be a messenger. The name I knew him by was Cello Charlie, because one of his attributes, an unlikely one certainly, was playing the cello in some sort of works orchestra. He lived in Lambeth, in a high-rise council flat, but he was mostly to be found in a certain pub, and sure enough he was there today, drinking a mother-in-law, or stout-and-bitter. I bought him another and we chatted of this and that, then I produced a ten pound note and we got down to business. He didn't like it much, but I uttered a threat or two concerned with his past life, and he gave in. My message would go through channels and he would ring me at my flat within the next three hours. This concluded, I left him, got a bus across the bridge, then

140

a taxi to my flat, where I awaited developments. While I waited my thoughts grew more and more bitter: the flat I hated now, for it contained too many memorials of Felicity Mandrake. Pots of this and that in the bathroom, a discarded bra hanging desolately in my wardrobe. There was even the lingering smell of her scent from my pillow.

I wandered around feeling sad, with a glass of whisky in my hand. Also, I was very conscious of time passing: I kept looking at my watch and counting minutes.

Within the distance, my telephone burred. Cello Charlie's voice said, 'Nine-thirty tonight. Duke of York's steps, at the bottom near the Mall.' That was all; he rang off the moment the words were out. Who the hell, I thought, do I look out for? But no doubt WUSWIPP would cope and I would be approached...I refilled my glass moodily, feeling strangely and unusually apprehensive, a sort of gut feeling that things were not going to turn out at all well. I went out for a meal in a Greek place, the handy-for-home one I used with Felicity often enough, and pecked at the food like an off-colour chicken. Then I went back to the flat, and it was lucky I did, because I found my closed line from Focal House burring softly but somehow urgently. It was Max himself:

when trouble was on, the man never went off duty. Checks had revealed that at the relevant time a large Japanese vessel, the *Sendar Maru* by name, carrying nuclear waste for the Windscale ponds, had been reported off the Western Approaches. She had not entered any British port and had subsequently vanished. She was currently being sought by naval frigates out of Portsmouth and Plymouth and by aerial search.

'Now hold on to your hat,' Max said.

'Bad news, or could it be any worse?'

'Yes,' Max said briefly. 'Just under forty minutes ago a small coaster entered Plymouth Sound and got past Devil's Point into the Hamoaze before anyone ticked over. She crammed on speed and crashed the enclosed strike-proof nuclear submarine pens in Devonport dockyard before the doors could be shut. Two Polaris submarines are in there having just completed refitting. No missiles embarked, of course, but the nuclear power units are in place with the reactor cores ex Windscale, ready for sailing.'

* * * *

I went to my rendezvous. The thing had started in earnest now and secrecy could surely be maintained no longer. All Plymouth would know come morning. Max had told me that the huge reinforced doors had been shut on the coaster after she had entered and her crew was imprisoned inside, and so were a number of naval officers and ratings and some dockyard workmen. Luckily leave had been given that night, so the naval personnel was not present in large numbers. Defence Ministry was deliberating the next move in consultation with the PM and cabinet. It had occurred to me that the doors might be opened up and an attack launched against the villains, but Max had squashed this: such tactics, he said, might precipitate the nastiness and in any case the coaster's crew would be in a good defensive position and would clearly be heavily armed. If anything went wrong and the base was blown apart with its nuclear reactor cores, it would be goodbye Plymouth, and a lot of our defence capability was sited in that part of the country. The coaster's crew had entered with *kamikaze* panache and it could be taken as read that they were prepared for the ultimate self-sacrifice...Max said, coming round to what I'd stressed at our last meeting, that a cave-in might well be in the air, or at least a compromise; but I was convinced that no compromise would be acceptable to CORPSE. Why settle for less when you can win it all? And

143

surrender still struck me as grotesque, unthinkable, even now. The co-operation of WUSWIPP might turn the tide in time. That seemed more and more to be the only hope.

I approached the Duke of York's Steps from the Piccadilly direction, past the Athenaeum with its erudite membership enjoying its after-dinner port and brandy and cigars. I recognised a man coming down the steps, wearing a dinner jacket: a Lord Justice of Appeal. Cigar smoke wafted, an arm was raised, and a taxi came alongside. All so peaceful, but the *Garsdale Head* wasn't far away. There would be men inside the Athenaeum who would know about her cargo and who would be guarding their secret until CORPSE leaked the facts; or until the panic broke in Plymouth. I went on past the graven image of the mounted Duke of York and down the steps. Across the Mall, St James's Park was dark, the lights of London from Admiralty Arch and Buckingham Palace seeming to leave the trees shrouded in night's peace. I lingered under a street lamp and lit a cigarette. One or two other figures also lingered, back against the wall. Two men in leather jackets, belts studded with metal, and washed-out jeans and bovver boots. A girl, dressed like something out of Edward VII's reign, but without the elegance. The girl had a piercing laugh. Farther along the Mall, in shadow, also against the wall, a couple all but fornicated. I wondered why they didn't go in to the park to do it, joining the hundreds of others I assumed would be there. Too far to walk, perhaps, too much Mall traffic to cross. Up the Mall from the direction of the palace a policeman came; down the other way a mobile sped, blue light flashing and siren bleating. There was a fair crowd of pedestrians but I failed to spot anything that could check with WUSWIPP. Naturally, WUSWIPP wouldn't advertise, but I would know, all right, when the contact manifested. I looked at my watch: two minutes after nine-thirty now. Thirty more seconds passed and then I knew my man had come: not quite at the bottom near the Mall but near enough. Right by my lamp-post an Audi drew up and from the driving seat a large person leaned back and jerked the rear door open then spoke through his wound-down window.

'O.K, Commander, get in.'

I got in. The Audi U-turned into the traffic stream at once, no lingering, moving fast for Admiralty Arch. There were two men in front, both bulky men wearing dark hats: London could almost have been Moscow. Another man was in the back, sitting like the others in silence, back in his corner, also big, also hatted. As the lights of Trafalgar Square shone into the car, I saw the metal reflecting dully: the snout of a revolver, aimed at me and held steady. I also saw the man's face, but I didn't recognise it. Circumnavigating the massive roundabout of Trafalgar Square, the car exited up the Charing Cross Road, past the lit-up porn shops and the sex-aid establishments, and the strip and the massage in the side streets running off. An awful lot of enterprise was going to be atomised when the *Garsdale Head* blew. Half-way along, the passenger in front spoke without turning his head.

'You wanted to talk. We're listening.'

I said, 'I'm asking for help.'

'That's unusual.'

'Yes, isn't it,' I said as pleasantly as I could. 'I'm not suddenly seeing WUSWIPP as a bed of roses, but if you want Progress in Peace, now's your chance. You won't get far in a dead world.' I paused; the threat was only to Britain, but I could see it extending in the fullness of CORPSE's time. I said, 'Today Britain, tomorrow the world...and I think you know what I'm talking about.'

'Yes. Go on.'

'What else is there to say? You know about the threat. I'm asking for WUSWIPP's help in putting a stop to it, that's all. Also, I'd be interested to know why you haven't reacted already. I imagine you and CORPSE don't see eye to eye, do you?'

The answer was a laugh in which the two men in front joined forces: the man next to me concentrated, in a humourless way, on his gun. The front passenger said, 'You should not assume we haven't reacted, Commander Shaw. Soon you will see something.'

'See what?'

'Patience.'

The tone was final, and I was in WUS-WIPP's hands now. I asked no more questions. The car moved on through the night traffic, the lights throwing flickering shadows on the three big men. Like my back-seat companion, or guard, the driver was unknown to me: the third man's face I had yet to see, but I didn't recognise the voice. We kept on going north and after a longish while we stopped in an unfamiliar street, a poorly-lit street of high-rise flats. Council, obviously. Once there had been some grass, but no longer. Bangers were parked haphazard among flasher vehicles, from somewhere a noisy musical instrument played loudly, even rising over the muted sounds of transistors and the telly from a thousand open windows: it was a balmy night. A few children

147

played, preferring the street to bed. On the walls of the nearest block slogans had been sprayed, advertising the National Front, the Socialist Workers Party, Trotsky, Marx, and Blacks Out. All on its own another urged 'Tories Thatch Off'. On the gritty concrete in the shadows a girl fought two men for her virginity, but the giggles indicated that she didn't mind really. In the car, the three men stared ahead intently, waiting. After we had been *in situ* for ten minutes there was a wild scream from above and I caught a glimpse of something flashing past the lighted windows: a body, arms and legs whirling. The screams lasted almost till it hit the ground. After that, an uncanny silence set in for a space until the awed persons still abroad began to approach the jammy mess in the road. As they did so the WUSWIPP driver started up and moved ahead towards the remains. I saw the face clearly in the headlights: Polecat Brennan, with fixed stare.

We drove on past.

★ ★ ★ ★

Brennan, the front passenger told me, had flown in from Spain during the afternoon. His intention, under CORPSE orders, had been to

148

get me. WUSWIPP, in acting so promptly, had saved my life. I should be grateful. I said I was, but could have coped on my own if necessary. They didn't respond to that, but went on to say that Brennan had in fact been planted in the CORPSE outfit to get the information required after the first word had come through to WUSWIPP that the rival show was about to take the road. Having been planted, it seemed, Brennan had taken root and grown into CORPSE ways. CORPSE had treated him as something of a big shot, which he wasn't used to. There was no knowing what he might or might not have revealed about WUSWIPP, though on that point it was hoped he'd talked tonight before being pushed into space: there would be information about that shortly, the man said. Brennan had had to be eliminated for the better maintenance of WUSWIPP discipline, an example to others. He had been lured to the high-rise flat, all very much under cover, and there would be no come-backs. There would be a whole-block search and questioning, naturally, but no one would have been able to identify Polecat Brennan from life, and the couple who rented the flat from the council, long-service WUSWIPP lower-echelon members, would by now have packed and flown to a safe nest.

I said, 'So thanks for ridding the world of Polecat Brennan by anonymous means. But what now? Do I get your further help?'

The man said, 'Be precise. What help?'

'Use your influence,' I suggested. 'You have a big membership in all countries. You can prevent the sailing of any more ships carrying nuclear waste.'

'How?'

'Use your loaf, and for God's sake don't stall, there's not much time left.' I had broken out into a sweat by now. 'Strikes, refusals to handle dangerous cargoes, stoppages by tugmen—you know as well as I do! If the ships are at sea, they can be contacted by radio...it's not beyond WUSWIPP's ingenuity to pass a safe-sounding code message. Bring the crews out, or such of them as are WUSWIPP's paid lackeys.'

'Mutiny on the high seas?' There was a laugh in the voice. 'Risky for those involved!'

I began to lose patience. 'Whose side is WUSWIPP on?' I asked sourly. 'Do I take it you mean to share the spoils with CORPSE?'

'That is not so,' the man said, and now the voice was sharp. I'd trod on a toe. 'We are of the Left, CORPSE is of the Right. There will be no sharing, no accommodations offered. Give us credit for consistency, Commander Shaw. And in case you are thinking of doing

150

so, do not use the word expediency. There is no expediency in obliteration and WUSWIPP does not wish to see a take-over of Britain by the Right.'

'Then—'

'It is too late, Commander Shaw, that is the point.' For the first time the man in the front passenger seat turned round and looked at me directly. I didn't know him, but I read truth in that face, truth and sincerity, or I believed I did, plus a desire to help if at all possible—which, it seemed, it was not. 'The *Garsdale Head* lies ready in the Thames and that is a fact of current life that is impossible to reverse. No one, not even WUSWIPP, can prevent what is already irrevocably set up.'

I told him, then, about the ship that had crashed the nuclear submarine pens in Devonport Dockyard. It merely confirmed his opinion, and he added that WUSWIPP's information was that other nuclear-waste carriers were already approaching British shores. There was only the one way: strike at CORPSE's operating base and get control before the man in purple could make the final signal. I said how right he was, but no one would locate the base in time, not short of a miracle anyway. CORPSE had the whole world to use.

'I agree with you,' he said.

151

'Can't you help through your agencies? WUSWIPP has many ears to the ground.'

He made a gesture of impatience. 'You are teaching your grandmother. Our agencies are doing all they can, but CORPSE is elusive. As you have said by inference yourself, what now remains for them to do is simplicity itself, child's play that calls only for a transmitter.' There was a massive shrug. 'A room in an attic, a field, a tree-top even. And CORPSE will have alternatives. If one should go, the others will remain. There is just one possible but not very useful hope, Commander Shaw, and that is that Polecat Brennan will have talked before he died.'

I said bitterly, 'It's a pity you were so bloody hasty, isn't it? A little more time—'

'A fast example was imperative. WUSWIPP is currently under strain, and many of our members could be tempted by CORPSE. And the persons who dealt with Brennan are clever at extracting information. I have every confidence in their abilities...but I have one reservation.'

'Well?'

'Whatever Brennan has said, if he has spoken, cannot be relied on. Why?' There was a harsh laugh; I knew the answer before he gave it to me: once they learned of his death at

WUSWIPP hands, CORPSE would be expecting Polecat Brennan to have squealed, and all
they had to do was shift berth to somewhere
else. The places indicated by Brennan could be
relied upon as being where the man in purple
would *not* be found. The most we could hope
for was that an investigation of the revealed
places might yield clues.

And time did not stand still.

CHAPTER 9

Dropped by the WUSWIPP car right outside
Focal House, I reported at once to the suite.
Max was there, chewing at a cigar and sipping
a glass of brandy amongst busy telephones. I
told him about my useless evening and his
response was sour and bitter.

'Haggling with the enemy is always useless,
Shaw.'

'WUSWIPP's with us on this,' I pointed out.

'So's my backside.' Another telephone burred and Max listened in silence, said 'Yes,' into
the instrument, then banged it back on its rest.
'Downing Street. Still yacking—the cabinet.
They can't agree on evacuation of any part of

the metropolitan area, but Devonport's different.'

'Because the news will break in the morning?'

'Because it's broken already, as it was bound to. You don't crash bases, as you should know—'

'Sorry!'

'—with total damn secrecy. All the Plymouth area's in something bordering on panic and it's feared the armed services and police will lose control shortly. A lot of people are getting out already and the roads are in chaos. The cabinet's on the brink of ordering official evacuation. By tomorrow morning, the press will be carrying it nationwide. You can't put a clamp on this sort of thing—' The same telephone as before burred again. Having answered it, Max said, 'That's it. Plymouth area to be evacuated except for armed forces, police, and essential persons to maintain civil government. There'll be a Prime Ministerial announcement on television, time yet to be decided.'

'London?'

'No decision yet, and when it comes it's bound to be no. Ever tried to evacuate London?'

'Is the government,' I asked, 'going to

concede, do you suppose?'

Max threw up his hands; I didn't like the inherent despair in that simple gesture. After that, the messages came in from all directions and they were far from happy: the roads out of Plymouth were blocked solid, and the harbour was filled with boats of all sorts beating it across the Tamar or through the Sound for the open sea. Looting was going on, the vandals risking their lives for a wonderful opportunity. Already the political extremes were mustering, and marching on the Lord Mayor. From the submarine pens there was total silence, no contact had been made with the world outside. Families had besieged the dockyard gates and were being held off by a reinforced naval guard with rifles, and Ministry of Defence police. A senior naval officer was doing his best, trying to reassure them that all would be done that could be. Out at sea an over-stretched frigate force plus smaller craft had intercepted a handful of inward-bound ships in the Western Approaches and in Scottish waters also; searches were being carried out. It would be a drop in the ocean, clearly. More messages following closely indicated just how small a drop: entries followed by crew abandonments to presumably prepared funk-holes had been made in a number of places, some obvious choices, others unlikely but no doubt effective morale-wise: one off Shellhaven in the lower reaches of the Thames, a potentially devastating threat to Canvey Island with its stored liquefied petroleum gas, oil and chemicals. Others off Greenock in the Clyde, in the Mersey, in the Tyne. One in Great Yarmouth...one in Whitby. One in the mud slap beneath the Severn bridge, another similarly situated beneath the Forth road bridge. One anchored in Cowes Roads off the Isle of Wight. There was just one piece of good news: the Navy had located the suspect Japanese mothership *Sendai Maru* and she was being kept under surveillance. Then another good news item: in the Clyde the port authorities had been right on the ball and the entire crew of the vessel off Greenock had been apprehended as they came ashore.

Max said, 'I suggest they be put back aboard and left to fry. They just might decide to talk.'

I said that wouldn't be good enough; they wouldn't talk, if talk they did at all, until it was much too late. I told Max I was going up to the Clyde right away. He wished me luck.

★ ★ ★ ★

I went north in a 6D2-chartered aircraft from

Heathrow and was put down in Glasgow airport. The plane's pilot was under orders to remain and await my instructions. A police car met me and rushed me down the upper reaches of the Clyde to Greenock, lying peaceful beneath the moon whose light fell starkly on the Tail o' the Bank, on the Polaris submarine base at Faslane, and on the hills around Lock Lomond to the north-east. Another nuclear submarine base under threat, this time in the Gareloch. It looked as though the whole of our sea strike force, or anyway its effective part, was locked in. The submarine service was today's effective Navy: the rest was of small account. NATO needed those submarines. However, I need not have worried on that score; also present when I reached the police station, where the danger vessel's crew were being held, was a Captain RN from the staff of Rear-Admiral Submarines at Fort Blockhouse in Portsmouth dockyard, and a Captain USN. They told me the NATO Polaris fleet, British and American—the latter in fact carrying Poseidon missiles—was being moved to sea from the Gareloch and would not enter port until further orders. To enter the Tail o' the Bank for the passage past Cloch Point to the Cumbraes and the Firth of Clyde, they would need to squeeze past the abandoned vessel: she had been left swinging at anchor between Roseneath Patch, a somewhat nasty submerged bank, and the entrance to the Gareloch.

I went with Greenock's police chief, and a little short man from the Foreign Office who'd just beat me to it, to interrogate the merchant seamen. They were all Dutch except for one man, the cook, who was a Norwegian. They hadn't much English between them and I had no Dutch nor Norwegian, so the Foreign Office man came in handy. He spoke both. I just listened while he interpreted their conversation for me, and in point of fact he wasn't overworked: those men, interviewed singly, had clammed right up. They admitted the cargo content and they admitted the explosive device that would scatter the load, and that was their lot. They simply shrugged off everything else. The master was a real tough nut, so was the first mate. They had dangerous faces, hard as iron, and a formidable way of speaking. Maybe they were part of the overseas *gauleiter* delivery; CORPSE would need some men with sea experience to run the ports, or such as would be left afterwards. When the man from the Foreign Office had got through five of the twenty, I spoke into his ear and suggested he might remove the velvet gloves and drop the hint that we could always put the crew back aboard their death-ship till they talked and shoot any man who tried to make it overboard before the end. He nodded, whispered back: 'Good wheeze,' and said he would try it on. Thereafter I noticed no change in the expressions of the crew. All the same, after the interrogations had been completed with a nil result, I decided Max might be right and asked the Foreign Office man if he would in fact authorise the order to have the bastards put back aboard and the ship surrounded with a sea-borne guard.

He didn't like that. To actually do it would be crude. He pursed his lips and held his head back, a short-arse trying to look down his nose. He said, 'Good heavens, no, my dear chap!'

'Why not?'

'Well, think of the trouble it would cause in Europe. Surely you've heard of Human Rights? We'd never get away with it, never!' He was quite indignant.

'Uh-huh,' I said, musingly. 'Cruelty, degradation, lack of respect for the dignity of the person...that sort of thing?'

'Exactly. The threat was simply that—a threat. I'd never dream of putting it into effect.'

I nearly burst a blood-vessel. I said, 'If I were

you I'd go back to London. There's—what—thirteen million or so people there, waiting for the *Garsdale Head* to blow. When it does, you'll see all the cruelty and degradation and whatnot that you need...you might even send a memo about it to the Human Rights people if you have time.'

★ ★ ★ ★

I decided I'd wasted my time: the Foreign Office is impervious to everyone, a law unto itself. Max might get the wheels in motion, but what we did not want at this delicate stage was interdepartmental friction. Also it was all too possible that those dedicated seamen wouldn't open up wherever they were put, thought there was the chance that the crew contained a weaker member who would break, and when the deadline was all but run even the Foreign Office might change its tune. In the meantime an idea came to me as, going out to the police car for the drive back to Glasgow airport, I felt the cold night breeze coming off the Tail o' the Bank: the vessel herself—she was the Dutch-registered *Johann Klompé*—could well speak louder than her silent crew. If I could get aboard...the risk was great in theory but, I felt, not necessarily in practice. True, CORPSE had threatened to blow if anyone boarded their death ships, but I didn't believe they would react so strongly to a first probe. They stood to gain all they wanted from just the big threat which might induce the British Government to surrender, and why lay waste so much of a country they wished to take over until they were convinced surrender would not come? Besides, they had plenty of other ships on station.

I reckoned it was worth the chance, but I knew I had to do it on my own responsibility and not involve 6D2 or the Foreign Office. In the nick I'd been told that the *Johann Klompé* was under surveillance from a circling naval cutter, and somehow I had to get past that cutter. As I was pondering, and keeping my police driver waiting, the US Navy Captain emerged, chatting to the officer from Fort Blockhouse. I heard him say that his gasoline gig was standing by to take him back to the Gareloch, and I reached a decision.

'I'd like to take a look at the Gareloch, and the *Johann Klompé* in passing,' I said. 'I'd appreciate a lift, Captain.'

'Sure,' he said at once. I dismissed my driver; I would make arrangements later with the nick. In company with the USN I went out across the dark waters of the Clyde, approach-

161

ing but keeping clear of Roseneath Patch and the silent coaster beyond. She was a compact little ship and looked very clean in the moonlight. Living quarters aft, also the engine-room, leaving all the fore part for her cargo. She carried a deck cargo in addition to what lay below hatches—on deck were cased goods of so-far unknown content. I noted that her starboard accommodation-ladder was down: the crew would have come off that way and there would be no one to restow the ladder. As we approached I chatted-up Captain Jefferson, USN, who happened to be one of the top controlling brass from the Poseidon fleet. As a matter of fact he'd been yacking all the way across, being a friendly man. He'd sure hate to think, he said, of New York harbour having such a threat in it. All Manhattan, Brooklyn and New Jersey would go up.

'Just like crazy,' he said, shaking his head. 'Can you imagine it, Commander?'

'Very easily,' I told him. 'Let's hope it doesn't happen.'

'They wouldn't try it on us, I reckon. Too big a land mass, and too far for CORPSE to extend effectively.'

'You could be right,' I said non-committally. I believed he was, in fact. CORPSE would probably be satisfied with Britain, would have enough on their plate, and by the time they were ready to consider expansion the world would have come to grips with the problem of nuclear-waste-carrying ships. I went on, 'Currently I'm more concerned with right here. I think I can do some good, with your negative assistance.'

Jefferson stared. 'Come again?'

I swept an arm towards the coaster, sudden death beneath the backdrop of the distant mountains. 'A look-see, that's all.' I explained my theories as to why CORPSE wouldn't blow at the first boarding, and he was with me. I asked, 'Do you happen to have a blind eye?'

He grinned, teeth beautifully white in the moon. 'Like Nelson?'

I grinned back. 'Just like Nelson. Strike a blow for freedom, why not?'

'Well...so long as my name doesn't go down in history.'

I took his point: I assured him he would not be implicated. He wasn't all eyes, especially when looking intently the other way to ensure that his coxswain kept well on target for the Gareloch entry. Just give me a start, I said, and he could raise all hell afterwards, and could use his four gold stripes and brass hat to keep the cutter well away from the *Johann Klompé* in case CORPSE should grow apprehensive about too many boarders.

I watched my time, and Captain Jefferson watched anything but me, and I slid over the gunwale aft at the precise moment that the crew of the guard cutter had the *Johann Klompé* between themselves and the gasoline gig so had no view of the latter. I went deep and aimed true, and surfaced almost on target. A few more strokes and I was hauling myself on to the lower platform of the accommodation-ladder. As I ran up to the deck dripping water, I became aware of distant consternation and heard Jefferson's voice yelling through a megaphone at the cutter's crew, something to the effect that Commander Shaw had gone arse over tit and they better had converge on the gasoline gig to look for him, which they did. Reaching the deck I became aware of a low hum coming from somewhere below, and a pronounced vibration in the plates. I went through a door into the superstructure, closing the door behind me. All the lighting had been switched off and I had to grope around for a switch. I found I was where I'd expected to be: I was in an enclosed alley with no ports. I didn't want the shore authorities to see the lights coming on, so thereafter I banged down deadlights before lighting up the cabins, saloon and other compartments. It was all very ordinary: clothing lying around, personal possessions, girlie magazines, bottles of schnapps, cigarettes—all just as though the crew expected they might come back. Curious ...but of course they'd stuffed their pockets with all they could manage—the nick had been like an off-licence. I went through the master's accommodation with extra care, and soon came upon his safe. This I had no means of opening, and if there was anything of any interest to an intruder, it would be in the safe, so I drew a blank.

I went down to the engine-room, the source of all power. As I went lower in the ship I found the vibration and the hum increasing. That, I guessed, would be the water-cooling system for the nuclear-waste flasks. I took a quick look around, then climbed for the bridge and chart-house: again, all very ordinary. The radio room beckoned and I went towards it; it focused my attention on things like signal transmissions and device-tripping codes. I was about to go in, or anyway to try the door which could well have been locked, when I became aware of a racket coming closer across the Clyde.

Pausing, I listened.

A desperate voice was booming out through a loud hailer, and it seemed Commander Shaw was required urgently. I cursed, but stepped out into the bridge wing.

165

I saw a boat lying off; a moment later a searchlight played on to the *Johann Klompé* and in its back-glow I saw a police inspector and the man from the Foreign Office, braver than I had thought likely. He was going mad, waving his arms and shouting. When he saw me, he became more coherent.

'You are to get into the boat immediately. I speak for the Prime Minister. Come on down.'

'Has there,' I called, 'been a reaction from our friends?'

'*Yes!*' he screamed. 'And two and two added up to you!'

I went down, and fast. One thing seemed proved: CORPSE had the claimed ability to spot intruders. I wouldn't get another chance, but we knew where we stood beyond doubt. As I stepped into the boat, the Foreign Office man gabbled at me: CORPSE had contacted Whitehall by radio and the message had come instantly to the Clyde. The intruder must be taken off or within thirty minutes there would be a local bang, the first in the series. I looked at my watch: I'd already been aboard not all that far short of thirty minutes and I began to feel a sense of rush all of a sudden. The Foreign Office man was quite frantic, keen to be away fast. He kept dabbing at his trousers with a handkerchief; the suit had probably come from

Savile Row, and a good deal of the Clyde had slopped over it.

★ ★ ★ ★

I was due for a surprise later, and a stroke of good fortune that I could well do with, though it didn't appear to be quite that at the time it happened. My police driver had returned in the interval to Glasgow, and I was provided with another car from local resources, and off we set, as next day's small hours slid into dawn, for the airport and my waiting plane. We had just joined the motorway from the A8 when my driver and I became aware of another police car behind us, coming up fast and using its light and siren. On the trail of some domestic villain, I thought, but no: the mobile, passing us, slowed to our speed and put on its POLICE STOP sign, and we pulled behind it on to the hard shoulder and two uniformed men got out, one of them an inspector, and marched back towards us. The inspector took the driver's side and the constable came to my window. Not a word was said but two automatics stared at us. When we'd taken that in, the bogus inspector uttered.

'Out and take it easy or you're dead men.'

I glanced at my driver, and nodded. Then I

turned to the armed man at my window. 'Okay,' I said. Both my driver and I tried the old trick, in the same instant: we slid the catches and rammed our doors open, crash. The man on my side must have been a rookie at the game; he fell for it, literally, going flat, and I was out and on him before he could stagger up. A boot in his face and he dropped his gun, which I picked up. When I saw the other man coming for me, I fired point blank and dropped him, dead with a bullet right through the heart. My driver hadn't been as lucky as me: his assailant had nipped back in time and used his gun effectively before running round to his mate's assistance. The genuine copper was as dead as the fake inspector, I found a few moments later. Keeping my gun on the fake constable, who had no doubt at all that I would use it as soon as I had to, I used the two-way radio and called Greenock nick. And watched all the cars speed past...sane people don't stop at shoot-ups, nor if they can help it do they stop anywhere near police cars on motorways. I had just put down the radio when I saw a figure sliding out of the fake cop car, and because I couldn't leave chummy unattended in order to apprehend the emergent person, I opened fire and dropped him. Screams came back and I saw the man trying to drag himself to safety, without success. He flopped down, moaning and blaspheming, in a pool of blood. I had to let him lie until reinforcements came in from Greenock. When they arrived I was able to investigate my wounded villain, and that was when I got the surprise, for a man known to be dead stared me in the face. Dead Polecat Brennan in fact, not dead at all though in a fairly sorry state from the bullet wound. To say I was flummoxed would be to put it mildly. You only die once, according to James Bond.

★ ★ ★ ★

Things, the Glasgow police told me later, were in a bad way down south. Too early for the morning papers, of course, but word from Plymouth had reached London overnight: some private telephone calls, indeed a lot of private telephone calls until the exchange had pulled out the plugs on orders received, had informed the lay population of London that a lot of people were coming home to mum and dad for a while, and the news had spread like the plague. It had reached down into the underground lavatories at Piccadilly Circus and the junkies and hippies had ascended like maggots to the surface and had demonstrated noisily in Trafalgar Square, although one of them, asked by a police constable what he was demonstrating about, had replied, 'Shit, daddy, I don't know, do I, man?' The Met were expecting crowds outside the Defence Ministry and at the entrance to Downing Street from Whitehall, where the police barriers were already up. The police stations all over London had been besieged with anxious enquiries. So far, I was told, no one seemed to have cottoned-on as to the cargo content of the *Garsdale Head*, but it was probably only a matter of time now. Meanwhile I had to be on my travels again: back south to London by air, plus Polecat Brennan in a stretcher with attendant nurse. Max, contacted by me, had pulled strings rapidly and though the Glasgow police protested routinely they were overruled and Brennan and the fake constable were handed over to 6D2, which meant me. Polecat Brennan and his mate were going to go under a very highly concentrated grill. We have some excellent grillers inside Focal House; and as a matter of fact Brennan had done a little talking already—to me, by special pressure, for there were things I had to know. When I reached FH and the suite, and after Max had been woken from some snatched sleep, I told him what Brennan had coughed and at the same time confessed my previous error of identity.

'The man I saw fall to his death...I could

have sworn he was Brennan. A good likeness, which was either a lucky break for WUSWIPP in finding him, or some good work from make-up—enough to fool me. And why? Well, according to Brennan, who was quite well aware of his "death", it was simply because WUSWIPP wanted me to believe he *was* dead. That, in its turn, was because—'

'Because the living Brennan's still working for CORPSE, and WUSWIPP wanted to keep him at it, unknown to you, for their own purposes. That's obvious.' Max looked sardonic.

'Not at all,' I told him. 'It's not the fact—not in the way you mean...which is, isn't it, that WUSWIPP's trying genuinely to put the skids under CORPSE?'

Max's eyebrows went up. 'Aren't they?'

'No,' I said. 'WUSWIPP's in with CORPSE. This is a joint attack after all.' Max showed immense surprise as well he might, but I went on: 'The apparent death of Brennan for reasons as given to me by the WUSWIPP representative was intended to convince me that WUSWIPP was still anti-CORPSE and would help in the fight against them if and when they could. All of which Brennan has now revealed ...he was in a bad way and he was indiscreet. I'd have pressed further, only he went out like a light and stayed there.'

171

Max let out a long breath. 'And now?'

'He may have come round,' I said. 'If he hasn't, I'll wait till he has, then I'll be going down to join the grill.' I changed the subject. 'Has anything emerged from Downing Street, anything positive as to government thinking?'

Max shrugged and answered, 'Not exactly positive. The cabinet's still in session and the Chiefs of Staff are with them. And the Commissioner...and the Chief Constables of immediately affected areas. I understand they're formulating contingency plans and as a first step the government's likely to shift inland.'

'Evacuation of London?'

'Impossible, as I've said before. Nasty if it happens, but there we are,' Max hesitated, and I saw his eyes go above my head to where there was a head-and-shoulders portrait of the Queen in Garter Robes. 'Buckingham Palace has been contacted.'

'And?'

'The Royal Family's returning there from Windsor. They won't leave again unless a general evacuation's ordered, which I repeat is impossible.' Max paused again. 'Got her father's guts...I remember the war.' I believe he was about to say more, but was cut short by the burr of his internal line via Mrs Dodge, loyally remaining at her post throughout the

172

night, the same as her master. Max answered; Brennan, it seemed, had come round.

I got up. 'Right,' I said. 'I'll go down and report soonest possible.'

'Are you going to put the boot in, Shaw?'

I said I was.

'You're a bastard sometimes, aren't you,' Max said, but there was a grin lurking round his eyes. He could be a bastard, too.

CHAPTER 10

The WUSWIPP man who'd arranged the death that wasn't Brennan's had told me that he hoped Brennan had talked before he 'died'. By now, of course, that was phony history but Brennan, the real Brennan, was now all set up, and talk, I determined, he would, wounded or not—I'd smashed his right shoulder and hip-bone with my bullets—and one of the things he was going to talk about was Miss Mandrake: I'd had the girl on my mind solidly, and was hating myself for not being able to do anything for her. In the circumstances we were faced with, she couldn't be a top priority but she was not far below so far as I was concerned. Once again the deadline hit me: we now had thirty hours left, and so had Felicity Mandrake.

I joined 6D2 Britain's top interrogator, a man known simply as Number Four, late major in the Intelligence Corps with service in Northern Ireland. We sat behind a plain deal table covered with ink stains and precious little else. Number Four loomed across it, heavy and pugnacious, really more like a military policeman than an Intelligence officer. He had big shoulders and a large square head, and big hairy hands that he laid flat on the table as bandaged Polecat Brennan was carried in by two of our tough squad, one an ex-sergeant of the Met, the other a former Guards NCO. These two big boys stood one on either side of Brennan as he was held upright facing the table. Behind, another man took up station, coming into the room with a fourth guard who stood back against the door cradling a sub-machine gun. It was all over-dramatised, but with a purpose. Brennan must have known we wouldn't use that sub-machine gun, but all the same he eyed it nervously. One thing he was positive about was that strictly we had no right to be holding him: as accessory to a killing he was police property and never mind Max. That cut no ice. I said, 'Whatever happens to you in our custody, Brennan, will not be made public. We

174

even,' I said, tongue-in-cheek, 'have a corpse disposal unit and you can take that both ways at once if you like.'

That seemed actually to rock him; when you've been brought up to WUSWIPP ideals, and then CORPSE ones, I reckon you really believe such extravagances, and Brennan had plenty of reason in the past to know that 6D2 were very, very effective. Also that we didn't stick to the rules, which was where we had the edge over the police and the rest of the Establishment agencies. I went on, 'Considering where you were during last night, you'll also know we have the entire crew of the *Johann Klompé*. Dedication's all very well, but some are more dedicated than others. There'll be talking very soon. Those who talk will get... let's say, preferential treatment afterwards. If I were you, Brennan, I'd consider that very carefully indeed.' I felt a touch on my shoulder: it was Number Four, who whispered in my ear. He whispered nothing of any significance, but whispers are a pretty useful softening-up agent. The man whispered about doesn't like it at all. I responded in more whispers, then Number Four nodded and got up.

He walked slowly over to Brennan and stood there looking sour and moving his shoulders like a rugby scrum-half. 'Two things first,' he said. 'Where do we find the CORPSE bosses, and where is Miss Mandrake?'

'That's all?'

'For now.'

Brennan said, 'I don't know. Try something else.' He appeared cocky, but there was a tremble in his lips: Number Four's very slowness and solidity and calmness had a kind of built-in effect of their own. He'd been highly successful in Belfast.

Number Four said, 'All right, I will.' He reached out his hands, stared at them, flexed the fingers, then looked again at Polecat Brennan. 'We shall want to know a whole lot of things: the names of persons already planted in Britain for the running of the country. The arrangements made for bringing in support —times, places, numbers. Their present dispositions. The method by which CORPSE knows when one of those death ships is boarded. Names of persons in other countries who might usefully be brought in by the authorities acting in co-operation with the British Government. You know the sort of thing we need, Brennan.'

'I don't know the answers.'

Number Four disregarded that. He said, 'Let's go back to Miss Mandrake, shall we, from whom all else could very easily flow.

I believe you know where she's being held, Brennan—'

'Things change,' Brennan broke in. 'Wherever she was yesterday, and I don't even know that, she might not be there today.'

'Possibly, but a starting off point's always useful, don't you think, Brennan?'

'I don't know where she is.' Brennan sounded sulky.

'I think you have some ideas nevertheless. When they emerge, they'd better be the truth—I'm sure I needn't elaborate. I'll just add this: time's remarkably short now, and we haven't enough of it to go in for long term persuasion. Know what I mean? Face against the wall, arms lifted, no sleep, continual noise. It's effective, but time-consuming.' Number Four paused, eyebrows lifted. 'You'll talk?'

Brennan said, 'No.'

Number Four gave a slight jerk of his head and the two supporting guards on either side of Brennan lifted him in the air, swivelling his body so that his head was towards Number Four. Number Four seized it, one hand below the jaw, the other behind the head itself. Each of the guards took a leg and made an angle of some forty-five degrees with Brennan's crutch. Then all three pulled mightily and stretched Polecat Brennan. He screamed. This was going way beyond anything that had ever happened in Belfast. The neck elongated so that his collar looked several sizes too large for him. Something happened to the wounded hip: I believe the leg came clear of the socket. There was a funny bulge in the bandages and plaster. Brennan went on screaming in agony.

★ ★ ★ ★

The medical section attended to Brennan on the floor of the grill room then put him back on a stretcher. He was a broken man in more ways than the obvious one, and he knew that if he didn't talk the other leg, and then the arms, shot shoulder and all, would go. So he talked, though he didn't talk much because he didn't know much. I believed him, so did Number Four. To my sorrow he didn't know where Miss Mandrake was: the last he'd known of her had been in the cell near the Ark's slipway. Nor did he know the whereabouts of the CORPSE operational unit; again, his last knowledge was of the Flood Fearer set-up. He did confirm that CORPSE could operate on a pinhead, one man and a boy as it were. And the hard information he did give was useful: it would prevent the inadvertent blowing up of the various bugged ships in British ports; and,

178

hearing what he said, I was thankful that I'd been prevented from mucking about in the radio room aboard the *Johann Klompé* the night before. The radio rooms, not unexpectedly, controlled the devices that sent the word winging to CORPSE when anyone boarded, and just in case it should occur to authority to inhibit or destroy the radio rooms themselves by outboard means, they were all set to go into automatic blow-up if there was any interference with them as radio units.

It looked more hopeless than ever: CORPSE had covered everything. On the face of it, we were beaten. When that awareness spread, surrender would seem virtually certain as the only alternative left.

★ ★ ★ ★

The fake copper was less useful than Brennan: he told us nothing. Never had I felt so frustrated.

I left Focal House while Polecat Brennann was being put together again and went out into a London that seemed all at once strange and alien. By now the papers had all carried the news from Plymouth, and London was in a state of shock even though nothing had broken as yet about the *Garsdale Head*, nor indeed about the various other waiting death ships around the coasts. People gathered on street corners, strangers yacking like old friends. No one seemed interested in work. The pubs were full, buzzing with strain and talk. There had been no Prime Ministerial broadcast after all and I wondered why. Was the cabinet even now facing the cave-in, the hand-over to CORPSE and WUSWIPP, but delaying the announcement for fear of what might happen in the streets? Once the decision was made, there would be a vacuum until CORPSE took over, a time in which it would be every man for himself, a time in which the government, still theoretically in being, would be a thing to disregard...I found a taxi, and went along again to stare morbidly at the *Garsdale Head*, seeking inspiration, a way of dealing with an impossible affair. I came upon a group of soldiers, men of a bomb disposal squad ordered by the Defence Ministry to remain handy, just in case.

'In case of what?' I asked the major in command, and he just shrugged: he knew his own uselessness, but authority had to do something however daft. Defence Ministry, he said, had ordered squads to stand by in all ports under threat, and they would all be as useless as his. I looked across at the Houses of Parliament, and Big Ben still ticking the time away to

180

countdown. This afternoon, Parliament would be meeting as usual, it not yet being the summer recess. I wondered how many of the Lords and Commons knew what was right alongside them. Not far behind, the good clergy of Westminster Abbey stood in equal peril, and so did the throngs of sightseers, the tourists from all over the world. I felt my fingernails dig into my palms: it was more than time for the government to act in preservation of life...yet I saw the dilemma only too clearly. You just could not evacuate London, at least not in anything approaching an orderly fashion, and the moment you shut down anything like Westminster Abbey and tried to clear the river area, you simply asked for panic. By now, Plymouth was in everybody's mind and two and two would be put together instantly. Already, to any thinking person, the static position of the *Garsdale Head,* on the mud still at low water, was odd to say the least. Authority could bet its last cent that the security would spring a leak soon. What about all the staff of the Port of London Authority, for a start, and the lightermen and so on? They weren't fools, nor were the crews of the other coasters capable of coming so far up river: they had eyes. The cover story was, to me, as thin as dog's-wool: it had been announced officially that the *Garsdale*

Head had been loaded below her marks, and had grounded on a mud bank, and the crew had been taken off pending an attempt to shift her. Many *would* believe it, no doubt...

I felt a touch on my back and I turned. I came face to face with Cello Charlie, peasant of WUSWIPP. For a moment I thought of nabbing him and grilling him like Polecat Brennan, but the thought didn't linger. Cello Charlie was of no account at all. Anyway, he seemed glad to see me: been trying, he said, to contact me by phone at my flat. I said I hadn't been around and asked what he wanted.

'Dunno reelly.' Charlie wrinkled his nose. 'May be nothing in it, not worth bothering like.'

'Let me be the judge, Charlie.'

He stared at me. 'Look bloody tired, you do. Not much sleep?'

'Last night,' I said, 'none at all.' Nor, for that matter, the night previous. It was hitting me now, so hard all of a sudden once Charlie had mentioned it, that I seemed scarcely to be registering. The *Garsdale Head* looked peaceful enough; maybe she was. It was all like a bad, bad dream and once more I had that thought (and again rejected it) that the whole bloody show could be a bluff, and CORPSE were relying on Britain packing it in just on the

182

threat alone. Meanwhile Charlie was picking his nose and muttering away to himself. I told him to say what he had to say and he did. The night before—while I'd been way up north on the bonnie banks of Clyde—he'd met a bloke in a pub, a Dutchman. Charlie hadn't so much met him, it turned out, as eavesdropped on him. The Dutchman had been talking to another man, a drunk Irishman, and from their conversation Charlie had deduced them to be seamen. They had been joined after a while by another man, a Japanese Charlie thought, or he could have been Chinese.

'Hard to say, like, with them. He was pissed like the Irish bloke, pissed as a newt he was. But he talked about a Jap ship, something Maru, and Maru means Japanese, don't it?'

'Yes,' I said, all ears. 'What about it?'

'Nothing reelly, just that it was somewhere near England, handy placed. Then this morning I read the papers, didn't I? Cor! Them poor sods down in Plymouth...don't bear thinking about.' Charlie picked his nose again. 'Paper I read said there was nuclear waste on board the boat what crashed in.'

'I wonder how they deduced that, Charlie?'

'Well,' he answered reasonably enough, 'don't ask me. Some Navy bloke said what he didn't ought to, p'raps. And the Japs...they send their nuclear waste to Windscale for re-processing, right?'

'Right,' I agreed. Charlie's phrase 'handy placed' was weighing hard. 'And you see a link with your Jap friend in the pub, do you?'

He shrugged. 'Just thought it worth mentioning, like.' Then he used the phrase again: handy placed. Think about it, he said.

I nodded. 'I will, and thanks. I suppose you don't happen to know where I can find this Jap, do you, Charlie?' I asked the question more or less sardonically, but I might have known. Charlie, after all, had seen service with WUSWIPP. He'd followed the Japanese after closing time, and now he gave me the address. Surprisingly, it was in Westminster: an expensive Edwardian block of flats that I happened to know. Not the sort of address where you'd expect to find Japanese seamen. Another thing intrigued me as well: why hadn't Charlie reported to WUSWIPP instead of to me? I put it to him. He said he had reported to WUS-WIPP and they had been supercilious about it, told him not to go worrying about will-o'-the-wisps or something, though they had noted the address; then he had remembered me, done some more putting together of two and two and linked me in with the horror story from Plymouth. I gave him credit for good thinking. He was short of cash, and a shortage of cash usually produces thought...I slipped him a ten pound note, chargeable to my expense account. He went away then, sliding fast into the crowd, making for his local.

I stayed on the bridge, pondering. There could well be nothing whatever in Charlie's story, in fact he could even have invented the whole thing just to make some quick money. On the other hand, he couldn't have known about the proximity of the *Sendai Maru;* there had been nothing about that in the papers. His tip might be worth the tenner I'd given him, but there was another angle that had to be taken into account: WUSWIPP may well have sounded supercilious about it, but I was pretty sure they wouldn't disregard it, and a talkative Japanese seaman living in Westminster would probably receive a visit before long if he hadn't already. A touch of circumspection was called for, but the premises might be worth a little distant surveillance.

I walked back towards Westminster, across Parliament Square and along Victoria Street. Passing New Scotland Yard I noted the comings and goings, the brass well and truly on the move. Farther on, I turned off left.

* * * *

185

The block had just the one residents' entrance, the others being service doors. There was a pub opposite, and I watched over a lager. People came and went, not all that frequently, but frequently enough to keep me on my toes as it were. No Japanese, or Chinese either. Coloured people now and again, looking prosperous: lawyers, doctors, businessmen—that sort. No familiar faces, but of course I knew only a handful of WUSWIPP people so that proved nothing, I could be too late anyway. The Japanese himself may only have been staying overnight; he was, I thought—if Charlie had been right in his assumption that the man was a seaman—unlikely to be a resident in his own right. I grew restive; what the hell was I doing here anyway? Wild goose chases loomed to mock at me. I almost heard the tick of my own wrist-watch, urging me to remember passing time. But I was stymied; there were no leads at all to work on, no way, just no way of getting at the CORPSE leadership, of inhibiting them in time, so I was clutching at straws. The reports coming in to Focal House up to the time I'd left had all indicated that everyone else was equally stymied. There had been an appalling paralysis in the air. Everyone's thoughts were really concentrating on what to do when the blow-ups came, or on the chances offered by giving in before it all happened. The whole situation was so impossible to deflect. Impatience took me by the throat and I got to my feet, the decision made to do something that might be dead risky since I might drop myself slap into a WUSWIPP or CORPSE pounce. I was still dead tired and perhaps my judgment was clouded, I don't know. Anyway, acting on impulse really, I went out, crossed the road and went into the block of flats.

I found a man in a small glass-enclosed cubby-hole and said I was looking for a man who'd found my wallet: a Japanese. I couldn't reproduce the name, I said, but he lived here.

'Not live, sir,' the man said. 'Not live. Just a visitor. That's to say, there's only the one Japanese gentleman in the block as I know of.' He told me the name of the relevant tenant, the host; the name rang no bells. Or it could have done: the name was Smith. He gave me the number and I said I would go up. He offered to telephone ahead, and although I guessed he would anyway, I told him not to bother. I went up in the lift, fourth floor, and outside a very solid door I rang the bell, not without fear. No answer. I tried again; still no answer. There was a letter-box, and I bent and pushed in the flap. I looked down a long, narrow hall. The hall was empty of life and I took a chance on it that the whole flat would be equally empty. From my pocket I brought a set of master keys, made specially by our own 6D2 locksmiths and guaranteed to open any lock, Yale type or mortice, in the British Isles and some overseas. As it happened, the very first one I tried, worked.

I went in, shutting the door behind me. I looked into all the rooms—sitting-cum-dining room, two bedrooms, kitchen, bathroom, W.C —and found all empty. I didn't know how long I would be left alone, of course, so I worked fast and searched for clues...clues to anything that might help, that might produce a lead from a vacuum of ideas. I chose the sitting-room first because it contained a kneehole desk. A nice one, well polished mahogany. One drawer only was locked. I riffled through the others first, pulling them right out to look behind, but found nothing of interest. Then I broke out the lock of the central drawer with a small pocket jemmy. Again nothing: receipts, a cheque book, some share certificates, a thousand-pound holding in National Savings Certificates, 14th issue. The name was still Smith.

Cursing, I banged the drawer shut.

There was a bookcase: bookcases can hide things that aren't books but it would be a long job. Anyway, I started taking out the books one by one. Smith was a man of wide tastes. His books covered almost everything from Alastair MacLean to a biography of Zinoviev, the Russian who had sent the letter that put the lid on Labour in the 1924 General Election. Philosophy and Economics, Drama, Archaeology, enough to constipate any normal brain. And travel books and books on sex...I stopped at a couple of books on Spain. A work on the gypsies of Andalusia, and, somewhat out of context amongst the non-fiction, a novel: *Death in the Afternoon*, by Ernest Hemingway. When I flipped the pages of the latter and a sheet of notepaper fell out, I believed I'd struck gold and I had. It was a brief note, an *aide memoire*. Brigadier B, it read, if anything went wrong, could be contacted in Torremolinos. The name of a hotel, and a telephone number, were given.

I memorised the contents, which was easy enough, and slid the paper back into Hemingway and Hemingway back on the shelf. All was secure, though it was one hell of a pity about that damaged drawer-lock—but that couldn't be helped now. I was on the way: 'if anything went wrong' and 'Torremolinos' and 'Brigadier B'. Brigadier B was Brigadier Bunnett, so much I knew from a list of Flood Fearers, a sort of parish roll of all Britons and other nationalities foreign to Spain living in the vicinity of Carena, supplied by 6D2 Madrid; these people might or might not in fact be Flood Fearers but among them would be those who were, and Brigadier Bunnett was for sure—he would have been the Brigadier who had broadmindedly saved the pastor's bacon over La Ina. So what with all that, and Cello Charlie's Japanese, and the mention of a Jap ship name...it just had to tie up. And I kicked myself hard: it was true that Senor de Panata in Madrid's 6D2 HQ had sent word through that all the Flood Fearers were clean—it was also true that the man in purple had said they were not concerned in Petersen's activities—but hell! No doubt they *would* appear lovely and clean, with backgrounds beyond reproach ...English gentlemen of leisure and all that...but now it hit me like a bomb: who in fact would be more likely to prove CORPSE's most manured breeding ground than a set of ultra-conversative expatriates disillusioned with the New Britain, whether it be under Jim or Maggie, Tony or Willy or whoever? They were ready-made for the job. Tailor-made, rather, a good fit. Patriotism was their watchword; to that, CORPSE would have managed to appeal, and the security cover would have been right up their street too: religion. Flood Fearers my backside: they, or anyway a hard core of them led by Brigadier Bunnett, were in it up to the neck, Flood, Noah, Ark and all...

On the desk, a telephone bell rang out, startlingly. An outside call, or the little man in the cubby-hole, having a busy day announcing visitors for Mr Smith? With WUSWIPP in mind, I opted for the latter, and I went for the window, leaving the phone unanswered, which might appear funny to the custodian but couldn't be helped. Like many of the older blocks of flats in London, a wide ledge ran just below the window and out I scrambled, managing to shut the window behind me. It was vital that I get away with my new knowledge, or anyway my well-founded theories, rather than start a fresh war with WUSWIPP, one I might well lose, since WUSWIPP seldom worked in less than threes. I went along the ledge fast to get out of sight should anyone look through the window, and I got round a corner to safety from prying eyes. Prying WUSWIPP eyes, anyway: I was in fact spotted through an adjacent window by a middle-aged woman standing stark naked by a ruffled bed. She screamed. The window was open and I climbed in, by which time she was sheeted modestly but very frightened and angry.

I apologised. I said I had no designs upon her, and no, I was not a Peeping Tom. As she backed for the bedroom door I followed, saying she could ring Scotland Yard, or Focal House's number, or Defence Ministry, and they would all vouch for me. That checked her, and she began to recover. I laid it on very thick, quoted the Official Secrets Act or what was left of it, and said she was never, never to breathe a word to anyone at all about the incident or HM Government would pounce and shove her in Holloway. To make certain, I insisted that she ring Scotland Yard and ask for the Commissioner himself, quoting my name. She was quite overcome. I left her feeling she had struck a blow for Britain, and in a sense she had, bless her. I went down the stairs after a cup of coffee, allowing time for WUSWIPP to vacate the premises, and sneaked past the man in the cubbyhole while he was dealing with other matters.

That evening, after some welcome sleep aboard an aircraft from Gatwick, I was back in Southern Spain and feeling sad again about Miss Mandrake, with whom I'd last been here outward bound. When I left Malaga airport for Torremolinos, Britain had just twenty hours to go. And, although at the time I didn't know this, my London flat had been wrecked by a bomb and a lot of shredded CORPSE or WUSWIPP body. Somebody hadn't been very clever with his explosives.

CHAPTER 11

I could be recognised, obviously, by someone put on watch; but I was not, so far as I was aware, known to Brigadier B. Either way, I didn't much mind: things often, in my experience, get done the faster by making a magnet of oneself, always providing one is ready for what hits you as a result. I would be ready, all right. I had fixed ahead for a Dormobile to await me in Malaga, and in this I drove out for Torremolinos as the shades of evening fell and the lights of pleasure city shone ahead. On arrival I parked and sat at a table under a palm tree outside a bar, and ordered Fundador. I observed the scene and again felt sad, for near here I had sat and drank with Miss Mandrake and the Ogmanfillers and I could only hope that deaths didn't have to go in threes. I watched armed *guardias* patrolling, and priests hurrying, and tourists of most nationalities getting tight on sherry and *vino*. There were lots of Ogmanfillers about, and many Germans, plus plenty of British eating chips with their sherry, but I didn't notice anyone as military-looking as a brigadier should be, though there was no knowing what Brigadier Bunnet had been a brigadier in; Madrid's list had not indicated which regiment or corps he had belonged to in his pre-brigadier days. I ruled out only the Salvation Army Catering Corps...had my grandparents been alive today and advertising for a Cook General, they might well have been surprised at what turned up. I drank more Fundador, then decided things needed forcing: time never stands still. I took the Dormobile out on the road for Carena and the Flood Fearer's church. En route I flipped the switch of the radio and twiddled until I got the BBC. I listened to the late news: the Prime Minister had at last got around to the expected appearance on the TV but it had been a total fiasco: the image had mouthed just a word or two, then the screen had gone blank. After some alarming crackles and streaks of coloured light, another image had shown: a man in a purple garment, with hood. No one, it seemed, had been able to obliterate him before he had got his message across in full. He had blown the lot and now the government was doing its best to calm the country and stop the panic by saying the whole thing was a hoax by persons unknown, probably the Opposition. As the man in purple had cut himself off and out, the Prime Minister had been seen briefly, badly shaken according to the parliamentary correspondent but managing to take a drink that might have been water but was, I fancied, more likely a stiff brandy. Purely as a precaution to help control 'undesirable elements who might try to make capital out of the situation' all army reservists would be ordered to report to their regimental headquarters for possible service. Navy and RAF also. In short, it was really general mobilisation and not before time. Selfishly, I was glad I was out of England, at any rate temporarily. I reckoned I would need to go back before the end came.

Driving fast, I reached the church. The steeple glowed in the moonlight, all cheerful and silvery and religious. As I emerged from the Dormobile I saw light behind the church windows, faintly. From 6D2's parochial roll I had learned that there was a handful of tarted up British-occupied cottages a mile or so the other side of the church, and it was really those I was interested in currently. However, that light beckoned and I approached the door gun in hand.

Cautiously, I inched the door open.

There was a woman inside, just one middle-aged woman in a hat, now rising from one of the thwarted and rowlocked pews. She stepped, or perhaps I should say disembarked, into the aisle and curtsied toward gun-damaged Noah. When she turned, she saw me. She gave a startled cry and a hand flew to her mouth. I apologised for the intrusion.

I asked, 'A parishioner, I presume?'

'Who are you?' she demanded. The voice was brisk; she had already regained control. She hadn't seen my gun; I had put it away before she turned, since her obeisances seemed to indicate genuine devotion rather than anything sinister. 'This is a private place.'

'The house of God is always open,' I ventured.

'God, perhaps. This is Noah's house.' She was very sharp. 'Will you please go away?'

'In good time,' I said. 'Are you the verger, by any chance? Or doing the flowers?'

There was a short, brisk laugh. 'In Spain, in midsummer? I was worshipping, if you must know.' Suddenly she seemed to crumple a little, though she looked basically uncrumplable, a stern English gardening gentlewoman and dog-lover whom I could see, when there wasn't a chronic water-shortage as in summer Spain, with watering-can in hand over the geraniums and lobelias. Then she said, 'I lost my husband recently.'

'I'm sorry,' I said, feeling glad she hadn't

seen my gun.

'Who are you?' she asked again. 'A tourist, I suppose. Isn't it a little late for sightseeing?'

'I was hoping I might find the Brigadier.'

'Brigadier Bunnett?' Her eyebrows went up. 'You wouldn't find him at this time of night even if he was here, which he's not. I believe he's gone home to England, but I'm not sure. Why d'you want him, Mr—er—?'

'Jones,' I said. To get her started I told her I was a private enquiry agent and was interested in a young girl named Sandra Shingler alias La Ina, lately one of the Flood Fearers' congregation.

She sniffed. *'That* girl. No better than she should be—I dare say you know. If it hadn't been for the Brigadier, Mr Petersen would have been sent packing at the same time. The Brigadier's too...too—'

'Human?'

'It's not the word I'd use, Mr Jones. However, I know what you mean. It was all a most terrible scandal, but of course it was hushed up—one doesn't talk about such things, does one? Especially when the church is involved. I shouldn't be talking now.' She turned away and marched back to the boat-pew in which she had been worshipping. She bent and picked up a pair of gloves which she drew on with an air of finality. 'I must go before I'm indiscreet. I feel very bitter about that dreadful girl, you know.'

'Naturally. I do understand.' I paused. 'Do you live near the church, Mrs—'

'Pumfret spelt Pontefract.'

'Ah. And your house—'

'Cottage. Primitive but very charming. It's fifteen minutes walk from here.'

'You walk?' I asked. 'Aren't you worried about bandits?'

She was very brisk again. 'Good heavens, no, the Spaniards are immensely chivalrous and would never harm an English gentlewoman, Mr Jones. I'm not in the least worried, so you need not suggest escorting me and I'll not ask you to.' Breeding stopped her adding the obvious: tongues would wag, never mind her age, and she was not of a similar persuasion to La Ina. But there were things I needed to ask, and one of them was what had happened to the Reverend Clay Petersen, pastor of this parish. I did so. Mr Petersen, she said, had been under strain due to overwork, and had had many worries over the building of the Ark. Materials and skills were expensive and there had been trade disputes in addition. Mr Petersen had taken a holiday, leaving rather suddenly, and since no one had been appointed in his place, she, Mrs

Pontefract, had taken it upon herself to care for the church in his temporary absence. She referred to the visit of the 'tourists', which she had heard about after the event; and also told me that subsequently an official party had called with a police escort and entered the Ark's covered slipway. This too she had heard about only afterwards, and understood that the department in Madrid responsible for the Spanish Merchant Navy had sent persons to check the Ark's construction for general seaworthiness whilst on the stocks. It was difficult to keep a straight face when this came out.

I asked where Mr Petersen had gone for his holiday. She didn't know. She added that his acolytes had gone with him, and that all work on the Ark had stopped.

'You don't find it strange that they've all gone?' I asked.

'I find it inconvenient rather than strange, Mr Jones. The clergy need holidays the same as the rest of us. Of course, it was rather sudden. I don't deny that.'

'And inconsiderate?'

'Well—yes. Yes, it was. However, there we are. It's the will of Noah.' She pushed at her headgear.

Noah had come out absolutely pat, and without any self-consciousness, in place of God, yet

Mrs Pontefract struck me as eminently sane; it was curious. No doubt Noah, as a good practical man who had taken sensible precautions in his day, was worthy enough; but I would not have thought him worshipable nor Mrs Pontefract impressionable, but, as she had said, there we were. And time was passing...I was about to put further questions to the lady when suddenly she frowned and seemed to be considering, taking some sort of mental stock of the situation. She had stiffened her back like a soldier faced with a duty that had to be done; I sensed that in fact she *had* found the total desertion of the clergy somewhat strange but loyalty had prevented her admitting it to a stranger who had no right to ask questions. But now she was screwing herself up to something, and I waited.

She said, 'There was something funny. You're a detective of a sort, I take it. Possibly you could help.'

'Just tell me about it, Mrs Pontefract.'

'Very well, then. Come with me.' She turned about and marched towards the looming figure of Noah upon his green plastic-foam waters. She stopped by the altar, which was covered with a green embroidered cloth, and bent, and ferreted about beneath the cloth. When she stood up, she had a shoe in her hand,

200

a woman's shoe with a heavy wedge sole. There were bloodstains on the fabric. Unnecessarily, for I had recognised it at once, she said, 'It's not that girl's. It's too small, she had big feet and in any case always wore sandals when she wore anything at all.'

'How did you find it?' I asked.

'I came in to say a prayer after Mr Petersen left. Before the police came. I found the altar cloth had been half pulled away and under it was this shoe. As you can see, there was some blood. I was shocked, as you can imagine. I put everything straight and pushed the shoe out of sight. It seemed the only thing to do. What do you imagine happened, Mr Jones?'

I shrugged, tried to keep my cool and not grab. I said, 'It's hard to say...but it looks as though Mr Petersen found another girl, don't you think?'

'Yes,' she said tonelessly, 'I do. It's dreadful, horrible.'

'Have you told anyone else?'

She shook her head. 'No. Because, you see, I don't *know*. Mr Petersen must be given the benefit of the doubt until we do know. It's all so dreadful for the reputation of our church.'

'Yes,' I said. 'May I examine the shoe, please?'

She passed it over. Miss Mandrake's shoe:

I held it tenderly. A struggle by the altar, below the brooding form of Noah and his naked wife? I slid my fingers in, I don't know why, and I found something: a segment of cloth had been pushed up into the toe. I pulled it out. It was white cotton, and Felicity had been wearing a white cotton shirt. There was more blood: shaky lettering, a message. Written in her own blood with some instrument unknown but of a finer point than a finger, the just discernible words, *Sendar Maru*. It was a hell of a pity the Spanish police hadn't found it much earlier.

★ ★ ★ ★

I kept the piece of cloth, with the blessing of Mrs Pontefract, while the shoe itself was replaced below the altar. I said there was something funny going on, and whoever was responsible for it might come back looking for the shoe and would be suspicious if it were missing. She was not, I said, to breathe a word about the piece of cloth or about me. She promised not to, and looked sternly British. I took a risk because I was convinced of her patriotism and dropped a hint about the British Government, and her back straightened even more, as I knew it would. She would be a good soldier to the end. At the church entrance I looked

202

back at Noah; some trick of the light before Mrs Pontefract switched off gave him the appearance of winking, or anyway leering. He wasn't a bad old so-and-so and his altar had been very productive this evening. Before leaving I dropped a British fifty pence piece into an alms box. It seemed the least I could do and I think Mrs Pontefract was grateful.

I drove back into Torremolinos, fast. It was a beautiful night, with a mass of stars and a moon riding high to bring silver to a brown land, the same moon that would be shining down upon the *Sendar Maru* and her lethal cargo. What had happened was very clear: Felicity, on being removed from that nether cell below the Ark, had overheard talk, and by her subterfuge had left behind the information as to where she was being taken. Either that, or the word that the *Sendar Maru* was now to be the operating base of CORPSE. Or both. In any case, any movements were positively decided: the *Sendar Maru* had to be boarded and disarmed, and I intended to be there present when the Navy went into action. Things looked like coming to a head and with luck we might just about have time. All I needed now was a telephone. Driving into Torremolinos, I made for a public call box. I by-passed Madrid: STD got me London direct within a couple of minutes and I spoke to Max's Number Two: Max was sleeping. The reaction that met my message was not reassuring: an investigatory boarding-party had been put aboard the *Sendar Maru* earlier from one of the shadowing frigates and nothing further had been heard of them. Signals from the frigate had been met with a massive silence, threats had been disregarded, and Defence Ministry, who were flummoxed, were stalling. Certainly, the *Sendar Maru* could be blasted from the seas by the frigate's rocket launchers, but would this be wise? The question sounded bloody silly, but the answer was no, it wouldn't, for very obvious reasons.

I said into the phone, 'I'm returning by the first available flight, and if necessary I'll board the *Sendar Maru* myself.'

I rang off; as I turned I became aware that the door was open. A voice said, 'That is very true. Commander Shaw, I presume?' The voice was British and hearty and held an authoritative military ring. I stared back at a tubby man wearing a walrus moustache and a white silk jacket, very well cut, above dark trousers.

I said, 'Brigadier Bunnett, no doubt?'

'Well guessed, my dear chap.' I looked at him sourly. He would have been too short for the Guards and too fat to fit into a tank, and

204

his voice didn't sound corps type: he had to be infantry of the line. Here was no Cook General but a tough fighter. He had no weapon but he had friends, whom he indicated outside the call box: six men, very British like himself though not all with a military air, and two formidable gentlewomen in the current climatic equivalent of English country tweeds. My guess, not difficult to make, was Flood Fearers. Mrs Pontefract must have been a dropout, there purely for Noah's sake. They all looked dedicated and all of them had their right hands in position for bringing out guns. So, for that matter, had I. But, as Brigadier Bunnett pointed out politely, no one was going to use a gun, not even me. There were members of the *guardia* around—I could see several of them—and they would react to shooting.

'They don't like it, old boy. Bad for tourism! You'll be in a Spanish goal before you can say jackrabbit, and Spanish gaols are filthy. You'd better just walk out smiling, that's my best advice.'

I took a deep breath and looked around: Torremolinos, late though it was, was busy yet. Shooting would bring panic, and priests would rise and flutter like crows. But I wasn't scared of arrest: 6D2 would have me out in a flash. I brought out my gun: Brigadier Bunnett was fast, much too fast for a man of his girth. A bunch of fingers like steel wire hawsers wrapped themselves round my wrist and my nerves seemed to twist in a knot. I dropped the gun and glared out at a ring of smiling faces, now came closer in. Brigadier Bunnett picked up the gun and stowed it away. Then, smiling still, be brought a knee up and smashed it into my groin and used a beefy fist a second later on my jaw. I didn't see what happened next, but later assumed that the Flood Fearers had closed in as good friends to carry home the dear old pal, the dead drunk fellow Briton, before he made an exhibition of himself. When I came round I was vomiting and feeling like death, with a blinding headache and great pain in the lower regions. And I was swaying about, which made the sickness worse. There was a hell of a lot of noise going on around me and when I opened my eyes I saw Brigadier Bunnett and his troops, the six men and the two ladies, and some glass through which I could see stars, real heavenly ones. I was in a helicopter, and dawn was not far off because the stars soon began to fade. There was not much room; one of the ladies was almost sitting on my face and I heard her voice booming out over the engine racket, something about Ascot. Later, a long while later I believe, Bunnett's voice rang out.

'There she is, and the frigates.'

Bodies heaved around me to take a look and soon the machine tilted and went lower. I caught a glimpse of a vast ship and two small grey frigates lying off, heaving in the deep-sea swell, bows pointed towards the Rising Sun of Japan that floated over the *Sendar Maru*, which was one of the quarter-million tonners by the look of her, riding light in the water. The ordinary sun of God streamed down, making a glorious cloud free morning of the last day for Britain. Lower and lower for touchdown on the ship's landing platform, while the frigate crews looked on helplessly. Brigadier Bunnett cocked a snook at them, laughingly. My frustrations almost choked me; there was the Navy, close at hand and well armed and able to cope, but without orders to do so. No one at home was going to risk it, but if I'd been the Senior Officer of the interception task force I reckoned I would have chanced it on my own. The *Sendar Maru* could quite possibly be destroyed before CORPSE could send out their signals... but possibly, of course, was the word that would be causing the fatal hesitation: the frigates' rockets would need to strike in the right spot first time, for the explosive-device-tripping signal could presumably be made in not more than seconds, and would go out the moment the rockets opened.

We touched down and I was hoisted to my feet and taken out to the deck under guard. The first person to welcome me aboard was the man in purple, still hooded and exuding confidence. I was marched aft, into the superstructure and down a series of ladders. On one deck was a large notice bearing Japanese characters and the English translation: BRITISH INTERIM GOVERNMENT CABINET ROOM, and an arrow. The ship seemed packed with personnel: toothy Japanese seamen, all armed, and a number of important-looking British subjects, or anyway Europeans, some in plain clothes, others in dark green shirts with ties, and insignia on the collars, and black trousers, and knee-boots. The corps of *gauleiters* or the new police, maybe, all ready to take up duty within the next few hours, or as soon as the *Sendar Maru* could make a nuclear-free British port after the signal had been sent.

CHAPTER 12

Before touchdown I'd asked about Miss Mandrake: yes, she was aboard the *Sendar Maru*. On my journey into the bowels of the ship I asked if I could see her.

'Not yet, old boy. Patience,' Brigadier Bunnett said. I asked him next about the boarding party from the frigate, and he consulted the accompanying armed guard. The naval men were all right, apparently. Not harmed, or not much anyway; they'd been greatly outnumbered and hadn't had a chance to show much fight. Brigadier Bunnett went off somewhere and I was taken down two more decks and locked into a small cell that sat smack on the double bottoms. I was left to brood and listen to the sounds of the secondary machinery; now and again there was vibration as the main engines were turned over to keep the *Sendar Maru* on station. After I had been left alone for a little over an hour, an armed posse came for me and I was taken up three decks to follow the arrow on the sign. I was admitted to a long compartment with three ports down its starboard side and a table running the whole length, or almost, with some twenty chairs, all occupied with men and women in plain clothes. Among them I recognised faces from the Torremolinos call-box and the helicopter. The assembly seemed to constitute the British Interim Government; indeed this was confirmed to me by the man in purple seated at the head of the table. I was taken to stand by him and he swept an arm around, making the introductions. I knew some of the names: well-known men who in the past had been noted for outspoken comments in political and military spheres, an outspokenness that had led to their premature retirements from public or army life. Of the others the professions, or former professions since all these people were superannuated and largely looked it, were varied and gave a wide spectrum of abilities useful in government. There was an ex-judge with a wizened face that, when he was wigged, must have given him the appearance of a rat peering out of a ball of oakum. He was possibly bound for the Lord Chancellorship and a seat on a somewhat singed woolsack. There was a solicitor, query Solicitor General. Brigadier Bunnett was a likely candidate for Defence, though he could be run close by a retired rear-admiral, a vigorous-looking man with a beard still fiery red and an autocratic nose. There were bankers, company directors, accountants suitable for the Exchequer or the Department of Industry, I supposed. There was also, curiously, a retired trade union leader, quite a big name in his day, which in fact was only round about yesterday: Ron Gudge. Mr Gudge has been, when active, very much of the Left, which only went to show: when powerless and on a fixed income, people's views shift.

Anyway, I had to allow that CORPSE had some formidable talent ready. When the man in purple made this point, I agreed, but said, 'Government isn't all cabinet, is it? Where do you recruit your civil service?'

'There are many now in the Civil Service who are with us, Commander Shaw—'

'A fifth column?'

'Yes. And when we form our government, many others will join us—you will see. The same applies to the armed forces and the police. We represent what many people have wished to see for many years past, and a *fait accompli* will bring in its own escalating support.'

This brought a chorus of hear, hears. The faces of the interim government stared at me, fish-like. There was a hint of the geriatrics, but in all truth this bunch were not much older than our current office-holders. There was, of course, a lack of governmental experience, but they could probably cope as well as anyone else in the brand-new situation that would have arisen. And I saw the logic of what the man in purple had said: so many people in all walks of life were sick and tired of what had been going on. They really would welcome change; law and order in place of vandalism and mugging and making life hell for old ladies in council flats; discipline in education; a full day's work for a full day's pay; respect for private property. These were just some of the things that CORPSE would have dangled carrot-like before the interim government and would promise the bemused masses when they filled the vacuum created by the nuclear holocaust. These things even rang a bell with me: they were what I would like to see too. But not at the cost, the price of CORPSE plus WUS-WIPP, the widespread death to come in a matter of hours now.

I said as much. I added, 'You'll not get the support you believe. What you'll get is hate, my friend. When the coastal areas die, there'll be a strike-back from the inland regions.'

'We expect this,' the man in purple said. I thought how bloody ridiculous he looked in his hood, sitting at the head of all the lounge suits and neat collars and ties. 'We're ready for it—

you know that, I believe. There are persons who will immediately take over control, moving to prepared strongpoints in their allotted regions. Support will come in from outside, airlifted clear of the radiation zones or brought in by sea via the unaffected ports. Come and I shall show you.' He turned to his cabinet, courteously. 'If you'll excuse us, gentlemen.' He got to his feet, and all stood politely, scraping their chairs back as we left the compartment.

★ ★ ★ ★

The place the man in purple took me to was deep down in the ship, below the waterline like the cell I'd been in: no ports here. We entered through a watertight bulkhead and the door was clipped down hard behind us once we were in. It was an extraordinary sight, a kind of War Operations Room. Along one bulkhead was a vast map of Britain; along another was a map of all the northern hemisphere. Men sat at consoles, wearing headphones and rapt expressions, and moving knobs that in their turn moved needles on dials. Above them was a platform with a desk at which a man in gilded uniform sat surveying his minions; at his side was a slim girl, also uniformed, and next to her a youngish man with what looked like an ADC's tassels. It was all rather like good old Dowding directing the Battle of Britain in the days of yore. Sounds of urgency filled the air: the muted shorts and longs of Morse.

I asked, 'Is this where you blow from, now you've deserted the Ark?'

'No. Not that.'

'Where do you blow from, then?'

'From this ship, but not from this room. When you got away from us in Spain, the decision was made to use the *Sendar Maru,* which originally we had not intended—we came to see it as more convenient although there were dangers in concentration. This room is our central control point for the support operation... from here we are in touch with all our incoming groups, and from here we shall direct their movements.'

'A headquarters ship?'

There was a smile. 'More than that, Commander Shaw. Britain is to be governed in the initial stages from the *Sendar Maru.* As you have seen, the interim government is already in being, and will rule from this ship. In effect, you are aboard the new Whitehall.'

'It's crazy,' I said.

'Quite the contrary, I do assure you. Everything has been provided for.' The man in purple took my arm in a friendly fashion and put me in the picture as regards the work-out after zero hour. At this moment, he said, men were assembling for take-off at remote and in many cases disused airfields in Germany, France and Southern Ireland and also in the United States and Canada. Others would come in from the Middle East—Libya, Egypt, Iran, Israel. It was to be quite cosmopolitan. The numbers involved were not in fact large; this was no Second Front. A good deal of reliance was being placed on the panic element, the shattering of morale, and the instinctive turning of the population to any firm authority emerging to fill a vacuum. That would militate towards the *in situ* bosses, the fifth-column *gauleiters* already a-creep towards the Regional Seats of Government with their by no means inconsiderable following. The inflying support groups would be strategically dropped in the places of most need, and they were largely the strong-arm mobs, the international thugs of WUSWIPP and CORPSE, together with certain technicians, specialists and what-have-you. And another vital point had not been overlooked, either: the centralised government computers upon which virtually all administration depended. One being the Department of the Environment's vast computer set-up at Hastings. For too long Whitehall had delayed the full provision of alternative manual methods which could have allowed a minimum service of administration to be maintained, and now CORPSE was about to throw everything out of gear either by wrecking the computers themselves or by ordering their fifth column to produce total frenzy. Order would go right off the beam: pension payments, driving licences, Health Service supply, ERNIE, salaries and wages in the public sector, rail operation, all that and more—the lot. Small beer in an attack situation of life and death, perhaps; but it would give the people pause and assist thoughts of surrender when they found they couldn't renew the colour telly licence. Crazy it all was; but possibly only to the conventional-democratic-government minded. It could work out. I was still there to see that it didn't happen. I looked at a clock high on a bulkhead where all could see it: the time was 0935.

★ ★ ★ ★

I was still not permitted a view of Miss Mandrake, though I was assured she was all right. From the operational control compartment I was taken to a room where all BBC broadcasts

216

were being monitored and I was able to form a mental image of what things were like in Britain. They were not good. The public had been informed of the facts in a broad sense and an inland rush was in progress, or anyway an attempt at one. The roads, in fact, were unable to cope and the police, in their attempts to impose control, had been attacked all over the country. Result, many serious injuries and an unacceptable number of deaths with many more feared. All army commands were assisting but were not doing much good—this was not precisely uttered, but I was well able to read between the lines. An emergency evacuee-billeting scheme was being set up in all inland regions like in the war, and though all the schools were so far doing their best to carry on and function normally, they were being turned into casualty clearing stations around the teachers and pupils. Mobs were on the march as was only to be expected, and there had been looting viciously carried out. There was a sharp increase in rape and mugging and there was a good deal of hysteria I gathered. The area around the Houses of Parliament sounded like death city already: virtually total desertion except for police and troops, nobly standing to their duty. Parliament had evacuated to overcrowded conditions in Lewisham Town Hall, displacing the mayor and his council—this was a temporary measure pending the taking over of an unnamed stately home in a hopefully safe area. The Royal Standard flew splendidly from the flagstaff of Buckingham Palace, and crowds had gathered at the gates where Her Majesty's Guard would change that morning as usual. There had been demonstrations of loyalty and these were continuing. You can't keep some Londoners down, and it would be those on whom CORPSE would founder. I said this to the man in purple.

'Possibly,' he said, which was quite an admission. He said it somewhat enigmatically, but I was paying more attention to the broadcasts as they came through minute by minute than to him. Some news was creepy in the circumstances: in Cleethorpes, Merseyside and Milton Keynes groups of workers had gone on unofficial strike against the threat, apparently believing that their manifestation of righteous indignation would influence CORPSE. On the other hand the National Union of Railwaymen had behaved magnificently, calling off a threatened official strike by a sizeable majority so as to keep the trains running out of the ports and the capital. The strike threat had had to do with an inter-union dispute over the entitlement of Inter-City drivers to privileges not available to other drivers and, with almost hysterical emotion in his voice, the announcer ferved away about democracy and unselfishness and the essential goodheartedness of the British work force which was capable of putting the national interest first in times of emergency. Because it all sounded like an intercessionary prayer-hint to the Almighty that we were not as bad as we were painted after all, I said Amen to myself.

The man in purple went back to my last comment. He said, 'There *are* persons in Britain who will stand out against us.'

'Rather a lot actually,' I said. 'Like the NUR, for example.'

The slit showed an understanding grin. 'Yes. And we don't want trouble.'

I stared at him and gave a hollow laugh. 'You don't?'

'We don't. It can be avoided, and this would be better for all concerned.'

'Cold feet at the last?'

'By no means. The threat is there, and it will be used...if necessary.'

I nodded; I understood fully. All along, I'd guessed that CORPSE would much prefer to gain their ends by persuasion rather than the inconvenience and danger to themselves of operating inside a cloud of radiation. Such was human nature, even CORPSE nature. But I

219

held my tongue and let CORPSE expound for themselves. CORPSE, the man said, had already induced a nice degree of panic and Britain was currently bedlam. The panic could not in fact be much worse after the blow-up, and that essential part of the CORPSE plan had already been achieved. Besides, surrender by the British Government would not lead to withdrawal of the death-ships: they would remain as the big stick. Indeed, there would be even more security for CORPSE that way. The threat, once blown, no longer existed and a strike-back could come. It was better to hold it as a continuing inducement to obey.

'You should have thought of that earlier,' I said.

'We did.'

'Really? And how, now, do you back pedal... how do you get the British Government to hand over to CORPSE short of the actual blow-up— which is something the tone of the broadcasts tells me they're not in fact inclined to do?'

Another smile. 'Yet,' the man said.

'Time's short.'

'Yes. Very.'

I lost patience: the strain was telling on me. 'For God's sake,' I yelled at him, 'stop this bloody stalling and tell me how you expect to get surrender, will you?'

'You and Miss Mandrake will get it for us,' the man said. 'That is why you're here.'

★ ★ ★ ★

It was simple enough, really: diabolical, but essentially simple. First, I was taken back to the compartment with the portholes for an informal chat with the assembled interim rulers of Great Britain. The idea was an indoctrination or impressment course, designed to convince me that resistance would be futile and very messy. Whitehall couldn't win this one, they said, and I was inclined to agree from the start. Nevertheless, they all had a concentrated yack at me and very earnest they were. I believe they were all half-way round the bend, but in quite a nice way so long as you could disregard the nature of the threat they'd all put their signatures to as it were. The ex-judge was very matey, and drooled on about his speciality, which naturally was the law and order angle. I began to feel I was in the Old Bailey and about to be sentenced, then I was handed over to a stout woman in a large hat, overdressed like the Conservative Women's Conference assembling for a garden party. She was an addict of hanging and the birch, and again I didn't disagree with her views, though I would have expressed
221

them less viciously and without such relish. I gathered that she expected the portfolio of the Home Office. Ron Gudge seemed to be the only sane one, out simply, I believed, to feather his own nest and get back at some former cronies who'd unfairly ousted him from his trade union pinnacle before he'd been ready to go. I could understand that; there was no bull about Ron Gudge, but he was going to be a right bastard at the about-to-be-formed Department of Trade Union Reformation. A kind of Selective Eradication Department, I felt it would be, rather than pure Reformation, with a lot of old cronies biting the dust before Mr Gudge was through. Brigadier Bunnett had another go at me too, along with the retired rear-admiral. I was good material, Bunnett said convincingly, the right sort for advancement within the new security organisation. Just the type they wanted. I would be invaluable, with all my experience and inside knowledge. I was almost promised a Secretaryship of State...

When indoctrination ended, I was removed under guard to the medical section. A superbly equipped sick-bay—a hospital in miniature with two wards, an operating theatre and the usual offices—was presided over by a Japanese doctor with a full staff of junior doctors and nurses, all Japanese. The senior Japanese told me to sit, and pointed to a thing like a dentist's chair. As I sat, this chair was suddenly flattened into the horizontal position and steel arms came out, bent and held me fast, one round my chest, the other across my legs. To my side moved two more Japanese, grinning mightily, and laid hold of my arms. The doctor came across to me and stood looking down. He held something in his fingers: an oversize pill.

He said, 'You take pill, please.'

'What's in it?' I asked.

'Not important. Just take.'

I said I would not take it. He nodded towards another sick-berth attendant who clamped his fingers over my nose. Then he yanked my mouth open and dropped the pill in, followed by a glass of water. My swallow was automatic; down went the pill, and it felt like lead. I could track its descent all the way down until it lodged somewhere in my gut. My nose was released and the chair mechanism was operated so that I sat up.

'All right,' I said, feeling vicious. 'So it's down. It won't stay there.'

'Will stay. Will neither come up nor go down further. Can be removed only by lengthy surgical interference needing opening of stomach in lay language.'

'Balls,' I said.

'Not balls.' The doctor was washing his hands now, quite finished with his patient. 'Under heat of stomach, pill melts a small bit, enough to allow slides to emerge and prevent regurgitation or passage into duodenum...slides like stabilisers from side of ship to stop seasickness. Very effective.'

'All right,' I said, 'now tell me what's in it.'

He did, with relish and toothy grin. The pill was a tiny radio receiver in part, a radio that needed to receive one signal only: the signal, transmissible from the *Sendar Maru*, which would blow the other part of the pill, the pill that contained enough nuclear explosive to disintegrate not only me and anyone who happened to be with me at the time, but the building I was in also. While I hoisted in this horrible information, and started to learn to live with it, I was reunited with Miss Mandrake, who was brought in from another room in the medical section. I was delighted to see her but too shattered to express it. I could do no more than gaze at her glassily. She looked as bad as I felt, and I guessed why. It was a good guess. She asked, trying to smile at me, 'Wired for sound, are you?'

I said yes.

'Me too,' she said, and I saw tears run. 'For

God's sake, what do they want now?'

I was unable to answer that one, but all was to come clear. A Tannoy began fizzing and a voice ordered Commander Shaw and Miss Mandrake to be brought back to the interim government cabinet room, which I was already beginning to link with the House of Commons, and, still under guard, up we went for a briefing session. The whole circus was present when the man in purple went into his spiel. Like the little bugs in our innards, like the whole concept of the death-ships, it was really very simple: we were to be helicoptered direct from the *Sendar Maru* to the Plymouth area, where the authorities would be advised to have an aircraft ready to whizz us to the nearest RAF station for Whitehall. We were to impress the government with the crushing power of CORPSE and urge immediate surrender upon them: they would soon be facing internal chaos as the governmental computers went, by hand of CORPSE fifth column, into paralysis of the administration. To allow a little more time, the deadline would be extended until 1800 hours. The man in purple was certain we would be convincing; so was the whole interim cabinet. I could understand their certainty well enough: I kept feeling that internal bug in my guts. The CORPSE brass crowded round with their good wishes, heartily expressed, all smiles and hand-shakes. It was much as though we were the opening bats in a Test series. The one sour note came from the man in purple, who said gravely that if we didn't succeed, everything would blow at once, including us. He had only to authorise the two separate signals, that was all. And, just to dispel any hopes that I might still nourish, he added that it would be advisable not to attempt any jamming. The British Government had already been advised that to do so would only precipitate matters. Any jamming would have the effect of tripping the explosive devices via the transmitting aerials of the *Sendar Maru*.

Five minutes later we were airborne, gaining height over the helpless frigate. Faces stared up from the deck at the helicopter. I didn't see any way out now. I was myself coming round to the surrender view. Better perhaps to live to fight another day...

★ ★ ★ ★

I felt that internal device digging. It was hellish uncomfortable in a physical sense, never mind the mental torment. When my body heat had brought the little fins out, it had grown worse. It was pressing into something. It was akin to an ulcer. I tried to put it out of my mind and failed. It was right there with me all the way; and my heart was bleeding for Felicity. She sat there beside me, tense and drawn as we watched the toe of Cornwall come into view. We came over the Lizard, raised Falmouth and the mammoth tankers laid up in the river. We had expected to touch down at Roborough, but having passed over the enclosed submarine pens in Devonport Dockyard with their entombed naval personnel, we were told to go on to Exeter instead. At Exeter airport we were pushed out on to the tarmac and the helicopter at once took off again, watched by grim-faced ground staff, and police, and a naval officer from the Plymouth command, and swung back towards the sea and the distant *Sendar Maru*. Felicity and I were taken to a waiting jump jet and as soon as we were aboard we lifted off for the capital. It was to be a direct flight, we were told, no time wasted: the word from CORPSE was being treated with respect. The jump jet's pilot put us down skilfully in the middle of Horse Guards Parade, the Harrier dropping like a bird down past the government buildings. The area had been cleared by the police, and beyond the blue ranks and the barricades a large crowd stared tensely, and a rising murmur came as we walked through to Whitehall and across to the Ministry of Defence escorted by a major-general. The whole thing seemed totally unreal, but the nag in my guts gave the lie to unreality. As we walked quickly away from the crowds and their anxieties, the major-general had gloomy news; the Prime Minister could not attend, having suffered a heart attack.

'Sheer strain,' he said.

'I'm sorry. Who's in charge?'

'Defence Ministry. Martial Law's been declared.'

'Since when?'

'Just an hour ago.'

I asked, 'What's the feeling, General? Surrender, or take what comes?'

'There'll be no surrender, Shaw.'

We entered the building; whether or not the expressed opinion was that of the major-general personally, or of the Chiefs of Staff and politicians as a body, I knew not. I had a strong feeling that if the brass all had internal bugs fitted, they might find their outlook somewhat sharpened towards getting rid of them; but I determined that I would put self, and Felicity too, aside in the interest of giving the Chiefs of Staff an objective report and assessment. I could only make a guess at how many lives were in the balance throughout Britain; it could run into millions. They had to come first. Yet putting them first might well mean that my gut feeling about surrender was right on target. I had absolutely no doubt in my mind that CORPSE could do everything they'd said they would.

★ ★ ★ ★

I faced the circle of faces, the current executive power in Britain: it was the *Sendar Maru* all over again. The same kind of faces, even down to the union men. Today you couldn't run Britain, even under Martial Law, without the say-so of the TUC and there they were to prove it and very dour they looked: they didn't like the military. However, they all listened intently to what I had to say and there was a gasp of horror when I told them about those internal bugs. That, I think, impressed them more than anything else had done with the ultimate determination of CORPSE. I could see those faces, or the brains behind them, thinking: at any moment a horrible disintegration could come and they would be too close for comfort.

A face asked, 'What do you advise, Commander Shaw?' The speaker was the Minister of Defence.

I shrugged and said, 'I'm not here to advise, sir. Only to report.'

'Oh come, don't split hairs.'

'I can't advise,' I said. 'I'm by way of being too personally involved.' I patted my stomach. The Minister took my point. I said, 'In any case I have no advice to offer. I see no way out.'

'But you believe these people will do as they say?'

'Yes,' I said flatly. 'I know they will. At 1800 hours, if you don't concede, they'll blow. That's fact.'

The faces looked frozen. Looked beaten, too. Very definitely I felt surrender in the air and never mind that major-general. Yet it was a decision so enormous that it beggared definition. Britain had never been attuned to the concept of surrender, even less to surrender without a fight. But this couldn't be fought and they all knew it; the moment any fight-back started, CORPSE pressed the tit and that was it. The honourable members now in Lewisham Town Hall had better take a fast vote, I thought, feeling the stir in my stomach and noting the time: just gone noon, and six hours left. Six hours more of British democracy whichever way the vote went. All those on-site nuclear-loaded vessels flashed through my mind: the Clyde, Plymouth, the Tyne and all the others, not to mention the

230

close-flowing Thames.

There was nothing more I could say. Beside me, Felicity burst into sudden tears. I took her in my arms, and the brass looked embarrassed. But the shakes in the girl's body, and the knowledge of that wicked inset device that was tormenting and racking her as well as me, put the steel back into me and I knew I had to fight on after all. I embarrassed the brass again. I said, 'Balls to surrender, gentlemen! We'll beat the buggers at their own dirty game. The risk's high but worth chancing.'

I was about to put a proposition, one that would involve a fake surrender and would probably not have worked in fact, when a telephone rang. An aide answered it. He listened, then put a hand over the mouthpiece, and said, 'For Commander Shaw.'

I asked, 'Who's calling?'

With an expression of puzzlement and alarm on his face, the aide said, 'WUSWIPP.'

Feeling tense I went across to the telephone amid a profound silence. I said, 'Shaw here.'

A thin voice said, 'Listen carefully, Commander Shaw.' It was the voice of an old man, brittle and wheezy, and it was one I didn't recognise, but I did recognise the name when he gave it. It was Zambellis. Mirko Zambellis,

231

perhaps one of the most eminent physicists of his day and still going strong. A Yugoslav…a stalwart of WUSWIPP, one of their backroom boys, a dedicated communist who had fought Hitler, forsaking the test-tube and the retort or whatever for the sniper's rifle and the hand grenade. And Mirko Zambellis was a very worried old Yugoslavian, it seemed, who didn't like the direction WUSWIPP was taking vis-à-vis CORPSE. CORPSE, he said, was fascist. I said I knew that, and had been much surprised at WUSWIPP all along. Zambellis rambled a bit and I had to cut him short. Brought back to the point, he asked me a very pertinent question: did I have a device planted in my gut? I asked how the hell he knew that, and he said he was still active in the cause of WUSWIPP and he, Mirko Zambellis, had himself dreamed up that dastardly bug, so knew all there was to know about it…

'Are you willing to risk your life, Commander Shaw?' he asked. I said cautiously that such was part of my job, and he went on talking calmly as though I'd given him an outright yes. He wouldn't tell me where he could be found, but assured me he would be in the right place at the right time, and he promised total success against CORPSE. That was all very well. When Zambellis rang off I found that my hands were shaking uncontrollably and the dreary political and military faces were swaying from side to side.

CHAPTER 13

I took a grip and steadied. I glanced at Felicity, pale and tear-stained. I addressed the brass and told them who and what Mirko Zambellis was. I said, 'Currently he's dissatisfied, to use no stronger word, with the WUSWIPP leadership. He's devastated to think they've chucked in their lot with CORPSE.' It was, I thought, a situation comparable with the Liberal Party during the Lib-Lab 'Support Jim' phase. 'He has an idea to save WUSWIPP from the devil—'

An interruption came. 'We're not here to pull WUSWIPP's chestnuts, Shaw.'

'And,' I went on regardless, 'at the same time to sink CORPSE. Take that in, gentlemen! This could be salvation at the eleventh hour. That is, if I'm willing.'

Clamour began, and was stilled as I lifted a hand. I felt lightheaded, pompous, in a unique position—which latter in fact I was. The

233

odd light-headedness induced silly thoughts in me: I could demand the earth and it would be granted now. A peerage would be mere peanuts. I expounded Zambellis's theory. Like all that had gone before, it was dead simple when put into plain language: Zambellis, father of the stomach bug, was currently in close contact with a transmitter that could blow it just as effectively as could the CORPSE directorate aboard the *Sendar Maru*. He had said that when it did blow, it would do much damage in its vicinity. Its vicinity would not be a pleasant place to be. If positioned right, it could blow the bottom out of the *Sendar Maru* and she would go down like a stone before CORPSE or the interim government of Great Britain could collect their wits. Once that happened, the threat was over. The big boys of CORPSE, plus Brigadier Bunnett, Ron Gudge and all the interim gentry, would be below the waves, either dead or ready to be picked up by the frigates on station. There were, I said, some snags: the blowing up of the *Sendar Maru* might, just might, trip the devices shipbound in our British ports. That, at any rate, was what CORPSE had threatened if the frigates, for instance, should open fire. But Zambellis believed that would not happen. The device-blowing equipment would not be attacked in itself; it would just sink, which was a different proposition from gunfire or such. A chance would have to be taken on that. The other snag was personal to me alone: Zambellis's suggestion was that I with inset bug be sent back aboard the *Sendar Maru* on some pretext, that I get myself reincarcerated in the cell below the waterline, and that a little before 1800 hours he blew me up.

There was more clamour. Deep in thoughts of eternity, I let them rave. When the clamour subsided, the feeling was very obvious: they didn't like to say it, but they all hoped desperately I would volunteer. Well, I would. I said, 'To refuse would be churlish. I'll go. If I didn't, I couldn't live with myself afterwards. There's just one thing. A request.'

They couldn't wait to say it: 'Anything you ask, my dear chap, anything.'

'Right,' I said, and once again, and it would be for the last time so far as I could tell, I took Felicity in my arms. 'Immediate contact with St Thomas's Hospital. An examination of Miss Mandrake, and an operation to remove that filthy device.'

★ ★ ★ ★

When I left the Defence Ministry we had

235

everything sewn up. I wasn't leaving it all to Mirko Zambellis. After Felicity had been rushed across the river to St Thomas's, I went into further conference with the Chiefs of Staff and the top politicians. I was to go back aboard the *Sendar Maru* as an emissary or mediator on behalf of the current governing body of Britain. I was to discuss terms, and was empowered to negotiate even to the extent of outright surrender. If, as a result of that surrender offer, I was able to get CORPSE to switch off the threat so that interference would positively not trip the various devices, and if I was able to announce this to Whitehall, then the frigates were to be ordered to open fire and blast the *Sendar Maru* out of the water. That way, I just might survive. There were too many ifs but it couldn't be helped. This decided, the *Sendar Maru* was contacted by radio and asked to pick me up at Exeter airport. Just before I left the conference, word came through from St Thomas's: they hadn't dared risk an X-ray in case it blew the device but an exploratory abdominal incision—a laparotomy—would be made and they would take it from there. It might be as simple as a partial gastrectomy or it might not; time would tell. The theatre staff deserved unstinting praise; it was impossible to say what might happen if the knife slipped, or even if it just touched against the device or its slide-out stoppers.

Back aboard my jump jet, I was hastened to touchdown at Exeter. The helicopter from the *Sendar Maru* had been hovering, and came down a few moments after I'd disembarked from the Harrier. I boarded into the guns of CORPSE and off we flew, no one speaking. When I reached the ship there was just a matter of two hours and a few minutes before the showdown came one way or the other. I was met by the man in purple and taken again to the cabinet room. There was still tremendous confidence in the air, which I found touching: in fact the bastards had had it, thanks to Mirko Zambellis, and their over-weening certainty was quite misplaced. Anyway, they welcomed me with courtesy: I was, after all, the ambassador for a country's life and a valued negotiator.

Brigadier Bunnett brought me a brandy.

I asked if it was safe.

He raised his eyebrows. 'Oh, you mean that little gadget? Yes, it's safe enough.'

'Thank you,' I said, and took the brandy in a gulp. It went down like fire and I was grateful. If I was offered more I would take that too; it would be better to go out as tight as a drum, I decided, though I would need my wits about me a while longer yet. We got down to business under the aegis of the man in purple. Once again I was apprised of what was arrayed against the British Government but I cut the exposition short. Whitehall, I said, was well enough aware by now.

'So?' the man in purple asked.

'As you've been informed, I've been sent to discuss terms.'

'Yes. Terms of surrender?'

'Not surrender,' I said, showing for the sake of authenticity a tough negotiating front. 'An accommodation, let's call it. What's CORPSE's price for withdrawing the ships from our ports and rivers, gentlemen?'

'There can be no compromise,' the man in purple said flatly.

'Oh, come,' I said, speaking as it were over the head of the CORPSE man and trying to reach the lay persons who would form the government. There must, surely, be some grains of commonsense and reality amongst that bunch. 'Nothing's so final it can't be discussed and moderated. The Prime Minister and cabinet are willing to meet you on certain points—'

'What points?'

This was not easy; of course, I'd been briefed so far as time had permitted before leaving the Defence Ministry, but what points could in fact be met, or conceded, in a situation such as this? The man in purple had been dead right: a compromise was impossible, really, CORPSE couldn't be given, say, Wales and Scotland, with Cornwall as make-weight in reserve if Wales and Scotland were not enough; nor could CORPSE be offered a share in government by the invocation of a kind of proportional representation. Nor, again, would the combined forces of WUSWIPP and CORPSE be bought off by the repealing of a handful of laws they didn't like or the promise of legislation along the lines they did like. Anyway, I waffled on in general terms about co-operation and mutual understanding and a total willingness on the part of the British Government to meet CORPSE and have full discussions with the threat withdrawn in the meantime. A truce, in effect. It cut no ice at all with the man in purple.

He said as flatly as before, 'No truce. We would stand to gain nothing. You are wasting time, Commander Shaw, and that is foolish for your people. Tell me this: are you empowered to offer surrender?'

He was a direct man and he held all the cards, or he thought he did. I glanced at the clock: I was getting nowhere, but the clock was, too fast. I said, 'Yes, I am.'

'Unconditional surrender?'

'Yes,' I said. There was not much of a stir from the interim government; they had been sure of this all along, ever since I'd come back aboard. In their eyes my return was of itself an admission of defeat on Whitehall's part.

The man in purple said, 'Kindly spell it out, if you please, Commander Shaw.'

'Very well. On your assurance, to be transmitted by your radio to Downing Street direct, that the threat is totally withdrawn, the Prime Minister is prepared to order all service personnel to lay down arms and disperse to their homes, and the police—'

'No, no. That is not what we require, Commander Shaw. The armed forces and the police must not be dispersed—we need them to control the population, to act under the orders of CORPSE. They must remain in possession of their arms and must retain their positions. The guarantee we wish is this, that they do not use their arms against CORPSE—that is all.'

I shrugged. 'That will be acceptable, I've no doubt. You can confirm with Whitehall direct if you wish. As to the rest of it, Her Majesty's Government will guarantee to hand over to the interim government as soon as satisfactory arrangements can be made for the shift of power.'

'Which means?'

I shrugged. 'So far as I know, it means you can put representatives ashore to meet the present government and officals and so on, and make mutually satisfactory plans for the hand over.'

'You repeat yourself, Commander Shaw.'

I said pleasantly, 'Yes, I know. But since you didn't seem to understand—'

'I wished to know the precise meaning of "satisfactory arrangements". You must be honest with us, Commander Shaw. Is there anything else the present government of Great Britain has in mind?' The voice had hardened.

'Only this,' I answered, and proceeded to exceed my brief. 'The offer of surrender is expected to be met not only by the withdrawal of the theoretical threat, but also by the immediate standing-down and removal of the death-ships.' I paused. 'To that extent, the surrender will not be unconditional, but I submit that you can reasonably expect no less.'

★ ★ ★ ★

That put the cat among the CORPSE pigeons: I believe the ladies and gentlemen of the interim government really had been banking all along on surrender, right from the start, and now that they had the cave-in confirmed and guaranteed the last of their worries had gone. They were against the idea of rejecting that handy surrender and they said so. Ron Gudge put it best. He said that union power was important and handled right they could get the unions on their side from the start. Unnecessary brutality, by which he meant the continuance of the threat once surrender had been offered, would cause a sense of grievance among the workers and they would get all manner of trouble. Strikes, official and unofficial, go slows, sit-ins. That sort of thing. The workers didn't like the stick, the big fist, he explained portentously and at length until I began to wonder if he was past his prime after all. He had only to look at the expression in the eyes behind the purple hood. Those eyes said clearly that union power would be the first casualty of the take-over. For my money, once he'd played his part in persuading the union leaders to co-operate in the first instance, poor Ron Gudge himself would be the next casualty. However, he talked on loudly about the workers and he seemed to impress his colleagues even if for different reasons. Many of them would have families in Britain, and all must have friends. The lady who was bound for the Home Office backed up Mr Gudge with a series of short, sharp statements

242

that emerged like barks. CORPSE must be seen to be civilised. One didn't shoot sitting birds. One had one's standards. One didn't put women and children at risk. And so on. I even began to wonder if these people would ever have stomached the blow-up at all. They had probably never believed it would really happen. There was a decided hint of mutiny in the air now. More by good luck than anything else I had struck the right note with my impromptu commitment of Whitehall to the physical removal demand: it had appealed to them. The overall menace would still be there, of course, but a demonstrable act of goodwill in bringing the ships out to lie off the shores of Britain would be a salve to their consciences as well as a good propaganda point.

They were adamant. The man in purple was clearly furious, but he had a need of them, at least in the early stages, and he conceded. A message would go immediately to Whitehall: the surrender had been accepted by CORPSE, and Her Majesty's Government as represented by the Prime Minister and full cabinet were to be flown to Exeter where they would be exchanged for the members of the interim government, heart attacks or not. In the meantime the *in situ* CORPSE heads of regions would take post, and as soon as they had reported back to the *Sendar Maru* by radio the nuclear-waste vessels would be boarded by their own crews and withdrawn three miles from the coast where they would remain for re-entry if required. This would include the vessel in the Devonport submarine pens. In return, Whitehall was to withdraw the naval frigates from the vicinity of the *Sendar Maru*, this withdrawal to take place immediately upon receipt of the CORPSE message. At that, my heart sank: some basic planning was thereby scuppered, for now I would not be able to get the frigates ordered in on a rocket-blast mission when CORPSE switched off at the main as it were—which they would have to do, I believed, in order to prevent any chance of the death-ship crews inadvertently tripping the devices by use of their radio.

There was one other disquieting item in the man in purple's list: to accommodate a slightly changed situation, the deadline was naturally annulled. It was no longer relevant. For me, however, it remained, and I was more than a little worried: it would be just too bad if I blew the bottom out of the *Sendar Maru* after the Prime Minister and cabinet had been brought aboard in place of Mr Gudge and associates...

★ ★ ★ ★

As Britain's only remaining hope my duty now lay below, in that cell above the double bottoms. I had to get myself put there, and the way to achieve that was to misbehave, so I misbehaved in a highly satisfactory way. I appeared to go berserk and I launched myself at the man in purple and got to him before the guards had gathered their wits. I got him down on the deck and before I was seized I pulled away that stupid purple hood. When I had done so I realised why he wore it: there was hardly any flesh and what there was, was purple like the hood itself. Burns—acid probably, for even the bone structure had been eaten away. He gibbered at me in German: I'd been right about the nationality. As the guards grabbed my arms and held me ready for him, he struck me viciously in the face, again and again and again. The interim government didn't like it, but they didn't interfere. They were flabbergasted, I think; until now, the man in purple had no doubt behaved like a gentleman fit to govern England. After a while he calmed down and replaced his hood. That gave him back his dignity and authority. The guards were ordered to take me below, and back I went, as planned, to the deep-down cell.

I sat on the steel shelf that acted as chair and

bed and mopped my bloodied face. From now till the end came, my role was to be a passive one. All I had to do was wait for Mirko Zambellis to transmit into my gut and, through me, to sink the *Sendar Maru*. If I had to die, I hoped I would die usefully; but I wasn't even sure of that, now. It all depended on the timing.

CHAPTER 14

There was a maximum of one hour and a quarter before Zambellis transmitted and each second was going to be agony. I found myself reviewing my life, all the way from my earliest memories. I hoped I'd chalked up a few good points along the way. I thought about Felicity in St Thomas's: by this time the surgeons would perhaps have operated or anyway would know the score, whether or not they *could* operate. I wondered what the sequence of events in Britain might be, at what stage the government would assemble at Exeter for the exchange. Most likely the frigates would have been ordered away from the *Sendar Maru* by now, and I was on my own.

I rather wished I hadn't got my watch. I could always smash it, of course; but I didn't. That would have seemed unworthy, cowardly. There might yet be something I could do, and a knowledge of time might well be vital, though in all conscience I doubted most mightily that I could do anything at this stage except act as the vehicle for the end of the *Sendar Maru*. That, of course, could still save Britain even if HMG had been embarked by that time. They could be done without; Martial Law was in being anyway, and the Chief of Staff would cope. But in the meantime, right now, there must be the most colossal feeling of hopelessness, and increasing panic, right throughout the country. I wondered if the government had made any public announcement of surrender. There would be points in favour both ways and no doubt there would have been plenty of argument in Downing Street.

The seconds passed. I was sweating like a pig. The atmosphere was close anyway. There was a quietness apart from the sound of the generators aft of my cell, and of the forced-draught system blowing air at me; I could hear no other sounds that might have given me some clue as to the passing events, such as helicopters touching down on deck, or boats scraping the plates as they made to come alongside the accommodation-ladder. Nothing. I was totally cut off, a being apart, a being on the point of fragmentation.

I wouldn't know a thing about it, but I knew right now, so there was no consolation in that.

The infernal device in my gut was hurting badly, seeming to cut into me with its fins each time I moved. As the time ran down I found my attention riveted on my watch: an impulse I was powerless to fight though I detested every movement of the hands. Fifty minutes left...

Eternity passed and then there were forty.

Again the past came to me: happy days, and not so happy days, but mainly the happy ones. So many memories of so many people, so many countries where duty or leave had taken me. Felicity...I'd not known her all that long, but she'd grown on me. So, in his way, had Max. Max wasn't so bad when he wasn't being an official bastard. He was always fair, and knew by instinct when a field man had had enough for a spell and needed a good, long leave and a good, strong woman to go with it. Life hadn't been too bad...maybe I was lucky to be going out while it was still good, before old age and the retirement pastures struck. I had never wanted to be a geriatric; once, I'd spent a leave, misguidedly and not for long, in Worthing. You couldn't move along the shopping streets for nasty little bags on wheels full of groceries and whatnot that could be lethal to a fast-striding active man. It certainly wasn't for me, and in any case didn't look like being so...

Thirty-five minutes.

I believe I passed into a coma. Perhaps it was a kind of protection sent by God to make the end easy—I don't know; what I did know when my watch showed four minutes to deadline was that I was hearing things, and what I heard was not the heavenly music of harp-strings being plucked on a cloud but the clang of footsteps on metal. Someone coming down the ladder from the deck above. They would be just in time to join me.

The footsteps banged along the alleyway and came to a halt outside my cell and then I heard the outside clips being taken off the door and a moment later it opened up and the man in purple came in with two armed guards. He didn't say anything, he just stared at me through his slits.

I said, 'Welcome. Are you ready for a surprise...like when you used to rummage in your Christmas stocking!'

There was the gleam of a smile behind the slits, but he still said nothing. I took another look at my watch: just over two minutes left. Zambellis was leaving it a little late, a little close

249

to 1800 hours. There was poetic justice around somewhere; the CORPSE boss would be the first, with me and his guards, to go. Wouldn't he be mad, when we reached the Other Side in company, down the dark corridor and out into the everlasting light, hand in hand!

He stared at me, eyes mocking away behind the purple, and light of a different sort began to dawn on me as my watch ticked on and the hands drew towards their full 180-degree angle. 1800 hours came, and went again. I was still there, so was the man in purple.

At 1801 he laughed. 'The surprise is yours, Commander Shaw. Zambellis is dead. His throat was cut soon after he contacted you.'

I asked, 'How come?'

'His telephone call to your Ministry of Defence was tapped. Just one of many. We knew where to find Zambellis. So the *Sendar Maru* lives on, unlike Zambellis, and our threat still has a stranglehold on Britain. And on your interior, Commander Shaw.' His voice changed, hardened. 'Get up, and come with me.'

I obeyed, automaton-like. I felt no sense of anti-climax at all, just a sense of postponement. And the bug was biting harder than ever. With the guns of the uniformed guards in my back, I climbed the steel ladders until I emerged on the upper deck. The day was fine as it drew into evening, and the sea was a flat blue calm. And it was empty: the friendly frigates had sailed away on orders from Whitehall, the last link gone now. There was still no land in sight, but as I stared out helplessly at that vacant sea I felt the vibration beneath my feet and when I looked up at the *Sendar Maru's* navigating bridge I saw much brass: the Captain and some of his officers. We were on the move. This, the man in purple confirmed.

'Where to?' I asked.

'Closer to the British coast.'

'The Channel?'

'Not the Channel.'

'Too much shipping? If there is, I'd be surprised. All shipping'll be standing clear of British waters till further notice.'

The man in purple agreed; monitored broadcasts had indicated this already. The Channel was becoming strangely deserted, he said, a vacant seaway now. But the *Sendar Maru* was bound for Scottish waters. More precisely, she would enter the Firth of Clyde by dawn, remaining outside the Cumbraes, somewhere off the isle of Arran, in the deep-water lane.

I asked why.

He said, 'A handy place to govern from, particularly if we should need to send the vessels with the nuclear cargoes back into the ports.'

'From which I deduce that they've all been withdrawn—and that you don't intend sending back the one off Greenock?'

He nodded. 'Just so. Also the one in the Forth. If we need to blow the others, Scotland will remain relatively free from fall-out and radiation. The *Sendar Maru* is capable of remaining clean after being battened-down against fall-out and we can survive indefinitely, for we can replenish food stocks at sea—and our nuclear reactor can power us indefinitely, of course. But government cannot be carried on very conveniently if no one can leave the ship for fear of radiation.'

'I take your point,' I said. 'Going back to Zambellis...has there been any change of plan?'

'As a result of what?'

I said, 'Of my dirty dealing. Are you still in negotiation with Her Majesty's Government?'

He smiled. 'Very much yes! Now there will be even greater urgency for surrender...and I am informed by my regional controllers that all is going according to plan. You yourself have helped to demonstrate physically to the British people that CORPSE has the power to do all it says, Commander Shaw.'

'Me? How?' I shifted a little, and the bug bit again, and suddenly a great fear swept through me. I said, 'Miss Mandrake—'

'Yes, Miss Mandrake. I failed to hear in time of the operation. I am told she came through it and that the device was removed. On hearing of this, I at once transmitted the signal that blew the nuclear content, with results that were remarkably if fortuitously effective against morale.' The man in purple paused. 'St Thomas's Hospital wished to rid themselves of the device as soon as possible, and a helicopter was sent to pick it up and then to fly it out for disposal at sea. It appears that my transmission took place while the helicopter was stupidly low over Brighton beach. It was very spectacular and there were many deaths.'

I took a deep, deep breath. Many deaths indeed. This was the holiday season and the weather had been set fair for many days past over the British Isles. In spite of panic, I would have been prepared to bet that there had been plenty of people on Brighton beach of a sunny afternoon, all staring up at the friendly helicopter with its military or naval markings. The man in purple was totally unconcerned; for him, it had just been a lovely piece of luck. He'd capitalised, he told me: his radiomen had cut in from the *Sendar Maru* on the BBC broadcasts, claiming responsibility for CORPSE. There was absolutely no point in my telling him what a bastard he was, but I was about to do so anyway when there was a hail from the bridge and a lot of Japanese chatter, and a gold-ringed arm was waved in the air.

I turned to look: distantly to starboard a fleet of helicopters was coming in. Six big machines, coming out of a heat haze, the Rising Sun of Japan approaching in blood-red blobs of fire.

'Her Majesty's Government,' the man in purple said.

★ ★ ★ ★

I was taken down below again, this time to a different section of the ship, to join the hijacked naval boarding-party from the frigate. The man in purple had wished at this stage to keep all his prisoners together and I dare say I had now lost my particular value to CORPSE and was just a number. I didn't expect to die by transmission just yet; CORPSE wouldn't wish to sink their own mobile government unit just to get back at me, though I supposed they could always throw me overboard and steam away from me and then blow me up like a mine once they were clear. That wasn't a happy thought and I sheered off it and thought instead about the defeated bunch who had disembarked from the helicopters while I was still on deck to watch. The muffled one in the stretcher had been the Prime Minister, boarding with an attacked heart. All the faces so familiar from the telly: Chancellor of the Exchequer with a face as desolate as a Return of Income Tax; Minister of Defence giving me a very bleak look indeed; Home Secretary, Foreign Secretary; Environment, Social Services, Energy, Trade, Industry and the rest plus Lord Privy Seal and so on. There were some backroom boys whom I didn't recognise, probably Ministers of State roped in with their cabinet masters, or maybe top civil servants, the ones who really had the knowledge and did the work for the politicians. They all looked like death warmed up. Some of them tied themselves in deferential knots when they met the man in purple, new ruler of Britain. Perhaps they hoped to get their jobs back one day, but if so I felt they were due for a disappointment. CORPSE would make a clean sweep. Apparently the interim government boys had been put ashore in the helicopters that had picked up HMG, as planned; by now they would be taking over in the name of CORPSE and making contact with the new regional controllers hived up in their RSGs. The man in purple had told me, while we were awaiting the touchdown of the helicopters, that the last broadcast to the people by HMG before leaving had ordered the armed services and the police to obey CORPSE orders. It was all systems go for CORPSE now...

Thinking all these thoughts, I looked around at my fellow prisoners. A lieutenant, a gunnery instructor, two leading-seamen, twenty able-seamen and a communications rating. And me. I hummed a tune: it was 'Soldiers of the Queen'. *For we're part of England's glory, lads...*

The lieutenant, whose name I'd learned was Dick Phillips, implored me to shut up. I was out of tune, he said, and I didn't disbelieve him. He added, 'Right now, it's inappropriate.'

'Why?'

He waved an arm around. 'Prisoners of war...'

'That's one way of looking at it, Dick.'

'So what's the other?' He sounded sardonic.

I said, 'Trojan horse. Slap bang in the enemy camp. Start thinking about it.'

On we sailed for the Clyde. Fast now: the vibration was intense and I could hear the water hissing down the ship's side plating.

★ ★ ★ ★

Being a Trojan horse was all very well, but

256

the soldiers of Troy had had an advantage over us: they could, and of course did, get out of their wooden horse. There was no way out of our prison accommodation, which I fancied had been a storeroom until it had been cleared out to accommodate prisoners. There were two ports, both very much too small to admit passage to the thinnest and most stunted man even if there had been a way of smashing the thick fixed glass, which there was not. There was ventilator trunking, but again no use as a way out unless you were a rat. The deck was steel. We were well and truly boxed in and I gave CORPSE credit for having seen to it that escape was impossible except by the obvious means, i.e, attacking any guard who opened the door, but that was too obvious to be viable. However, during the evening and night something curious and remarkable and lucky happened: after I had been incarcerated for some while, the door opened and food was brought under very heavy armed guard, the arms being sub-machine guns. The food was Japanese and fishy and it was left in plastic containers for us to feed from without knives or forks or even spoons. We had more or less to tip it into our mouths or go at it like cats; and it was filthy. I believe it was off, though at first I thought it was merely Japanese and as I was hungry I ate to keep my strength up. I didn't manage much, neither did my companions. An hour or so later sickness set in, real gut-tearing sickness. Never had I been so revoltingly ill. We were all like fountains, gushing. And with me, much blood and a good deal of pain and after a while something came up and stuck in my throat so that I almost choked to death. My plight was seen by Dick Phillips, and he staggered over and thumped my back, hard. Then he got his fingers down my throat and probed around and after a racking few minutes of blood and agony, out came that little metal bug with one of its slide-out stoppers gone. The metallurgists of CORPSE had made a balls, or I had a larger throat system than other people.

Anyway, there it was. Up till then I hadn't told the naval party about the bug, but now I did. They hoisted in the fact that they were close to death, since there was no way of getting rid of the bug, but they took it well. I got groggily to my feet and shoved the bug out of sight in a corner of the deckhead, where it lay concealed by the ventilator trunking. I said casually, 'You never know, do you? The most unlikely things, if kept, can come in handy one day.'

What happened next was terrifying: the *Sendar Maru* gave a bit of a roll, probably as the helm went over for a change of course to stand clear of a vessel crossing ahead. There was a sliding sound, then a series of metallic clanks like a stone dropping down a drainpipe. The bug had evidently gone through some chink in the trunking and had descended willy-nilly and we all expected instant cremation. However, bangs seemed not to harm it and after a while we breathed again. I was in some considerable pain from the thing's re-emergence, but I felt very much easier in mind, and grateful for that filthy supper. After that, I slept. The atmosphere was foul thereafter, but the sleep was very welcome and refreshed us all. As dawn lit the ports I got up and looked out: there, right on our ETA, fine on the starboard bow, stood the great rock of Ailsa Craig at the mouth of the Firth of Clyde, whitened from its age-old use as a seagulls' lavatory. As the *Sendar Maru* swung to starboard to enter the Firth, I lost my view of Ailsa Craig. Up the bright blue stretch of water we went, with the engines eased a little now. Soon we came up to Turnberry, with its expensive hotel and golf course. Even at this early hour, even with Britain moving under the CORPSE shroud, a handful of lunatics strode the fairways with bags and trolleys. I could see them clearly, could imagine them yelling 'Fore!' as they loosed their balls. On past

Turnberry, with Arran looming immense but to me invisible to port beneath the great craggy peak of Goat Fell. On towards the entry to Inchmarnock Water and the Kyles of Bute, also to port, and the town of Ardrossan coming up on my side. Then the vibration died and the hiss of water ceased and we lost way, and soon, by picking out a couple of leading marks, I saw that way was off us.

I wondered: what next?

* * * *

'Next' was a boat coming off from Ardrossan a couple of hours after we had hove-to some distance off shore, keeping to the deep-water channel on account of our draught although, as I had noted on first seeing the *Sendar Maru* from the air, she was high in the water due to not being loaded down to her marks and in all probability was not in any danger of grounding. That boat approached below the portholes and I saw what was in it: an admiral and a general in uniform, and two provosts in their civic robes and chains, plus minions. The admiral was probably the Flag Officer, Scotland and Northern Ireland, the general his military counterpart from Edinburgh. In this I was correct; all we prisoners were brought on deck shortly after the party had boarded and we were told who they were and that they had come to pay court to CORPSE. When we appeared, the admiral at once demanded the release of the naval personnel—he wasn't worried about me, I was a 6D2 responsibility if that organisation still existed at all. The man in purple granted the admiral's request without ado. CORPSE intended to be correct in its attitudes; the naval men had merely obeyed orders and until such time as they refused to follow CORPSE directives they would be treated properly as would all other service personnel. And much to my astonishment, I was chucked in with the rest. All was going well for CORPSE and the boss had no further use for me. Or so I thought, and I was wrong.

The man in purple took me aside before we went down to the boat and spoke in friendly fashion. 'You will see that it pays to be on the winning side, Commander Shaw.' He paused. 'All the incoming reports are excellent. The take-over is proceeding reasonably peacefully— but remember this: the nuclear-loaded vessels are handy for bringing in if needed.'

'I'm remembering,' I said. 'So?'

'So there is something more required of you, Commander Shaw.'

'Well?'

The man in purple said, 'Your organisation—6D2. It will be disbanded in its present form, of course, but while it remains in being it constitutes a threat to the new government, since it is outside the Establishment. In other words, I cannot be certain of the reaction of 6D2 Britain—'

'Or of 6D2 America and—'

'All the others, yes. You have put your finger on it. We could face trouble, but we shall not. It is you who shall ensure that we do not.'

I asked, 'Why me? You say you have the power. Why not put the army or the police in and shut down Focal House?'

He smiled through his ludicrous slits. 'I respect your organisation, Commander, and will have a use for it—when it is reconstituted. There will be a place for you. Even CORPSE has a continuing need for such men, and 6D2 will be incorporated into CORPSE once the old guard have been disposed of.'

I asked, 'Can you elaborate?'

'Certainly. The man you know as Max...he is expendable now. A man of set mind and outlook, a man who will never change enough to accept CORPSE. You will go to London and replace him. If necessary you will shoot him. You, Commander, will be the new Max, the new executive head of 6D2 Britain, and you will reshape the organisation along acceptable lines. Do you understand?'

I understood very well indeed: the bastard thought he had the drop on me because of that bug, supposedly in my stomach still. I would be an excellent dummy, and could be killed at the drop of a hat, or a switch anyway. Of course I would play ball, thought he! I could only hope no one would find the bug somewhere down the ventilator shafting. So long as it remained hidden, so long as the CORPSE boss thought I was still loaded, I would be considered a very safe man indeed since there was now nothing particular I could achieve by suicide, like the sinking of the *Sendar Maru*. It was too late for that now even though the bug remained aboard —Zambellis was dead. The man in purple gave me a parting reminder once again before I went over the side to the waiting boat: if 6D2 gave any trouble, or if anyone else did, back into position would go the nuclear-waste ships and the interim government would withdraw aboard the nuclear-sealed *Sendar Maru* until the fall-out blew away and Britain lay prostrate.

With this ringing in my ears, I went down to the boat. Once away for Ardrossan, I pumped the admiral and the general and the civic dignitaries. Law and order was being maintained largely because the mass of the population was stunned by the immensity of the CORPSE threat and by the sheer speed with which the elected government of the land had handed over power. The backlash would come.

'Then what?' I asked rhetorically. The man in purple had already given me my answer. He expected the backlash and had prepared for it in advance.

★ ★ ★ ★

It was certainly a stunned land. Everyone looked like a zombie, walking around in a dream. There was a crowd watching when we came ashore at Ardrossan, but it was a silent crowd that stared out across the Clyde towards the *Sendar Maru*, immense and lethal. Even the backdrop of the rearing peaks of Arran failed somehow to dwarf her. The admiral and the general and the provosts were met by a man wearing the CORPSE uniform as aboard the *Sendar Maru*, a Scot—one of the *in situ* boys, the *gauleiter* corps. He was Commandant MacKechnie, he said in rich Glaswegian. He was polite and deferential; CORPSE had a need to inveigle themselves with the ex-Establishment for a while. But behind him he had his uniformed other-rank thugs, hard-looking men

264

with holstered revolvers hanging from black plastic belts. He accompanied us to a car waiting outside the landing pier; I had arranged with the brass for a lift into Glasgow, where I would find air transport to London, but Commandant MacKechnie had made other arrangements as a result of orders from the *Sendar Maru*. As the brass drove away I was led to another car that would take me to Prestwick.

'Flight arranged?' I asked.

'Aye.'

MacKechnie came with me and sat dourly in the back of the car. There didn't seem to be much traffic on the road as we headed south and away from the *Sendar Maru* now doing a slow patrol up and down off Ardrossan, keeping in deep water. I found the whole ambience extraordinary; there was normality yet there was not. Prestwick airport was functioning as usual, but was not as busy as I would have expected at this time of the year. Perhaps not unnaturally: the holiday spirit was certainly in abeyance by now. Just before I was escorted to my flight, which was a special one for me alone, a nasty little incident took place: three raw-faced Scots, surging along in advance of a strong smell of whisky, saw Commandant MacKechnie's CORPSE uniform and grew drunkenly belligerent. MacKechnie was jostled.

I sensed his fear that belligerency would spread; many people were looking on and showing their feelings. But CORPSE, though thin on the ground yet, were in command. A group of thugs shoved through from behind and smashed the Scots on their heads with truncheons, and like three switched-off lights they went out and were dragged away bleeding. Incident over. Feeling murderous, I walked through for my plane. Commandant MacKechnie watched my take-off. The aircraft headed out for Gatwick, where a helicopter waited to ferry me into London and Focal House. All so normal; the sort of routine I'd followed so often in past times. But when I went down from the roof it was all different. Not physically; but as to atmosphere. The staff had changed—the same people, but grown different almost overnight. They wore a hunted look, and no doubt with reason: the new masters would be watching and sorting out. Junior staff hung about in groups, doing no work but drinking a lot of tea. I was stared at as I went along the lushly carpeted corridors to the suite. In the suite I found Mrs Dodge, her face tear-stained. She was alone; the first thing she told me, because she knew I wanted to know, was that Miss Mandrake was coming along well but still in hospital. I let out a long, long breath of relief and asked,

'Where's your bevy of beauty, Mrs Dodge?'

'There's no work,' she said. Her voice was flat, almost entirely without tone. 'I told them not to bother to come in. Transport's so difficult, you know...ever since the panic started.'

'Max?'

She said, 'He's at home, Commander Shaw. He's been relieved. *Sacked*,' she added fiercely and bitterly. Her loyalty was intense. I broke it to her gently that I was the new Max and for a moment she brightened just a little, but then grew hostile. 'So you've joined them,' she said. 'I would never have thought it of you.'

'I've not joined them,' I said, and trusted to her efficiency to have ensured that her office was free of bugging devices. 'I'm here to lead the strike-back, but you'll keep that under your hat, if you please, Mrs Dodge. So far as anyone else in FH knows, I'm CORPSE's man and 6D2 becomes a CORPSE agency as of now.'

Many emotions had a chase across her face; she almost got up and hugged me, I believe. She didn't know what to say, and said what came most naturally: 'Would you like a cup of tea, Commander Shaw?'

I said no, I would prefer a glass of whisky but I wouldn't linger even for that. I had to see Max soonest possible. Out I went again.

CHAPTER 15

6D2 still had some cars left and I equipped myself with a Jensen. When I took it over in the underground car park I was saluted by ex-CSM Horridge.

'A sad day, sir. Sad for Britain.'

'Yes. And 6D2.'

'Yes, sir. The suite'll be missed, sir.' He lowered his voice. 'Is there any gen, sir?'

I told him I was the new Max, or in his terms the new suite. He was as frigid as Mrs Dodge had been, but I couldn't tell him that my appointment was to be turned to advantage: Horridge was a first-class man but he liked his liquor and just might, in the likely circumstances of being pushed around by the CORPSE boys in a pub, lose his cool and be indiscreet. I couldn't take the risk with so much at stake. I felt his hostility like a stab from a bayonet as I drove out into the city. I had a bet with myself that his notice would be going in pronto. Driving through the city, westbound for Chelsea, I was surprised to find little superficial evidence in the streets of the superchange that had hit Britain. There were the usual crowds, police and traffic wardens patrolled as ever, and the traffic lights were working, and there were jams though there didn't seem to be any buses. The sun shone and it was hot and London simmered gently, its stone buildings acting as huge night-storage heaters and pumping back the absorbed heat. The crowds were as colourful as ever, jeans and cheesecloth proliferating. At the Horse Guards in Whitehall the Queen's Guard was mounted yet, but in the background, under the arches by the stables, a quick glimpse of lurking CORPSE uniforms showed what was behind the facade. CORPSE was again in evidence at the gates of the Houses of Parliament, and again outside New Scotland Yard, yet again outside Buckingham Palace. Then I saw commandeered bus-loads of them and assumed the incoming waves of support had started arriving to back up the fifth column inside London.

I found Max in a blue silk dressing-gown, smoking a cigar and staring from his study window like a pugnacious Churchill glaring defiance across the Channel. When he heard me he swung round and pointed the cigar at me.

'We've lost,' he said. He sounded personal about it, as though the whole thing had depended on 6D2 and 6D2 were the letters-down.

This was bunk and I said so and he snarled at me to shut up.

I said, 'I'm your replacement, Max.'

'I'm aware of that. CORPSE must be crazy.'

'I'm glad of that observation,' I said quietly.

'Why?'

'Because it means you trust me. It means you know I've not ratted and am not likely to.'

He grunted, but gave me a sharp look. 'Correct so far. What's your next step, Shaw?'

'To get CORPSE out of Britain.'

'Quite. How do you do it?'

Unbidden, I sat down. Max gave me another sharp look, then crossed his study to a cupboard and brought out glasses and a whisky decanter. He poured and handed me a stiff drink. I told him then about the current situation of the device ex my stomach. I said that the first transmission would sink the *Sendar Maru* in the Firth of Clyde and that would be the end of the big threat. He gave an un-Max-like whistle and looked a good deal happier. He asked how I could get that transmission made and I said that currently I had no idea, since Zambellis had been murdered.

'Did they smash up his equipment?' he asked.

'I don't know, they didn't say.'

'It's a long shot, isn't it? Zambellis dead,

transmitter possibly *kaput.*'

'It's a long shot all right, but it's all we have.'

'Possibly an ordinary transmitter might do it...but then I suppose you don't know what the tripping signal is, nor the frequency of the thing?'

'No,' I had to admit.

Max threw up his arms and scowled at me. Then something struck him. 'This man in purple, Shaw. He's got you where he wants you because he believes the device still to be inside you—right?'

'Right,' I said, 'but—'

'Then why can't he blow his bloody HQ ship up himself, for God's sake? All you have to do is to step badly out of line, and be positively seen to be a danger to CORPSE, and he presses the tit—doesn't he?'

'Yes,' I answered patiently, and explained why that wouldn't work except maybe as a very last resort. There would be extreme danger to the Clyde coasts when that device blew, since not only was the *Sendar Maru* herself nuclear powered but she was said to be carrying some of the nuclear waste for the Windscale ponds and could in fact have been the parent-ship for supplying the small death-ships with their cargoes after they had cleared from their official

271

loading ports as per manifests. If she still had some of that cargo aboard, and if that lot blew in the Clyde, the effects of the resulting fall-out would be too appalling to contemplate. True, Mirko Zambellis had said that my stomach bug would merely sink the ship straight down and that there would be no explosion big enough to trigger the devices aboard the death-ships, and I was prepared to believe he had known his job. Something could still go wrong, though, and I didn't care to chance it at this stage. And Her Majesty's Government was aboard the *Sendar Maru,* while the interims were lording it around Whitehall. Another point: I feared that a lot of the *Sendar Maru's* superstructure could, depending on her position at the time—she could be in comparatively shallow water for her draught if we were out of luck—remain above sea level when her bottom fell out. She had to go down like a stone in very deep water or CORPSE would still blow the nuclear-waste ships, and they were all too close for comfort even though they had been withdrawn from the ports.

'Then what do we do?' Max asked impatiently.

I said, 'We get a line on Zambellis's laboratory and hope it's still intact. I reckon it will be—the CORPSE thugs who killed Zambellis

272

won't have rampaged around the equipment in case they happened to trip something nasty. Much too chancy. And if the set's okay, then it's quite possible his transmitter will be found lined up ready on the right frequency, and it's also possible that just a touch on the key will do the job.' I forestalled the coming remark: 'A long shot as we've agreed, but all we have. And I'm going to try it.'

'And the *Sendar Maru?* How do we get her out of the Clyde for your purposes—and get the damn cabinet off first?'

I grinned and said, 'Oh, by acting clever... the CORPSE boys are not fully organised at the moment. For one thing, I'm pretty certain I had no tail on me from FH to here. How are you fixed for contacting persons who'll remain loyal to HMG?'

'I can manage,' Max said briefly. 'What's in your mind?'

I said, 'I was told when I went up to Greenock—when the *Johann Klompé* came in—that the nuclear submarine fleet had been ordered to sea from the Gareloch, with their Polaris and Poseidon missiles. They'll still be at sea right now. And those submarines are the one bit of Britain that is right outside CORPSE control. They're independent, out of sight, unattackable, and lethal. All they need is orders. Orders that can be picked up by the *Sendar Maru*—if you get me.'

★ ★ ★ ★

Max got me: the *Sendar Maru* could hopeful-ly be sent right out to sea by a nicely-worded last-ditch signal calculated to put the fear of God into CORPSE unexpectedly. The Polaris fleet had so far remained without orders simp-ly because no one wanted to use the missiles where they might send radiation over Britain, and I had no doubt at all that the man in purple had realised this and was confident they would not be used. Now they could remain in their nice safe submerged nests and merely have their awful power, equal to CORPSE's own, invoked in a good cause. It might not work— CORPSE might not believe they would really be used against the Clyde even at our last gasp—but it would be interesting to see what happened. Of course, we had not yet found salvation for the shipbound cabinet, but something might emerge. If not, they might have to be sacrificed for the greater good. In the meantime I had other matters on my mind and on leaving Max's house I drove to Scotland Yard. I sought an interview with the Commis-sioner, and this was granted. Once again, I had to chance bugs, relying on CORPSE not yet having had the time to fix things behind the Commissioner's back. The Commissioner was, of course, loyal. He had made a pretence at co-operation, but didn't expect to remain in his job for more than another day. I asked him to busy himself in the meantime and do what I wouldn't have a hope of doing, which was to find means, like Max, of contacting other loyal persons in Foreign Office security, or possibly via Interpol's network, and dig out all he could about Mirko Zambellis, deceased. Firstly, where he had died, and if this had not been in his laboratory, where his laboratory was. Secondly, names and current whereabouts of his associates. The Commissioner promised to do all he could and would arrange to report to me. Not, I said, by telephone to FH or my flat: loyalties inside FH must now be regarded as suspect, which was why I couldn't make use of our own files Zambelliswise. That name would spread and I wouldn't last long. I was in a particularly vulnerable and tricky position, I said—vis-à-vis CORPSE, I had to be whiter than white. And I added that the line to my flat was out of action via an explosive device, as was the flat itself. This, he knew. I said I intended getting accommodation at my club, and the line there could be considered reasonably safe.

From Scotland Yard I went back to Focal House and set about my whitening. I called a conference of heads of departments and formally confirmed my appointment in Max's place. The new order, I said, was a fact in being. It was up to us all to smoothe the transition and I knew I could rely on all present, et cetera. I tried to assess the expressions and reactions, find the loyal faces and the time-servers, sort the sheep from the goats. I didn't get far. Most of them looked just one thing, and that was scared stiff. No one knew where or when the axe would fall, the bullet come. Fear and the awful suddenness had in fact made time-servers of all the admin side at any rate.

I felt utterly depressed, utterly useless. I brought the session to an abrupt end and went back to the suite and found Mrs Dodge moping too. I was going to be at a loose end until the Commissioner contacted me and I knew that wouldn't be for a while yet. Meanwhile Miss Mandrake was recuperating in St Thomas's and suddenly I couldn't wait to see her. All else could wait, Britain included. I was on the point of telling Mrs Dodge that I could be contacted at the hospital when something funny happened. The security telephone on Mrs Dodge's desk burred and she answered. It was the

Foreign Office, for me. I took the call.

'Shaw here,' I said.

'Ah, Commander Shaw...this is Mellowes.' I knew Mellowes; a good man, straight as a die, in fact one of the people I expected the Commissioner to contact about Zambellis; I hoped he was not about to be indiscreet enough to mention Zambellis on the telephone, but I needn't have worried. He went on, 'Someone's been put on to us by our consular section. Name of Barnsley. I'm sure you understand. This person would like to meet you and I've suggested the Captain's Cabin off Lower Regent Street in one hour's time.'

Mellowes rang off, no time even to say he hoped the time was convenient. It was, if I neglected Miss Mandrake. I had no idea who Barnsley was, I didn't understand at all, but duty was duty and Mellowes had been mysterious enough to interest me. I decided reluctantly against St Thomas's and went down and took a taxi to Lower Regent Street and walked through to the Captain's Cabin, a congenial pub that I knew slightly but where I would not be known, and bought myself a whisky and looked around for Barnsley or for anyone who might look like Barnsley looking out for me. *Mr* Barnsley, I took it to be.

I was dead wrong, and when I saw her I

clicked. Barnsley...quite clever really, I supposed. Staring at me from a corner with a glass of something on a table in front of her was Mrs Pumfret spelled Pontefract, next door to Barnsley on the map of Yorkshire. She looked mightily out of place in the casual camaraderie of the Captain's Cabin, the Women's Institute come to town, hat and all. And gloves, as in the Flood Fearers' church in distant Andalusia. She made a sign, and indicated without pointing, since ladies didn't point, an empty chair. Obviously, she'd been keeping it for me, but I pushed through the crowd and asked politely if the chair was engaged, and she said no, it wasn't, and do sit down.

I sat. I said, 'I thought my name was Jones.'

'Isn't it?' she said. She looked surprised. I said it didn't really matter but how had she contacted me? It turned out that she had rung 'the Government' which to her as an expatriate seemed to mean the Foreign Office and had asked for the Mr Jones who had been on a secret mission in Spain; from there the rest had followed: one up to the FO, I thought, they'd ticked over remarkably fast.

'Well?' I asked. 'What do you want me for, Mrs Pontefract?'

'It's about that girl,' she said.

'You came to England because of her?' I

leaned closer. 'Look, Mrs Pontefract, you know what's happening here in England. Or didn't you get to hear, in Spain?'

'Yes,' she said. 'I knew. That's why I came. I came to strike a blow for England. If her own daughters can't rally round in a time of danger, well, it's very sad, that's all I can say.' There was no self-consciousness about her utterances; nor was there any unction. She was just a good old-fashioned patriot at heart and never mind the expatriation. When danger threatened, the Empire, which lived on in the mind of Mrs Pontefract, stood to. She was much ruffled by her reception at Gatwick, where CORPSE had taken over immigration and Customs, or anyway were very obvious in the background with nasty uniforms reminiscent of Hitler—she had been a Wren 1939—46. However, she hadn't come just to rally round. She had come to make a report to me; and she made it. It wasn't directly about La Ina as it turned out: it was to do with La Ina's lover, the Reverened Clay Petersen. Mrs Pontefract had entered the Flood Fearers' church for purposes of worship early the day before, and who should be there but the missing pastor. He had been doing something to the altar, she didn't know what, and hearing her entry he had turned, and had suddenly fired a gun at her.

'It was dreadful,' she said. 'Really dreadful.'
Her grip tightened on the handbag in her lap.
She was living the moment all over again. The
bullet had missed her and she had dived behind
the gunwale of one of the pews. Then a terrible thing had happened, though really it was
only retribution for sacrilege and attempted
murder: the sudden noise, she thought it must
have been, had dislodged Noah with wife and
angels and the great figure had come crashing
down, minus its lower portion. Noah had come
in half. Joining his two portions had been a long
pointed steel shaft, and this had entered Mr
Petersen's skull and killed him stone dead.
After a period of trepidation behind the gunwale, Mrs Pontefract had steeled herself and
had remembered my visit, and what had been
below the altar cloth, and England. She had
emerged and she had gone through Mr Petersen's pockets.

She handed me what she had found. It was
small, oval, and plastic, like a mock-up of a
bantam's egg. A bantam's egg that had been
'blown' by a collector of such: there were small
holes at each end. I turned it round and round,
curiously, though fearful that it might explode
at any moment. Mrs Pontefract held out her
hand and said, 'I'll show you, Mr Jones.' She
removed a safety pin from somewhere around

her breasts, opened it and dug the end into one of the holes. She fished around for a moment, then pulled. A very thin metal rod came out behind the pin, a rod with a tiny hook at its end: it could have been an aerial. I brought out something I always carry just in case: an optician's lens. I screwed it into my eye and made a close examination. The thing was beautifully made and the join was still not very noticeable, but it was there all right, around the middle. I fiddled and pulled and twisted; after a while I found movement, and I unscrewed and laid bare the two halves. It was a tiny transmitter.

Frowning, I put it together again.

I asked, 'What made you wonder about this, Mrs Pontefract? What made you think I might be interested?'

'Aren't you?'

'Yes,' I said. 'But to outside appearances it must have looked fairly ordinary and never mind the steel rod. So what?'

She reached into her handbag again. 'There was this too,' she said. She passed across a sheet of paper and said it had been wrapped round the bantam's egg. It was a very interesting document, containing a mass of figures and numbers forming very obvious code groups, and the plain language version of the message had been written in above the groups, Petersen

having probably written out his message first
and then coded it up for transmission. It read:
Zambellis dead also wife and daughter transmit-
ter found and retained. I met the eye of Mrs
Pontefract.

'Well done,' I said inadequately.

'Have I helped?'

I reached out and squeezed her hand.
'You've been wonderful. You may have helped
more than I'll ever be able to tell you.
England,' I added, 'will be grateful.'

She seemed immensely pleased.

★ ★ ★ ★

I went to see Max again, by taxi. I'd told Mrs
Pontefract to lie low and not breathe a word.
She assured me no one else had been anywhere
around when the lethal half of Noah had dropped on Mr Petersen and the Spanish authorities
had not been in evidence for some while; and
although the body could perhaps have been
found by now, no one would know she had
been present at the time of death. She was in
the clear; as soon as she had recovered her
equilibrium she had shut up her cottage and
driven to Malaga and the Gatwick flight, and
she wouldn't be going back. Not yet, anyway.
And she was very disillusioned with the Flood

Fearers. Mr Petersen had behaved abominably.

When I reached Oakley Street in Chelsea, I paid off the taxi and walked on for Max's house in Cheyne Row. But I went no further than the corner: I saw the CORPSE uniform at the top of the steps leading to Max's front door. House arrest had set in, and for my purposes Max was a dead duck. I went back down Oakley Street and found a taxi in the King's Road, and was driven to Scotland Yard again. The Commissioner was in conference and I had to wait. I waited in growing impatience and much anxiety: I believed I had Zambellis's stomach-bug transmitter in my pocket, and thus possible salvation for Britain, but what I still didn't have was the frequency or the particular signal that would blow the device, though once again I thought it was possible that just a plain bleep could do it. I waited an hour for the Commissioner and when I was taken to his office his face was pale.

'You won't have long with me, Shaw,' he said. 'I'm being relieved of my appointment. One of the CORPSE mob's taking over.'

'I'm sorry,' I said, and meant it. 'Have you any news?'

He had: Max had been in touch, but the call had been cut before he'd finished. That must have been when CORPSE had moved in for house arrest. Anyway, Max had used his private methods in time and contact had been made with the Flag Officer, Submarines. A mendacious signal had already gone out; it had gone in naval cipher in the interest of authenticity, but we all knew that CORPSE would by now have access to the deciphering tables. The signal had been made to the Pentagon, intimating that the British contingent of the NATO Polaris-carrying submarine force was about to be ordered to stand by to send off the missiles into the Firth of Clyde and it was up to the Americans either to assist with their Poseidons or detach as they might decide. The Commissioner passed me the naval communications frequency as used by the submarine fleet and a Top Secret code group that, should I have a need to be in touch with the submarines at sea, would, by its use, authenticate me as the caller. After this I felt slightly more confident, the more so since the Commissioner had other information to impart from his own sources: Interpol had been in contact, he didn't say how. A communist named Josip Humo, another Yugoslav and a close friend and associate of Mirko Zambellis, had reported to the *guarda civil* in Barcelona: he had found the butchered body of his good friend Zambellis, also the equally butchered bodies of the family, right there in Barcelona, and he was willing to help. Currently he was in 6D2 HQ in Madrid, and no risk was being taken of trying to get him into Britain. Somebody had to go to Madrid— me. I felt there was at least some chance that this Josip Humo might know the stomach-bug frequency, but there was too much risk in trying to get it sent across by radio: CORPSE might go into premature action right there in the Clyde if they picked it up. And the Commissioner had a big over-riding worry: once the members of the CORPSE directorate aboard the *Sendar Maru* were in possession of the breakdown of the signal to the Pentagon, would they not bring the death-ships back into the ports?

'Probably,' I said. 'It's something we have to chance. It's all a question of timing now.'

I left the Yard with a worry closely associated with that of the Commissioner: it was also a question of how long it would be before CORPSE brought me in and put me back aboard the *Sendar Maru* for questioning. I hadn't done anything yet to assist them, apart from the purely propagandic pep talk I'd given the heads of departments in Focal House. I decided the one thing I could do was try to get myself to Madrid, in company with Zambellis's little bantam's egg. It could be presumed—or anyway hoped—that the transmission could reach the *Sendar Maru* wherever she might be when the big moment came. And since CORPSE hadn't yet taken over the Continent, I would have freer personal movement.

In the meantime I hadn't an idea in my head as to how I was going to get Her Majesty's Government off the *Sendar Maru*.

CHAPTER 16

The difficulty, of course, was to get to Spain. I felt I'd lost my status by now; to try to fix a flight via Focal House would be useless. CORPSE would be on to me straightaway, and with them Spain would ring far too many alarm bells. I went into a call-box and rang Gatwick pseudonymously for a flight, in the first instance, to Paris. Just a little deviousness... and I would use my reserve passport, in the name of Watts. But I need not have bothered. By order of the new government, all unauthorised outward flights had been cancelled until further notice. Which I might have guessed, I suppose.

Thinking sourly of the alteranatives, such as

rowing boats at dead of night from a deserted shore, or sprouting wings, I turned to leave the call-box and came face to face with the CORPSE insignia.

'Commander Shaw, I think?' The voice was gutteral: another German.

I said he could think what the hell he liked, and he smirked. Of course, he'd been put on to me by a tail from the Yard, though I'd seen nothing suspicioius. I asked what he wanted.

'You will accompany me to your office in Focal House,' he said.

'Why?'

'You are required to take a telephone message,' he said.

'All right,' I said, and made a guess: the submarine operational signal had been cracked already. I obeyed orders; the CORPSE man led me to a car and off we drove for Focal House. There seemed to be more and more CORPSE uniforms around in the streets now, and I remembered that operations map aboard the *Sendar Maru*. The contingents would have been coming in all morning and more of the fifth column would have been emerging from their dirty little holes and reporting to their quartermasters for kitting-up and to their adjutants to be detailed for duty. I saw one or two nasty little incidents that sickened me: in Victoria Street a squad of uniformed men marched along the pavement in a solid phalanx that got out of the way of no one and an elderly woman was sent flying into the road where she was narrowly missed by a lorry. The lorry, in swerving, ran over a London policeman crossing the road to intervene. My CORPSE driver went right over the blue-clad legs. Along the Victoria Embankment an old down-and-out was being frogmarched past the end of Horse Guards Avenue, and as though keeping time with the step a CORPSE fist descended monotonously and rhythmically on the top of his head. He was crying. A little farther on a girl was being dragged for obvious purposes into the bushes of Embankment Gardens by two of the CORPSE stalwarts. No one appeared willing to interfere. Reaching Focal House we all went up in the lift to the suite, where Mrs Dodge was sitting in company with a fat man in plain clothes and the bulge of a shoulder holster beneath his jacket. She looked scared and miserable, but pleased enough to see me again. She introduced the fat man. 'Colonel Calibris,' she said dully. He looked Greek, and was. One of the celebrated Colonels, perhaps. He didn't say what he'd come for, but I soon found out when a telephone burred and Mrs Dodge answered it, shaking a little as she did so.

'For you, Commander Shaw,' she said. 'From CORPSE.'

I took the instrument and recognised the voice of the man in purple coming along the radio telephone hook-up. The voice said, 'Good afternoon, Commander Shaw.' In point of fact it was early evening now.

'Good evening,' I said. 'Can I help?'

'I believe it would be in your best personal interest if you did, Commander Shaw.'

'I get the message loud and clear,' I said, 'but I reckon I'm safe at the moment. In case you didn't know, a Colonel Calibris is here.'

'I do know.'

'I'm being relieved?'

'No. Not yet. There are matters for you to attend to, and Colonel Calibris is there to see that you don't step out of line.'

'I feel that's a nice safeguard,' I said. The man in purple didn't agree. Colonel Calibris would be withdrawn before any transmissions were made into my guts while as for me, he said, there could, of course, be no withdrawal. I asked, 'How do you know I've not had an operation?'

'I know this because there has not been the opportunity for you. Your comings and goings have been noted from time to time, and mani-festly you are not in bed. Now Colonel Calibris will ensure that there is no operation performed.'

'All right,' I said, 'now shall we get down to business? What is it you want?'

'There has been a signal. I think you know about this.'

'Oh?'

The voice grew testy. 'Do not stall, Commander Shaw. Time is growing short—'

'For you, yes.'

He went on regardless, 'You know of the signal. The firing of the missiles is not to take place. You know what will happen to you if you fail to have the order to the submarines negatived. I need not remind you.'

'No,' I said, 'you needn't. But the Polaris submarines are way beyond the control of CORPSE, aren't they? I'd go further: CORPSE is one hundred per cent at their mercy—'

'But you—'

'Suppose,' I said loudly, 'I'm prepared to sacrifice myself just to get rid of you—what then? Remember I was going to do just that until you had Zambellis killed!'

There was a silence; Mrs Dodge was looking as though she were about to faint. Colonel Calibris maintained a blank expression. Breathing sounds came down the telephone from the Clyde, interspersed with crackles and fizzes.

290

The man in purple, though not responsible for the atmospherics, was stymied. I found that satisfactory. But he was not done yet: further threats emerged. Those nuclear-waste ships would be ordered back in within three hours if I failed to negate the Polaris missiles. Their crews would be withdrawn under heavy guard against any interference, though interference was not expected as the coastal areas were largely empty and would empty altogether when it was known that the death-ships were returning, and known it would be because the announcement would be made from the *Sendar Maru*. And they would be ordered back in whether or not I had been blown up in the interval. I said down the phone, 'That may be. But you'll be a goner in any case, when the submarines blast off.'

'Not so. The *Sendar Maru* will be withdrawn to sea.'

'I see. When?' I was all glee; it had worked!

'When I so decide, Commander Shaw, and *where* I so decide. And—'

'What about the members of the cabinet?' I asked, and tried to strike a bargain. 'How about putting them ashore? I know they're only politicians, but one or two of them are popular. You still have to consider public opinion, haven't you?'

There was a cynical laugh, but no comment on the value of public opinion to CORPSE. Then he said, 'They will be safer aboard the *Sendar Maru*, Commander Shaw,' and rang off. He was, according to his interpretation of events, correct; but I was going to be much inhibited by those politicians' presence aboard the Japanese ship and if the worst had to come to the worst they were going to be very unsafe indeed. Once the *Sendar Maru* was in deep water and I blew the bug she would go down like a brick with no time to get boats away. Zambellis himself had said the bottom would be blown right out of her. However, the tongue-in-cheek signal had done its work well: the *Sendar Maru* would be nicely away from Britain ere long. Poor bloody British Government, I thought sadly, they're the one snag left. I turned from the silent telephone to face Colonel Calibris. And also to face the revolver that had now appeared in his hand.

Calibris said, 'You will now obey your orders. You will make signals to the British submarines, ordering them to withdraw.'

'I can't,' I said. 'I haven't the means now. You'll have to do it yourselves.'

'That will not be possible. We do not know the routines, the laid-down procedures.'

'No,' I said cheerfully. 'You don't, do you?

One detail wrong and the Commanding Officers will know it's not genuine. I really don't know what you're going to do about it, Colonel Calibris, nor how you're going to be absolutely certain of your own safety when I blow up. You have a dilemma. Frankly, I fear the big boss in the *Sendar Maru* could transmit at any time from now on out. Don't you?'

He was putting a good face on it, but I could see he was a worried man who didn't like his job. I turned away from him to speak to Mrs Dodge, asking if I could borrow her typewriter. I made some remark about sending a memo to Defence Ministry about Polaris submarines, just a bit of bull, then I picked up the heavy office machine and swung it and smashed it very hard into the face of the Greek colonel. His revolver went off and a bullet smacked into the ceiling. Calibris was staggering about, blinded with his own blood, and I kicked the wrist that held the revolver and it spun away across the floor, whence I retrieved it. There was no more fight in Calibris; his teeth had gone, his lips were split, his nose had a crunched and very bloody look and his eyes were bunged up and swelling visibly around the sockets. There was nothing much wrong with the typewriter. Mrs Dodge had her hands over her ears and her mouth was open: field work had never until now come right into the suite. Blundering around, Calibris cannoned into a wall and slid down it to the floor.

I reached down and jerked him to his feet. I said, 'There's a washroom next door, and some first aid wherewithals. You're going to use them, then you're going to help me leave the country. If you don't, you die.' From my pocket I brought out the bantam's egg, and once again blessed Mrs Pontefract's sense of duty. I believe from the look in Calibris's eye when he focused through his swellings that he knew what it was, but I made sure by telling him. And I added, 'I'm prepared to make the sacrifice, Colonel, believe me. I'll transmit and blow the two of us to Kingdom Come, and you won't have a chance of getting far enough away when I do it.'

* * * *

I left instructions with Mrs Dodge that if CORPSE should contact Focal House and ask after me and Calibris, she was to stall them; I knew I could safely leave it to her to dream up the right responses. I left Focal House within twenty minutes of typewritering Calibris, who was looking rather better but not much: blood was oozing through the bandages

294

and his mouth was a mess, but still. Ice had reduced the eye swellings and he could see after a fashion. The problem still was time, though I was banking hard on some elasticity. I didn't believe the man in purple would in fact blow the bug for a good while yet. In the living state, I might decide life was valuable enough to make me collaborate with him. As for the death-ships, sure they would come in, but there again I doubted if they would be triggered off until the very last ditch and I wasn't really anxious about them always provided I could use that little transmitter to sink the *Sendar Maru* before CORPSE got too worried about the Polaris potential. I shepherded Calibris down to the underground parking area where he had a CORPSE-commandeered police car and we set off with siren blaring and blue light flashing for Gatwick. We got through fairly fast; the traffic was thin on the ground by now, I didn't know why, but deduced from the number of closed signs on the filling stations that current events had interrupted the petrol flow. At Gatwick I kept very close to Calibris, who contacted the CORPSE airport control and demanded a flight to Madrid in the name of the interim government. His appearance caused a stir but he knew that if he aroused any suspicions about me I would transmit: so he was authoritative and loudly dictatorial, and very convincing. That plane was laid on right away, the CORPSE minions falling over themselves to please Calibris and through him the big bosses. Once airborne, Calibris shook like a leaf. He certainly couldn't get away now, and in Spain he would be cut right off from base and totally out on a limb, with explosive me. As a matter of fact I had no further use for him; once we were at 6D2 headquarters in Madrid I turned him over to our strong-arm section and asked them to lock him up till further notice just in case he came in handy at a later stage.

Then Josip Humo was brought in, still seemingly upset about what had happened to Zambellis. They had been close associates, good mates. He would help all he could against the men who had killed the Zambellis family.

He did, too. I showed him Zambellis's egg-like transmitter. He had worked on it with Zambellis, and he shared his friend's views about CORPSE and the WUSWIPP link-up.

'So you know the frequency?' I asked. Humo had good enough English.

'Yes, this I know. And how to transmit.'

'And you'll do it?'

'Yes,' he said. He was a little rat-like man, but there was sincerity and a kind of passion in his eyes: he had liked Zambellis a lot. 'I

296

shall do it gladly.'

I mopped my face; I was sweating with relief and with the build-up of tension. Now that I had the means the shortness of time struck home more than ever and I couldn't wait: CORPSE might surprise us all yet by blowing the death-ships, whatever my earlier thoughts on that subject had been. I asked, 'If you transmit from here, will it reach to somewhere off the north of Scotland, say—around fourteen hundred miles from here?'

'No.' Humo shook his head. 'Zambellis's transmitter has not the power of that aboard the *Sendar Maru*. The range is 200 miles only.'

'But Zambellis was—'

'Zambellis intended to fly to Plymouth.' I fancied for a moment he was about to weep. 'He would have been leaving for the airport when he was murdered.'

I said, 'Right. That being so, we leave for closer waters pronto. I assume you can transmit from the air if necessary?'

Humo said that would be perfectly possible. I was airborne again, with Josip Humo, within the half-hour, re-armed with a 9mm Stechkin APS having a fully-automatic capability. Everything had been laid on by 6D2 Madrid and I had been given a private plane, an executive jet with a range of around fifteen hundred miles, the crew of which had been placed under my personal orders. I told the pilot to lay off a course far enough to the westward of the Irish coast and to keep low over the sea to ensure the minimum chance of being picked up as an unauthorised flight by the British ground radar. Notwithstanding this, he was to come in later so as to take me over Scottish waters north of the Firth of Clyde, where I would begin the search if the *Sendar Maru* had not been sighted farther south or off the west of Ireland. En route, I racked my brains for the simple, safe answer. There was as ever the horrid question: did I or did I not blow up the cabinet? And pressing upon me hard was the knowledge that if the man in purple had got the word that I had flown to Madrid he might transmit and blow—not me, but the *Sendar Maru* with the British cabinet still aboard. I had much faith in Mrs Dodge's ability to keep CORPSE happy about me, but the CORPSE staff at Gatwick could have contacted the *Sendar Maru* though in point of fact they had not known my identity. It was fifty-fifty. In the meantime Josip Humo was all ready with that bantam's egg. Currently he was caressing it like a pet lap-dog, his eyes strangely luminous as he stared down through night skies from the jet's window. He was looking forward to a big thrill, a big bang that would shatter the killers of Zambellis. But I still didn't want to shatter the British cabinet. They hadn't quite deserved that and never mind the lily-livered way they'd trooped aboard the helicopters for the *Sendar Maru*. No doubt that had been done in perfect faith, in their eyes the only course left for the salvation of millions of Britons; and I had to concede that such widespread death and devastation would hardly be a vote catcher.

There had to be a subterfuge, but what?

★ ★ ★ ★

We came up off the west coast of the Irish Republic and as the first light of dawn brought up the sea below, I searched for the *Sendar Maru* but without success. When we were approaching County Mayo we altered north-eastwards towards the Clyde, which was standing empty of the Japanese vessel. There was no knowing what course she might be steering, in which area of sea I should choose to look for her, but I had a gut feeling she would be north or north-west, either somewhere around the remote Scottish islands or off Cape Wrath, or heading out into the Atlantic below Iceland perhaps, even as far as Greenland, losing herself in an immensity of sea until Britain saw sense and came to heel, heel being the calling-off of the Polaris fleet and its terrible destructive power. And as we cleared the Clyde northwards my pilot began worrying about his fuel.

I said, 'We'll be all right. There's plenty of choice at a pinch.' This was true: Barra, Benbecula or Coll in the Hebrides, Glenforsa in Mull, Port Ellen in Islay, even the Orkneys and Shetlands. The one thing we couldn't risk was going far out over the Atlantic. In the meantime I was getting nowhere, and getting there rather fast. The *Sendar Maru* was a needle in a haystack...and the pilot was of course dead right to consider his fuel. My journey began to seem pointless and as we approached Stornoway, with no sign of the Jap in the seaway of the Minches, I made a decision for good or ill and told the pilot to go in and land. At the very least—always assuming the airfield wasn't in CORPSE hands—he should be able to refuel. As we made our approach run I saw a biggish helicopter parked, and it began to give me the glimmering of an idea. I was out of the jet as soon as it had taxied clear of the runway. Faces stared down from Air Traffic Control and two men ran from the airport building to meet me and without preamble I asked if CORPSE had taken over yet.

'Aye,' one of them said. 'There's two

bastards up in Air Traffic Control the noo.' He
then looked as though he might have been too
forthcoming.

'Just two?' I asked.

'Aye.'

'They'll not be bothering you for long,' I
said, reassured by the involuntary use of the
term bastards: I was not dealing with converts
or the fifth column. I was surprised the Scots
airfield staff had been subdued by just two
bastards, but CORPSE had plenty of backing
and so far as Stornoway was concerned they
were now the bosses nationwide. 'That helicopter...I'd like to borrow it. I'd be glad if
you'd have it fuelled up to capacity.'

The Scot frowned. 'Who're you, then?'

I said, 'I'm part of the strike-back and more
than that I can't tell you for now. I'm asking
you to trust me.' Over the men's shoulders I
saw movement and I went on, 'I'm about to
prove I'm not CORPSE if that's what's worrying you. Don't look now, but your two bastards
are coming out to give me the once-over.
They're about a hundred yards behind you.'
I thought of Mrs Pontefract and I asked, 'Are
you willing to strike a blow for Scotland?' The
answer was yes; and I told the Scots to carry
on talking to me and give me cover just for
a moment. I brought out my automatic and I

301

lined it up clandestinely on the CORPSE men from between the two Scots and when the CORPSE uniforms were nice and close I blasted them out of existence, emptying the slide smack into them. The Scots, too, were almost swept asunder by the closeness of the discharge and I fancied I smelt a smell of singed cloth. They were very shaken men when they turned and saw the mess, and I apologised for what might seem to them a dirty deed, a shooting of sitting ducks from a hide as it were, but I needn't have bothered.

'It's a'richt,' one of them said. 'They were English.'

The remark made me feel at some disadvantage myself, but those Scots and the rest of the airfield staff proved very helpful indeed. They were one hundred per cent committed against CORPSE now and they acceded readily to my requests: use of the helicopter, and use of their radio installation. I went up to Air Traffic Control and I set up the naval command frequency for contact with the Polaris fleet. I had no means, of course, of enciphering my message so I had to take a big risk, but shrugged it away with the knowledge that the *Sendar Maru* had the capacity to break the naval cipher in any case. I made my signal as from Defence Ministry; the addressee was the lurking threat to

CORPSE and all its works, somewhere beneath the North Atlantic, and the message was an order to the nearest Polaris submarine to indicate its exact position immediately and then maintain it until further notice. All this, I authenticated by adding the Top Secret code group that had been communicated to me by Max via the Metropolitan Police Commissioner and memorised.

Then I sat back to await the response.

It was not long in coming: the nearest of the Polaris fleet was HMS *Renown*, cruising submerged off the North Irish coast and currently thirty miles from Malin Head, bearing 275 degrees. I did a quick calculation and then made one further signal: *Renown* was to surface in two hours as of now and stand by for the approach of a helicopter.

CHAPTER 17

I went down from Air Traffic Control at speed, leaving instructions with the airfield staff to shut up shop and make themselves scarce: I would myself have no further need of Stornoway, and I felt the staff were in imminent danger now from CORPSE. I retrieved Josip Humo from the 6D2 jet and told the pilot to take off for Madrid again as soon as he had finished refuelling. Humo and I then ran for the helicopter and were airborne within seconds. Under a bright and rising sun all too reminiscent of Japan, the machine swung away to the south-west and raced at something like a hundred knots over the peaks and crags of the Outer Hebrides, down towards North Uist and then away for the north Irish coast to search the area of water thirty miles north-west of Malin Head. In a little over two hours out of Stornoway we were over the reported position of the *Renown:* I saw her, long and black and lethal, wallowing on the surface in a slight swell, with water washing her casing, streaming over her and falling away again.

The helicopter came down to hover over the fore part of the submarine. I gave a wave to the captain, who was standing in the conning tower with two of his officers and a number of ratings, hair streaming in the down-draught from the rotor blades. First Josip Humo was winched down, then me, to be taken in hand by a naval party and set on our feet on the casing. There was a good deal of strain in the air, and many unasked questions hung: the *Renown's* company were among the last outposts of free Britain, and they would all have families at risk and the risk was as great as ever even now. In accordance with orders I had already given, the helicopter pilot at once turned away and sped low across the water to put himself down in Northern Ireland and get lost. I had considered an air search for the *Sendar Maru*, but not for long: the Jap could be anywhere, and the helicopter would not have fuel enough for any useful quartering of the sea. It should be possible to find a way of inducing the *Sendar Maru* to approach the Clyde, and when she got there she would find the *Renown* across her track. That would be faster than any search could hope to be. And in any case, when I climbed to the upper reaches of the conning tower, thick and tall and black, and identified myself to the captain, a Commander Foster, he had news for me. Foster was tense, his voice sharp with anxiety, with an obvious feeling that the sands were running out. He asked the questions that the ratings had not asked, and I filled him in briefly, then he gave me the news— good news up to a point: the *Sendar Maru* had transmitted a number of plain-language messages in the last hour or so and the *Renown's* communications officer had been able to get a fix of her position and plot her course. She was steaming easterly from a position in latitude fifty-five degrees north, longitude eleven degrees west.

'Almost due north of the Bloody Foreland, off Donegal,' Foster said, 'or around a hundred miles to the north-westward of us, and closing.'

'How fast?'

Foster shrugged. 'An estimated twenty knots. Contact can be made within the next two hours, if that's what you want.'

'It's what I want,' I confirmed, and then came the bad news. I asked what the transmission from the *Sendar Maru* had been about. Foster told me they had ordered the nuclear-waste ships in and they would be blasted off at noon if the Polaris fleet had not surfaced and set their courses for the Firth of Clyde for surrender and demilitarising. Foster's face was as pale as death itself; he had been under immense strain, bearing a tremendous responsibility. I glanced at my watch: it was a little after 0800 hours. I wondered where the *Sendar Maru* was bound. To all appearances it looked like the Clyde, though I doubted if she would enter before she had blown the nuclear-waste vessels in the non-Scottish ports, and maybe not even then in case the Polaris fleet, not having surrendered, went into the last strike-back. Anyway, according to those fixes, she was coming

306

fast towards the *Renown's* position: maybe her communicators hadn't been listening on the naval command frequency when I had sent my messages...maybe many things. It was at least possible—even likely I felt now—that she had no idea of the *Renown's* current position across her inward track towards the Clyde. And I had to act before CORPSE did. Quickly I told Foster what I wanted: the *Renown* was to close the *Sendar Maru* at full surface speed and then stand by to take off the members of Her Majesty's Government. Foster seemed surprised. 'You really think they'll release them?' he asked.

'Under threat, yes.'

'The threat being?'

'Your Polaris missiles. That is, the missiles from the other submarines of the Polaris fleet... which you'll have ordered to be homed on to the *Sendar Maru*. That's what you'll tell CORPSE.' *Renown*, as CORPSE would realise, would by then be too close to the Japanese vessel to be able to use her own missiles as a threat since the arc of fire could not be brought down to such short range; but the man in purple would know that in theory at any rate he stood at the mercy of the more distant, still submerged submarines. 'CORPSE won't want to lose their HQ ship, the nub of

307

the whole operation.'

'They have a good counter-threat, haven't they? They'll simply blow those bloody nuclear-waste vessels!'

'I wouldn't bet on it,' I said. 'The cabinet's not all that vital to them when all's said and done...but a radiation-free Britain is!'

'You're going to the brink, aren't you?'

I gave a hard laugh. 'So will CORPSE be. It'll be a case of whose nerve is the first to give. I've an idea it won't be mine. I have something of a trump card.' I told the submarine captain about the stomach bug, and its current nesting place low down in the *Sendar Maru's* guts rather than mine. Before the death-ships blew, I would sacrifice the cabinet. He seemed quite a lot happier after that.

★ ★ ★ ★

At 0932 hours we brought the huge shape of the *Sendar Maru* up ahead of our north-westerly course, which had taken us nicely into deep water and well clear of the land. *Renown* closed; soon the two vessels were no more than a mile apart; and I left the upper platform of the conning tower to take up my position below. There, I could listen by telephone to the proceedings without being seen myself from the

Sendar Maru, where binoculars would shortly give the bridge personnel a good view. The Japanese ship moved on, Foster reported, passing north of us, and a signal was made from the conning tower by lamp, ordering her to heave to or the missiles would be ordered in, sprouting up from the wastes of water to bring total destruction to the CORPSE command. The *Sendar Maru* maintained her course and speed. We all waited, scarcely daring to breathe now. I visualised scenes of fury aboard that enormous ship, the man in purple weighing the odds and reaching a decision behind his stupid hood. He wouldn't be wanting to balls up the whole operation at this stage when in fact—as he would think—he had won and had only to consolidate. By my side in the lower conning tower stood Josip Humo with Zambellis's transmitter in his hand.

'Ready?' I asked.

'All ready.'

Things began to look bad for the cabinet. Then some of the tension broke: Foster reported down his telephone that a curfuffle had arisen below the counter of the *Sendar Maru*: water was boiling in white foam and after a while drifted forward as her engines moved astern to bring her up.

'Round one to us,' I said to Josip Humo. He

made no response, he was too keyed-up. My voice had sounded brittle in my own ears. A moment later I heard the clack-clack of the Aldis lamp above my head, making the next signal, which Foster reported down to me: *All members of Her Majesty's Government are to be transferred to me immediately and in safety.*

Nothing happened.

There was a curious stillness, as though both vessels were somehow detached from the world, things apart and in a kind of time-suspension, though in all conscience time was passing fast enough...then as the distance closed more a great voice boomed at us from across the water, a voice immensely amplified by a powerful loud-hailer. I recognised it as that of the man in purple.

'You are being foolish. You make threats. So does CORPSE. Stand down your Polaris fleet and sail back into the Clyde peacefully, or I shall blow up the nuclear-waste ships now in their stations.'

The telephone from the upper platform whined in my ear again and I answered. It was Foster. In a strained voice he said, 'You probably heard that.'

'I did.'

'Well?'

I said harshly, 'Chuck it back at him. Repeat

310

the missile threat.'

'This is the brink, Shaw.'

'I don't think so.' I felt my hands shake on the telephone, felt a horrible stir in my guts as they began to turn to water. 'I say again, repeat the threat. And add that once the cabinet's aboard the whole Polaris fleet will assemble in the Clyde and demilitarise.'

'CORPSE won't take that. What would be the point of taking off the cabinet only to sail them back into CORPSE hands?'

'Just try it,' I said. 'He won't take the big risk now, he has too much at stake. Leave him to assume that we'll bargain again in the Clyde, asking for assurances as to the bloody cabinet's safety thereafter...or something!' I felt my nails dig hard into my palms as I gripped the telephone, and I shouted along the wire at Foster. 'Get cracking, will you, for Christ's sake, use all the bull you've got!'

There was no answer; the phone clicked in my ear. Then I heard the lamp sending out the message. I shook. Whatever I had said to Foster, this was indeed the brink. I had the devil's own job to stop myself giving the final nod to Josip Humo. Was the goddam cabinet worth all this, worth the risk? The answer was most probably no; but even so, I couldn't bring myself to kill the wretched politicians so long

311

as some hope remained. On more practical grounds, they did have a use: without them Britain would have no government, at any rate for a while, and vacuums are nasty, asking to be filled by wild men.

More waiting, more desperate nail-biting. No more amplified voices from the *Sendar Maru*. Then Foster came on the line again: there was a movement along the upper deck of the Japanese, a group of men and women being herded like sheep, and the gripes were being slipped from two of the boats which a moment later were lowered on the falls to the embarkation deck.

I found myself soaked in sweat. Up the telephone line, my voice hoarse, I said, 'Stand by to submerge as soon as they're aboard.' I put a hand on Humo's shoulder. I said, 'Don't jump the gun. Wait for my order, all right?'

He nodded. That bantam's egg looked lovely; it was salvation for Britain. With the high command gone, the heart of CORPSE would follow. I listened to Foster's continuing commentary as the boats filled with HMG and were lowered to the waterline and slipped. I visualised them moving across towards us under power, coming fast through a friendly blue sea. They came alongside and then I heard the men from Whitehall clambering out on to the casing, still with plenty of worries for the future: so far as they knew, CORPSE ruled yet. Down the phone Foster reported he would be submerging in two minutes. I told Humo to stand by. As the last of the cabinet clanged down the steel ladder of the fore hatch into the submarine's interior, the first orders were being passed to take the vessel down deep. There was much subdued noise, a sound of electrical efficiency. I nodded at Josip Humo, and he turned and went up the ladder: he wanted, he said, to watch Zambellis being beautifully revenged. I went up with him; it didn't matter if I were seen now in the binoculars from the *Sendar Maru*. As the hull of the *Renown* sank lower so that the waters swirled around the base of the conning tower, not yet shut down, I stood with Foster and Humo looking out at the *Sendar Maru* and I was about to pass the final order to Humo when somehow he managed to fumble the bantam's egg transmitter right on the lip of the conning tower bulkhead, and lost his grip. It went straight into the sea, splosh.

I went mad, so did Foster. Josip Humo had tears streaming down his cheeks. Then something happened: the *Sendar Maru's* loud-hailer came back to life and once again I heard the man in purple, this time addressing me:

'This you will not win, Commander Shaw.' That was all he said, I'd been recognised and I knew what was to happen next, and he didn't need to say any more. I yelled at Foster to get the boat down pronto, but it happened just seconds before the hatch was shut and in that twinkling of an eye I registered the whole awful sight, one I shall never forget: seemingly from the bottom of the ship a vast flame and a cloud of smoke arose, ripping up through the sea, to be followed by an almighty roar, and, just as Zambellis had promised, with no time for the death-ships' transmission to be made, the *Sendar Maru* went down like a gigantic mountain dropping at speed into a volcanic upheaval, her main deck and upperworks intact so that her remote control apparatus would be unlikely to have been automatically triggered off. She had gone within no more than seconds, and then we had the conning tower sealed and were submerging. We surged sideways, buffeted by giant's hammers that seemed as though they must smash through the hull. Everything slid, and lights went out and came on again, and then, as the disturbed sea quietened, we lay more restfully and Foster took us down deep and began moving out of the area towards the Clyde. Above us, as we heard later, a great cloud of fall-out formed, but was carried away

314

on the wings of a wind blowing from easterly, out into the wide Atlantic.

★ ★ ★ ★

When I reached London, the party was already over for CORPSE. *Renown* had been in immediate contact with Defence Ministry after the sinking, and the news had spread. The interim government had panicked; some, including Brigadier Bunnett, had died in gun battles with the army. Some had been taken, others would be taken soon. The *gauleiters* and the rank-and-file of CORPSE, shattered and leaderless and without a command base, had largely been rounded up after a series of bloody battles nationwide. During the day the whole Polaris force entered the Clyde, returning peacefully to the Gareloch. The rescued cabinet had been flown south as soon as they had disembarked at Greenock from the *Renown*. Good old British law and order was once again emerging; and the death-ships had already been sailed for Windscale and the storage ponds with the now useless tripping devices and priming explosives rendered safe by their own crews at gun point. CORPSE was no more; WUSWIPP would live to plague us again, but that was something for the future.

I went at last to see Miss Mandrake in hospital.

She was doing fine, she said, and she looked it. Just a question of stitches to come out and a scar to be healed. Max, walking away from a disintegrated house arrest, had been to see her. 6D2 was in being again, and back under his overlordship. All was well except in the hastily set up camps where the CORPSE thugs were being held. There, much misery and dis-illusion prevailed. Under the eye of a staff nurse I gave Miss Mandrake a polite kiss on the cheek and left St Thomas's for Focal House. From there I got Mrs Dodge to put out a call for Mrs Pontefract. When we made contact she sounded very pleased with the way things had gone and I could sense a blush along the telephone wires when I lavished praise on her and told her the country would be found not ungrateful. The next night I took her out to dinner, with Max, and we left the choice of location to her. She chose Brown's Hotel in Dover Street; so English, she said, but in the event was disappointed to find so many Americans eating.

'If anybody really *does* want to show ap-preciation of the little I did,' she said, 'I'd so much like to have Noah restored.' The Flood Fearers, she went on to say, were basically good

people and now that Mr Petersen and Brigadier Bunnett and their accomplices had gone,
religion would return to normal. Next day she
went back to Spain.